The Sins of My Fathers

JULIAN GRAY

cloiff books

Cover design: John Featherstone

ISBN-13: 978-0-9931663-5-8

For
Patrick and Clive
who were brothers

CHAPTER 1

I used the key I was given as a boy and went in through the lower entrance, making my way through the basement, past the unfinished stone blocks that Rob had left behind. It was dark upstairs, the doors shut, the curtain over the front door keeping out the draught. I swept it aside to allow the light in. I tried the living room, the study, the dining room, opening the curtains of each of them, letting in the winter sunshine. The kitchen was light enough, but cold. The stove that used to warm this, the kindest room of the house where we three were a family beyond all doubt, was dull, chill metal.

This was a new development. Louis had always kept the stove going, even after Rob died. It was an article of faith for him.

He was upstairs, sitting in bed, wrapped in a heavy, brown dressing gown, sipping a cup of tea, Radio Four on loud. He had an old Teasmade - had it since the seventies - discoloured yellow plastic. The tea was the same disgusting colour - I don't know how he drank it.

"I wasn't expecting you this morning," he said, looking up and switching off the radio. 'Thought for the Day' was just starting. Rob had always switched over to another

1

station when that came on. He didn't take kindly to moral lectures. They used to laugh about that, sitting in the kitchen together, eating the toast that Louis made in the mornings.

He put his teacup down in the watery saucer, held in a trembling, ancient hand. I hurried forward to take it from him before he spilled it over the covers.

"Can I get you some toast?" I asked, "You can't have been down to the kitchen today."

When I came up again, ready to offer Marmite soldiers, the same as he made for me when I was small, he was out of bed, struggling to put his underpants on.

"Thought I'd get dressed, have the toast downstairs" he muttered, gritting his teeth as he wobbled next to the bed. He couldn't reach down far enough.

"Let me help."

This happened a lot. After all, he was in his eighties. A nurse came to see him two mornings a week to help him with the bath, someone else for a bit of cooking and cleaning, but he'd been getting up later and later as the illness took hold. I wondered how much longer he could stay in the Hampstead house. When Rob died he could have sold it, but he hung on.

I could never get used to seeing his naked old man's body, his wrinkled belly and ribs, the blue veins near the surface criss-crossing his legs. I looked at his scrotum, stretched out, sagging low, the penis flopping against it. I felt like an invader.

He grunted as his leg twisted to slide his trousers on, then again as he fastened his belt.

"So, darling boy, what do you want?"

He's been getting more direct recently, less time to waste as his life runs out.

"Let's go downstairs," I said.

We sat in the living room overlooking the street, the thin sun casting its light across the carpet. I watched as he ate his toast. His face was lined, mottled with brown, the result of too much time spent in the sun, the places he'd been. Can you get liver secondaries from skin cancer? He'd travelled all over the world after the war, for his job. I remembered him coming back from those trips, the front door opening, me running to meet him, the bags in his hands dropped to the floor as he scooped me up, laughing. Rob laughing too, finding his way past me in his arms. All of us in that embrace.

"Are you going to tell me what it's about?" he asked.

I'd come to confront him. All the secrets and lies I'd been told in my childhood, just to protect them. Karen had insisted it was time, that I shouldn't put it off any longer. He wouldn't last for ever, she said, and if not now, I could lose my chance.

Louis was the one who broke the silence.

"I'm on the way out."

He sounded calm. Held his hand up to stop me speaking. To stop me objecting, stop me saying that must be wrong, that there had to be hope yet.

"The doctors yesterday. They told me. It's certain. Chemo's stopped working. Palliative care only. Someone's coming over this afternoon."

"I'll stay," I said, "here with you. I can stay here. You don't want to be on your own - at night I mean. I can –"

"You've got your own family to worry about. I'm not that bad yet," he said. "Wait 'til we see what the hospice people say."

After that first day with Louis I visited him regularly, helped with his care, took him to all his appointments, got him onto the Heath when the weather was right. Eventually he started to talk. He said he wanted to start at the beginning, that I should know about him and Rob if I was to understand. It was his last chance to set the record straight. He assured me he'd have enough time.

I wasn't so sure about that. He was fading faster than he realised.

Louis had never explained much about himself, but in those last weeks the stories poured out of him, all the things he'd stored up for years. Why did he decide to speak? Did he want someone to hear the record of his life with Rob before he died? I could see it was my chance, my final chance, to know the truth. But I also know he told people stories to make them believe things that weren't true, do things they didn't want to do.

But would he do that to me, his son?

CHAPTER 2

The day after Rob met Louis, he took him to meet his mother. Louis thought it was a good chance to get to know Rob: intriguing and free-thinking in ways he found strangely exciting.

The house was in the Vale of Health, not far from Hampstead Hill Gardens where Louis lived with his parents. Rob guided him through to a conservatory overlooking one of the ponds on the Heath. Hot sun shone through the glass onto dense green foliage and the windows were raised to allow air to circulate. The warm earth, moisture and flowers produced a musty perfume.

A tall woman with luxuriant brown hair rose from a wicker armchair and turned towards them. Louis put out his hand as Rob introduced him. He noticed a collection of silver bangles on her bare arm as both her hands softly enclosed his.

"How lovely," she said, a smile spreading over her face.

"I met Robert at the Albert Hall. Mr Pollitt was speaking."

"Yes, I know. Such fun, and so many nice young people there. I expect he's brought you to see my pictures."

Rob had mentioned nothing about pictures, but Louis, too polite to mention this, was drawn back into the house by Vita. Her long dress flowed behind her, creating a wake that pulled Louis along.

He led them to a room lined on two sides with white shelves strewn with oil paints, brushes, boxes of coloured tiles, stones, tinted glass fragments and jars smelling of turpentine. The floor was covered in brown linoleum, splashed with paint, the walls written on in a child's handwriting, a blackboard scrawled with coloured chalk. He stopped to look at a large table on which mosaic tiles made a swirling pattern.

"It's for the garden," Vita said, then pointed to canvasses stacked against the wall.

"Show them to him won't you dear?" she said to Rob. "I'll make you both a cup of tea."

Alone with Rob, Louis was shown the canvasses: a picture of a mulberry tree, a moorland scene, birds in a cage, crudely drawn but showing the same swirling motion and bright colours of the mosaic.

"They're very nice," Louis said, as Rob kept up a chatter about the paintings. It was hard to focus on the images with Rob so close. If Vita came back she'd see his unease, sense his desire.

Rob was talking about the tree and birds in the garden that had served as subjects for Vita. As a child he'd played in the studio as his mother worked, cutting mosaics or painting. He used to draw on the blackboard he said, and pointed to a corner where his height was recorded on the wall as he grew, each pencil line dated.

The last canvas showed the silhouette of a woman standing alone at the end of a long staircase, surrounded by imprisoning blocks of red and purple colour.

"That's a sad one," Louis said.

"Yes, Vita sometimes gets lonely. Willi hasn't visited for ages," Rob allowed the canvasses to fall back against the wall. He looked up at Louis, his face framed by dark hair that came down to his collar. Rob was one of those people who normally smile as they speak, but now he seemed serious as he thought of his mother.

"He'll kiss you if you stand so close," Vita said with a laugh as she came in with a tray.

Rob laughed too as he started back. "Oh shut up Ma."

The exchange of words jolted Louis with a mixture of fear and excitement, and he felt himself turn red. It was exactly what he wanted to do: kiss Rob. But he'd spent years suppressing and hiding such feelings about other boys. He couldn't believe Vita had, in an instant, just lifted the taboo. Perhaps it was just a risqué joke.

Mother and son still smiled as they went back to the conservatory to have their tea. They talked about Vita's painting. She'd learned to paint in Vienna.

It was another world, and a wonderful one. Louis thought of his mother and father in their living room, surrounded by gloomy dark furniture and heavy curtains, blocking out the light. The pictures on their walls were undistinguished oils, so brown with age it was like peering at what lay behind a dim screen. The sadness in his parents' home was palpable, and he realised he was happy for the first time in months. Here in the conservatory with Rob and his mother, he could see white clouds above, feel sunshine breaking through, sending life and energy into him.

The tea had a perfumed quality, but he decided he liked it. Rob sat next to him on a stone bench listening to Vita talking about painting, about Vienna, about the flowers and plants that enveloped them. She punctuated her conversation with little darting questions directed at Louis, delicately probing for details of his life which he did his best to answer. Her strange mixture of warmth and intrusiveness was disturbing. But for Louis the presence of Rob was everything. Their shoulders touched as Rob laughed, drawing him in with his welcoming spirit.

Last night's Albert Hall meeting had been a gathering

to discuss the war in Spain. He'd found himself in a seat next to Rob. Louis said it was time to accept defeat, time for the International Brigades to come home, stop the needless slaughter. Rob said the opposite: they should continue to fight for what was right, against the fascists. Louis insisted Rob explain himself. How could he know what the war was like? Then Louis played his trump card: his own brother had fought and died in Spain. He burned with the conviction that this gave him the right to prevail.

Rob was chastened and sympathetic when he heard about Christopher and suggested they go across the park towards Oxford Street. But when they were walking together through the dark, Louis said no more about his brother, feeling he'd overdone it by mentioning his death. They talked of other things, the kind of things that mean nothing in themselves, but which serve as an excuse to get closer to someone who is new, someone you like, and to look at them and imagine how it might be to touch them.

Waiting for the bus, Rob said he was thinking of joining the Communist Party and had been impressed with Pollitt, the General Secretary, who'd made a powerful speech urging continued support for the military efforts in Spain. As Louis gazed into his animated, passionate face, he stopped opposing him. He had a growing sense that Rob was different from the other men he knew, but he wasn't sure.

And then Rob had invited him to come to Vita's house the next day.

It was five o'clock by the time they finished in the conservatory and Rob suggested a stroll on the Heath. Louis had been preparing to say his goodbyes, but then was quietly thrilled that Rob wanted to spend more time with him. So when Vita announced she needed to get back to her studio they set off on their own.

"Who is Willi?" Louis asked as they headed towards

Kenwood. They wanted to see the view over London and then go to Parliament Hill.

"Didn't I say? Sorry. He's my father."

"Where is he?" Louis asked.

To look at, Rob was so unlike his mother. Where Vita was tall, angular with dark skin and high cheekbones, Rob was shorter, with a softer face. The only thing he shared with his mother was dark hair, which Rob wore longer than any other man Louis knew. The father must have differed greatly from Vita.

"Oh, he doesn't live with us," Rob said, waving his hand as if to dismiss the question. They'd reached the top of the hill and were going along the path to Kenwood House.

"I know a way through the forest. It's much more interesting," Louis said.

He led them through a gate and into the trees, pleased to have led Rob off the main path into a place only he knew about. They came to a circular clearing with a large oak tree at its centre. A gust of warm wind gently shook its leaves.

"We used to play inside that tree," Louis said.

"You and your brother?"

"We could fit in the hollow bit. We were goblins!" He laughed at the memory and fingered the stone in his pocket.

Rob stopped and faced him. "How did he die, Louis?"

"They told us it was a bomb from a German plane. The Jarama Valley in February last year. It's a useless fight you know. Whatever we think, whatever Harry Pollitt says - they can't win."

He felt miserable, his grief about Christopher surging up again. He resented it. Why did he have this cancerous thing gnawing at him? It spoiled his pleasure in the company of his beautiful new friend, whose dark eyes brimmed with concern.

"This stone," he said, taking it from his pocket. "He's

got the other half. We found it in the tree when we were kids. Christopher said it was a good luck charm and kept it under his pillow. He broke it apart when he left for Spain and said we'd put the halves back together one day."

"I'm sorry I made such a stink last night," Rob burst in. "I didn't know about your brother."

"That's all right. But you're wrong about Spain. It's no good continuing now the Germans are involved. It only means more deaths. They need to come home."

As they continued along the ridge he felt Rob's hand slip into his, trees shielding them from the view of passers-by until they descended to an area of open grassland. Rob's touch sent a thrill through him. It was an effort to speak.

"Weren't you going to tell me about your father?"

"He's a sort of doctor. In Vienna. They met there."

They stood looking out over London, their hands now separate but resting next to each other on the railing of a small viewing platform.

"He's a believer in free love," Rob added, with a laugh.

"Free love?"

"Yes, and free things in general. He's been in trouble over it."

"Well, I expect it would be nice if everything were free."

"When I was thirteen, they sent me to Monkton Hill," Rob said. "Vita met the headmaster, O.J. Lorenz, when he was living in Austria. He was ruddy awful."

"I remember the fuss about Monkton Hill in the papers. I've never met someone who was there."

Louis' own education had taken place in a cold, windy institution in Dorset. The boys were forced to wear shorts, come rain or shine, to encourage an outdoor, pioneering spirit.

"I heard at Monkton you didn't have to go to lessons if you didn't want to," he said.

"Yes, and we used to run around naked."

Louis wasn't sure if this was a joke, so just smiled. They talked on for a while. Rob's father didn't live with them. He stayed in Austria running his clinic, then had moved to Berlin and now, Norway.

"He's famous," Rob said.

"What for?"

Rob laughed and didn't answer. He said his mother looked forward to Willi's occasional visits, but talking about his father clearly embarrassed him and he changed the subject, instead telling Louis more about Monkton Hill.

"The teachers used to give us massages. Loosening up our muscular armour, they called it."

At that point he moved behind Louis and reached to put his hands on his neck muscles.

"Bend down. On your knees. You're too tall for me."

The knees of Louis' trousers sank into the soft grass. Rob's hands felt delightful as his thumbs rubbed and kneaded.

"You'd need to take your shirt off for me to do it properly."

There were people nearby and a middle-aged woman glanced at them. Rob's fingers moved under his shirt to his shoulders, but could go no further. Louis was reluctant to unbutton it.

"I'm not very good at it. Vita knows how to do it right," Rob said, stopping. "I can ask her. You're quite well armoured, I'd say. She'd enjoy breaking that down."

He stood up as Rob's hands fell away. "I'm not sure I'd want that," Louis said, shrugging his clothes back into shape and brushing the knees of his trousers.

Rob tried to take his hand again, but Louis shook him free. There were people around. "Come on, let's get to Parliament Hill."

They ran together down the slope until they reached a fountain where they stopped, breathless and laughing. There was no-one nearby.

"I don't know what those people can have thought," Louis said.

"Who cares."

Louis pointed to a railing. "That's the Ladies pond over there."

"I know."

Then he felt Rob kissing him. He leaned back against the fountain's edge, lowering himself as Rob's lips and tongue pressed into his, pulling Rob towards him. Rob's fingers found their way to the buttons of his shirt and he pushed his hands under the fabric and around to Louis' back.

"There's a hole in the fence, just there, see?" Rob said, breaking off. "Come on."

They squeezed through a gap in the railing. The light was fading now and Louis looked back, seeing the last rays of evening sun on the green slopes of the Heath behind them. Then he turned to follow Rob into the dark woodland surrounding the pond. He wondered whether there would still be bathers, but Rob said the main gate had been closed an hour ago.

They crunched across the leaf litter and reached the forbidden place, shimmering water reflecting the sky above. They stopped for a moment, listening and looking, anxious that a bather might have stayed on, or had scrambled through the fence like them for a late evening swim. But they were alone.

"Come on," Rob said again, tugging his hand and leading him to a wooden pontoon in front of the bathing hut. There were rubber mats lying about and he pulled Louis down onto one. Louis' excitement made him tremble as they kissed and he ran his hands over Rob's body.

He realised what Rob wanted him to do and began to loosen his belt. Rob unbuttoned him.

"I'm not sure I want to know about this, Dad."

Louis was losing his inhibitions as he got older. He and Rob had always been very discreet about their physical relationship when they were with me. Their bedrooms were separate and in public they never showed their affection for one another, even after attitudes began to change. A lifetime of subterfuge was hard to shake off.

Louis stopped in his tracks, looking up at me as if coming out of a dream of the past.

"Sorry," he said. "I was forgetting myself."

"That's all right," I said, patting him on the arm. "I know you and Rob loved each other."

I felt a bit mean for stopping him. Then I wondered how I was going to manage this flow of memories, divert them towards the things that troubled me.

"Fair enough," Louis said. "I'm too old now to worry about sex. It's a relief when you stop being driven by your prick. You'll find out, one day." He paused, then added, chuckling, "If you haven't found out already, that is. How are things with you and Karen, anyway?"

This was provoking, but I decided to ignore it.

"Everything's just fine between us and thanks for asking."

Afterwards they sat together, legs dangling over the decking as they watched the water. Louis picked up a few stones and threw them into the pond. He was both confused and happy. They leaned against each other and Rob stroked his head, planting kisses on his neck while he did the same, running his fingers through Rob's dark hair. Louis felt as deeply happy as he could remember.

Rob was right; he was suffering from muscular tension. His whole being since Christopher's death was imbued with a tense readiness, although for what he couldn't say. He'd been unable to focus on his studies. He failed his university entrance exams so now had to take them again in a Marylebone tutorial college, a year taken out of his life.

He kept up with news of the war in Spain out of loyalty to his brother, and attended rallies and meetings where the men who had inspired his brother and others like him to volunteer, still spoke about the progress of the fighting. He was angry at what had happened, but also proud of Christopher. He realised, too, that he enjoyed the attention he got as the brother of one of the fallen. He even congratulated himself with the honesty with which he admitted to this pleasure, reasoning that many others would not have possessed such self-knowledge.

Then he got involved with the Peace Pledge people and in November he'd given out white poppies at Belsize Park tube station to bowler-hatted commuters. Most of them avoided his eye; others shook their heads and pointed to the red poppies they already wore. When someone, usually a woman, dropped a coin in the collecting tin, he'd get a brief surge of satisfaction, but these moments were rare.

His parents withdrew into themselves after it happened. His father, a doctor, had become increasingly wrapped up in his work. Grief crushed his mother.

And now he'd met this gorgeous young man. Rob had drawn their bodies together and, it seemed to Louis in this moment of intense happiness, had invited him into his soul. The sense of connection with another human being overwhelmed him, and Louis decided this must mean he was in love.

"I expect you think that was very foolish of me," Louis said.

He was eating an apple I'd sliced and peeled for him. Apple skin upset his stomach, already painful enough from the illness.

"I was eighteen years old, and I'd never been with anyone before, boy or girl. Hardly touched anyone in that way." He stopped speaking, trying to remember. "In fact, yes, that's true. Boy's school you see, so no girls, and touching another boy like that in those days, well, you can imagine."

He paused, then continued. "Well, I suppose it did happen. I mean between boys, at school. But I was very shy. And very frightened too. Frightened of what was in me. Frightened of what might happen if I showed myself for what I was."

"You had good reason," I said, thinking of the times Louis had lived through. "But you really did love Rob, didn't you?"

"Well I certainly thought I did then."

He saw the look on my face.

"No, don't get me wrong. I adored him. But at that point I hardly knew him. I was inexperienced. That's the only way I can explain it."

He chewed some apple as he fell into thought again for a few moments.

"That first time was overwhelming, as if an electric current had suddenly passed through me. It blew a fuse."

"How do you mean?"

"My parents. You didn't know your grandmother did you? She was a Scot, a Presbyterian."

He was pointing to a photograph on the mantelpiece. It showed my grandmother before she married, a formal picture with her family, her four brothers like a row of stone statues standing behind their parents who stared unsmiling at the camera, as if made of flint. My grandmother and her sister sat on either side of them, all of them in their best Sunday clothes.

I hadn't known her, but I remembered grandfather. He'd seemed a kindly old soul. He used to get on his knees, slow and stiff, to show me how to fit together pieces of Meccano.

"They were very conservative. Not like Rob and his mother. As far as my parents were concerned sex between men was a terrible sin. I suppose I thought it was too, although of course I wanted to sin very badly. But it goes deep, that sort of upbringing. I was sure Rob must have been in love with me once we'd been together that first time. Can you believe it? But I couldn't explain it any other way. Why else would he give himself to me like that, risking everything, or so I thought?"

Louis was shaking his head at this memory. "Funny to think of me like that, having such ideas. I hadn't pieced it together, didn't realise it was possible for things to be different, even when Vita behaved the way she did, showing me she knew about Rob and didn't mind. I knew so little."

"Well…"

"You don't have to say anything. It was my parents who kept me so naïve. Rob always said it was their bourgeois morality. You remember how he used to talk? One of his favourite phrases: bourgeois morality. My poor parents. But, in a way, he was right. Christopher wouldn't put up with them."

"That's a shame," I said.

"Yes, it was. He refused Officer Training Corps at school, much to my father's disgust. Then he cranked it up, joined the Left Book Club, the communists, who then led him to Spain."

"What happened to the stone?" I asked.

"The stone? Oh, I see. That old thing. I must have it somewhere. His half was returned with the rest of his effects. Used to be in a glass jar over there."

Louis was pointing at the mantelpiece but there was nothing there, no jar, no stone. He continued. "He was sentimental you see. Two halves reunited. I suppose we will be soon, reunited that is."

I wanted to get Louis off the subject of his brother. The memory could still bring him down. I felt it too, the loss of this mysterious, glamorous uncle. His photographs showed so much life, so much energy, all cut short.

"What did they think of Rob?" I asked. "Your parents?"

Louis laughed. "I didn't tell them about him, not for a long time, at any rate. I can't imagine what they thought I was doing. I spent all my time over there. It was my second home."

CHAPTER 3

Louis was lying on a raised treatment couch in a small room at the back of Vita's house. The weak bulb of a table lamp cast shadows on the walls. A sweet aroma hung in the air.

She spoke: "Now lie back and I'll start with your head. Try not to wriggle too much. Breathe in and out, slow and deep."

An extraordinary sensation diffused down his neck as Vita used a metallic device to scrape the surface of his scalp in long stroking movements. She began at the crown and spread downwards towards his shoulders. The sensation made his eyes water and his body gave an involuntary shiver.

He heard her put down the device and her fingers passed over his forehead, making circular motions at first, then smoothing softly out towards the side of his head. Gradually she worked around to the area near his eyes, her thumbs pressing his cheekbone. The power of her hands was unexpected, and his temples throbbed with pain, although this dissipated as she made wider circles. His lower cheeks and lips came next, and she pushed and pinched them, pulling his upper, then his lower lip from side to side, hurting him again until he became used to the sensation.

After half an hour or so, in which she repeated the process three times, moving from scalp downwards and ending at his chin, she bent to kiss his forehead.

"Finished."

He sat up, feeling a remarkable lightness in his head. His face was different, swollen but somehow looser.

The thing she'd been using was shaped like a helmet, made up of ten curved metal wires with rounded ends. She'd been pulling it back and then pressing down again, pulsating the instrument to create the sensations that had entered his brain and sent shudders along his spine.

"Vita massaged my head the other day."

They were lying in the long grass on the slopes of Parliament Hill, Rob chin in hand, looking at Louis. People were nearby. If Rob had been a girl, he could have moved his body over hers, pressed her hands into the soft ground, looked down at her. The thought drifted through Louis' mind and he found the idea strangely exciting. But Rob had warned him about that sort of intimacy in public places.

"And I expect you loved it," Rob said, smiling. "Everyone does."

"As a matter of fact, I did. It hurt at first, but afterwards it felt wonderful."

Vita had suggested that she give him a head massage to help loosen his 'facial armour.' He could see if he liked it and, if he agreed to more, she'd use him to teach Rob.

"Just your head was it?" Rob asked.

"Yes, that was quite enough. Apparently she wants you to learn. I'll be your guinea pig."

"Ha, we'll see about that."

"I'm pleased you've given up that talk of joining the communists," Louis said.

"I don't know why you should care." Rob rolled over onto his back so his eyes looked up at the scudding clouds in the sky. "I didn't like them. They're fanatics."

They'd been wandering around the Heath extension that day. At one point Rob had pulled him into some bushes. A man glanced over at them and pretended not to notice, calling his dog to his side as he strode on, staring ahead and ignoring their giggles. After that they'd walked to Parliament Hill. It was late August and the weather was turning.

"What does Vita think about you?" Louis asked.

"What do you mean? I expect she thinks a lot of different things."

Rob's superior air annoyed Louis sometimes.

"You know what I'm talking about. When did she find out? Come on, don't pretend, you know what I'm saying."

Rob laughed. "I told you, she believes in free love. That applies to me too. I can do what I like."

Louis still wasn't sure if he believed this, even though Vita by then had given ample evidence that she knew Rob and Louis were lovers. Rob's easy acceptance of this state of affairs both surprised and intimidated Louis. Part of him even felt it wasn't the right way for a mother to behave, but he knew he couldn't say that to Rob without seeming ridiculous. His own parents would have had a fit if they'd known. But then, he reflected, Vita was an artist and an unmarried mother. She was bound to be unusual.

Vita's plan was put into action. Now on his visits, more often than not, he'd have a massage session in the dimly lit room, Vita at first demonstrating her techniques, then allowing Rob to copy them. Rob's fingers were nothing like as strong as Vita's, and his movements were uncertain. Vita encouraged her son to press and pull more vigorously, while Louis lay on the couch, his eyes closed, mostly enjoying the pummelling sensations.

After his head, the teaching progressed to his hands and arms, then his feet. He looked forward to the sessions, anticipating the delightful sense of lightness they produced throughout his body.

By now it was September and after the afternoon massage session Rob and he would go up to Rob's bedroom to make love. Was he imagining it, but was his pleasure in this becoming more intense? Rob said without doubt it was due to the loosening of his muscular armour.

"One day, we'll move on to a full body massage," he said with a laugh. "That'll send you through the roof."

He also noticed the mornings he spent at home were more productive. He was revising for his Cambridge entrance exams, hoping to be accepted to study modern languages. Science and maths had bored him at school and he'd failed them, but now he had a new energy for his studies. He'd go up to Cambridge in the autumn of 1939 and emerge in 1942, ready to take on the world. He'd become a translator.

Around that time, he experienced unusual dreams.

In one, he was hiding in thick jungle vegetation when he saw a brightly coloured tiger padding through the undergrowth. Colourful fruits hung on green foliage around the magnificent, powerful beast. Then, he was the tiger, hunting for food. At first, he thought he was creeping up on some unsuspecting animal prey, an innocent doe perhaps, feeding on grass in a clearing, unaware of her approaching death. Then, he - a tiger - was eating the fruit himself, dipping his snout into a huge orange melon, savouring the sweet wet flesh.

When he told Rob they were in bed together. He laughed as Rob's hand slid over him.

His brother appeared in another dream. Louis felt a mixture of pleasure at Christopher's company and curiosity about where he'd been for so long. Christopher was evasive, but finally admitted he'd been in South America. He offered to give Louis his half of the stone, but Louis wouldn't take it, just wanting to know why he'd left, why he'd gone away, whether he'd now be staying. He always woke from it feeling cheated.

He shared this dream with Rob too, and they talked more about his brother. He told Rob about the times they'd spent roaming the Heath. He and Christopher kept their treasure in the hollow tree near Kenwood, wedged into the crevices, matchboxes containing string, rubber bands, dried beetles, an ancient postage stamp with Queen Victoria's head. Rob wondered if anything was still there, so they went to look, finding an empty matchbox. Louis wasn't sure if it was one of theirs. He couldn't quite believe it would have lasted that long. But Rob said it must have been and took it home to put it in his cabinet of curiosities.

When he was ten, his parents had given them bows and arrows with real, steel-tipped heads. Now, he realised how dangerous these were but, uncharacteristically, their parents had simply told the boys to 'be careful where you point them.' They had aimed at targets on trees at first, but then took pot shots at birds. One of Christopher's arrows pierced a pigeon as it sat on a branch, right through its breast. It fell to the ground, its wings flapping as its life drained away. The boys ran to it and watched its dying struggle. After that, they stopped aiming at wildlife.

The Heath ponds were the venue for sailing model boats which their father made in his workshop in the cellar, complete with canvas sails. He showed them how to judge the wind for direction and speed. Then they set the rudder so the boats could reach the other side without mishap, scudding along in the breeze. If there was a sudden gust, or the setting was wrong, the sailboat would flip onto its side. They'd have to wait for the boat to drift to the edge. It was dangerous and not allowed by the park authorities, to wade into the water, but there were times when they did it anyway. Nine times out of ten the boats flipped over, until Christopher got the hang of it and could send his across safely as Louis waited, excited, on the other side.

"How did you learn of his death?" Rob asked, propped up by some luxurious pillows on his bed.

Louis gave a deep sigh.

He'd been home from school for half term and had gone to bed early. The repeated ringing of the doorbell woke him, so he dragged himself out of sleep, wondering why his parents weren't answering. Two policemen at the front door asked him who he was. He said his name and they looked briefly at each other. Was his father there? Confused he went to look, finding him in his bedroom, fully clothed, lying on top of the bed, asleep. Anxiety mounted inside him.

His father sat up violently with a shocked look on his face. His staring eyes tried to focus on Louis.

"What's happening, Dad?"

"Chris, it's Chris."

Louis didn't hear him. "There are policemen at the door."

"We had a telegram."

"What do you mean?"

His father bent forward and he began to cry, something Louis had never seen.

"What's happened to Chris?"

Raising up his tearful head his father told him.

"He's listed as missing in action. They say Chris is dead. Blown apart."

Louis couldn't remember what happened or what he'd said. A wave of horror came over him and it was impossible to think or feel.

At one point his father said "Are you all right?" He heard this as if from a distance; it was a crazy thing to say. No, he wasn't all right. A bomb had gone off in his head and he was collapsing inside.

His father had to go to the men at the door, leaving Louis on his own. Was he all right? No, he was not all right. He'd never be all right, never.

His father accompanied the policemen to fetch his mother, who they'd found wandering in the street in what the policemen called 'a distressed state'. She was outside the hospital, crying incoherently, imagining the body of her son was there.

Rob listened to this tale in silence and then stroked Louis' hair. Louis wasn't sobbing or weeping, just telling Rob the facts of how he'd learned the news, relieved to have told the story to someone else for the first time.

In the days and weeks after Christopher's death he had experienced an intense anguish driving something sharp and hard into his chest. Despite being together with his parents, each of them was locked into a lonely grief, wandering around the house, bumping into each other, tears in their eyes, unable to say anything, unable to give or receive comfort. They were beyond comfort. Nothing could help because nothing could be changed.

Christopher's body was never found, although he'd left a satchel behind in his lodgings which was returned to them weeks later. Louis thought there would never be a time that he'd stop thinking about him. Someone, a friend of the family, tried to help by saying these things pass, time heals. But Louis angrily pushed the advice away. He never wanted to let go of Christopher.

But these feelings reduced over time. When he met Rob it had been more than a year since the death. By then the grief had become something that surfaced when things reminded him of Christopher - when he walked near the boating pond or once, when he found an old arrow under his bed.

But his mother couldn't recover. She convinced herself that Christopher existed on another plane. She began attending a spiritualist church in Willesden, trying to get in touch with her dead son.

After a while Louis ran out of things to tell Rob about Christopher, but he still wanted to know more. He rolled over in the bed, propping himself up on his elbow.

"Tell me more about what he was like when you were children."

This was difficult for Louis and he hesitated, sat up and looked past Rob at a mirror on the wall.

"My brother was very loveable when he was small," he began. "The photographs of him show it. He was tubbier than me. You've seen photos of me haven't you?"

Rob nodded, smiling. "You were sweet."

"Well, not everyone agreed with that. I was thin. My ears stuck out. Christopher, though, was a little prince. I don't think you've seen any of him have you? There's one taken when he was two years old, pursing his lips and looking around as if he's on a throne. He knew he was irresistible. And I always knew he was my parents' favourite."

"Oh, come on, that's not true."

"You've got no brothers or sisters. You don't know. They sent me away to school."

"And so?"

"And so they kept him at home, didn't they? I had a hell of a time, but did they listen?"

"Did you tell them?"

"Of course."

"What did they say?"

"I don't remember," Louis said, "and we should go to sleep now. I've got exams to think about."

He lay down, turning his face to the wall, pretending to sleep while Rob breathed steadily beside him.

But Louis did remember. He remembered how, aged eight, at the end of a summer holiday, he had begged his mother not to send him back to school. Why couldn't he stay at home like Christopher? He liked playing with his brother. He missed him when he was away at school.

Christopher had asthma, his mother said, so he needed

to be at home. Boarding school would do Louis good. He needed to learn how to get on with other boys, stand up for himself. Didn't he like games? Didn't he understand the sacrifices they were making for him? It wasn't a cheap option, she'd have him know.

But his eight-year-old self couldn't see it that way. They allowed Christopher to stay at home but he was sent away. The unfairness of it enraged him. He screamed at his mother, red in the face, tears running down his cheeks. She called his father who took him upstairs and locked him in his room to calm down. In a fury, he kicked at the door until a crack appeared. Then he smashed his model boat onto the floor, stamped on it to break the mast. When he saw what he'd done to this most precious toy he flung himself, sobbing onto the bed.

And the next day, they sent him back to school.

He remembered these things, but was also ashamed of them. So he stopped telling Rob any more. Even the little that he had revealed was more than he had ever confessed to any other person.

CHAPTER 4

On an afternoon in early October Louis put his coat on and marched along Pond Street and across the Heath to Vita and Rob's place. Leaves had fallen and were blowing into the pool below the house. Going in through the garden gate he found Vita there, a pair of shears in her hands. Rob was out, she said, but he'd be back soon.

Vita's approach to gardening was almost wholly destructive. She saw it as a war between herself and the shrubs and climbing plants that threatened to overwhelm the beds and fencing around the edge of the garden. She cut, chopped and hacked away at the growth of ivy and honeysuckle that wrapped itself around every trellis or convenient post. If she managed to clear a patch of earth, she'd insert some newcomer - a primrose stolen from the Heath, a geranium seedling donated by a neighbour, or a poppy, her favourite - and wait confidently for it to die. She regarded the earth as poisonous. Plants that did well, despite this imagined toxicity, could become her friends and allies, fellow survivors, and she sang the praises of even the most straggling, nondescript new vegetable growth as long as it showed signs of life, until it became large and invasive, at which point she slew it without mercy.

He watched her for a while, her brown arms bare, hot with effort.

"Make me a cup of tea, darling?" she asked, stepping back from the flowerbed. "I'm all muddy."

"Of course."

"And make one for Wilhelm won't you? I'm trying to get him used to our British customs."

Louis looked behind them and saw a thickset, middle-aged man, seated in a deckchair near the door of the conservatory who waved to them and smiled as Vita pointed to him. He had a book on his lap and stood as Louis approached.

"Wilhelm Reich," he said, holding out a thick and hairy hand to grip Louis firmly.

"Louis Nicholson, sir. I'm a friend of Robert's."

"Yes, yes, I know about you." Reich had a heavy German accent. His face was wide and red, with a broad nose and fleshy lips.

"I'll bring you a cup of tea," Louis said.

Reich frowned at this and lowered his voice, leaning towards Louis. "If you can get for me a coffee, small like this," he held up his fingers to indicate the size, "I will be a friend for your life young man. The English tea they feed me - I cannot tolerate so much grey liquid," and he gave a little, conspiratorial laugh.

"I'll see if I can find something," Louis said and went indoors to the kitchen where he saw that Rob had come back and was already making drinks. He crept up and put his arms around him, making him laugh.

"I'll spill the tea!"

Louis kissed his neck, taking in Rob's fresh, warm smell.

"Who is that man?"

"Oh, that's Willi. He's here for a few days meeting people." He paused for a moment. "He's in trouble."

"Your father? He sounds German."

"No, no, no. Vienna."

Louis said he needed to make coffee for the visitor and Rob showed him where it was.

"He likes it small and strong," he said. "It's the way they drink it over there."

The coffee, which Louis brought to him in a small sherry glass, delighted Reich, and Rob and Louis settled down to their tea on either side of him on the steps as Vita approached them.

"I see you've got what you wanted," she said, eyeing the coffee in Willi's large, hairy hand. "Always the way," she added, smiling.

Reich grunted. "I must have some reward after the time I have had."

"Willi is having a miserable time," Vita explained. "We should all look after him," and she placed her hand on his head as he sat, stroking him. Reich leaned his head into her like a cat taking its comfort. His lips brushed her palm.

"I will have to leave, you know," Reich said, prompting Vita to withdraw from him, pain on her face.

"I must. I cannot stay here. They have driven me from pillar to post in Scandinavia. Now it's the Britischer's turn to kick at me."

"But surely you can be with me a few weeks longer?" Vita said.

Louis noticed Rob looking with alarm at his mother.

"Are you on holiday here then?" Louis asked, instantly feeling stupid.

Reich jumped up, spilling what was left of his coffee. "Ha!" he cried, and strode off to the other end of the garden where he stood, looking at the shattered remains of plant life Vita had left strewn over the grass. Louis found this reaction hard to understand. Was the man angry with him?

Vita was on the verge of tears. "He's only just arrived."

"He'll go to America then," Rob said.

"They say he has unresolved hostility. He's as gentle as a lamb! If only they knew him, who he really is, what he's really like."

Vita was in the grip of distress and Louis could only half understand what it was all about. He felt he was intruding, but he was reluctant to return home to his cold bedroom and books.

"I'll go up to your room Rob," he said, hoping Rob would take the hint and come with him. But when Rob moved to his mother's side, putting his arms around her waist, he left them and went upstairs alone to lie on the bed.

When Rob joined him later, he told him Willi was a psycho-analyst in Vienna where Vita had met him. He was part of a circle of artists and intellectuals who had lived through the Great War and its immediate aftermath and then tried to revive the cultural and intellectual life of the city. Vita had gone to him as a young woman, seeking treatment for a nervous condition which he had diagnosed as related to sexual repression. He treated her with body psychotherapy, similar to the massage therapy he and Vita had been practising on Louis.

"Did it help her?" Louis asked.

"Well, she thinks so. That's what she tells me. But then she fell in love with him."

Falling in love with your analyst: Louis had heard of that from his father, who'd been scathing about psycho-analysis. Completely unscientific, potty, he'd said. This comment had been prompted by press reports of Sigmund Freud's arrival in Hampstead from Vienna. Freud had taken up residence not far from Louis' house. He was said to be very ill.

"And they had another son," Rob blurted out.

"What?"

"My brother. In Vienna. Vita and Willi's child. I've never met him and I don't suppose I ever will. He's called Kurt and she had to give him away."

"That must have been terrible."

"When she was expecting, Willi tried to make her get rid of him, but she refused. She hoped Willi would leave his wife if she had the baby, but he wouldn't. She wasn't in a position to look after him alone so Willi arranged for Kurt to be taken in by his sister, so his aunt brought him up. Vita never got over it."

Rob paused for a while.

"I was a replacement. As soon as she returned to England, when Willi visited, she made sure she got herself pregnant with me. And this time she refused. She wouldn't give me up."

Louis couldn't fathom this. What was Reich doing at Vita's place? How could she put up with him?

"She's hooked on him still," Rob said. "I don't try to understand it. He's an unusual man."

Reich was in England on a visa, meeting English psycho-analysts to see if he could gain their support for a move to England. He'd been living somewhere in Denmark or Sweden, Rob thought, but he couldn't stay there anymore. Nor could he go back to Austria.

"So he's a Jew then," Louis said. The papers had run stories on what had happened in Vienna after the Nazis had marched in earlier that year. Children had been arriving in London alone, their parents putting them on trains to save them.

"Yes, but they won't have him here. That's what he was saying in the garden. I'm not sure why. Perhaps he's not very popular with the others, but he's always been nice to me. Anyway, he'll have to join his wife now - she's in America already."

During the night, Louis lay awake next to Rob who slept, his smooth, naked back touching his side. He didn't often stay the night there, but his parents were away, so wouldn't notice his absence. He'd been looking forward to it. Vita, as ever, had been entirely supportive of the idea.

His mind turned over the story of Vita and Wilhelm Reich. They were oddly matched. Reich was built like a bull next to Vita's lanky frame.

He heard a wooden sound, knocking. At first it sounded as if someone was tapping on the bedroom door. Then he heard grunts and groans; it was a couple making love, Vita and Willi, in the bedroom next door. The banging and knocking increased in volume and speed and Rob stirred beside him. The older couple were oblivious to the noise they were making. Louis went to the door and then into the corridor, as the movements became more energetic and the noise louder, Vita's cries of pleasure were accompanied by more grunting and a man's moaning voice. As Vita's cries peaked and then subsided, Reich gave a heroic shout of release. It occurred to Louis it was loud enough to wake the neighbours.

He felt Rob at his side, standing naked in the corridor.

"Come back to bed," he urged. "They've been doing that every night." He continued muttering through a bleary-eyed sleep haze as Louis followed him back into the room. "Keep waking me up."

They returned to bed and to the renewed silence of the house at night. Rob snuggled next to him and reached over to his groin, but Louis gently brushed his hand aside. He found the violence of the man's orgasmic explosion disturbing. Sex, for him, should be more private. Reich and Vita were treating it as a public performance. And Reich was married too. Despite the moral overhaul he'd received at the hands of Vita and Rob, he found himself disturbed at the adulterous relationship. It was something he associated with divorce cases in the newspapers.

The next morning, drinking tea in bed with Rob, he decided to find out more.

"So Willi has a wife has he?" he began.

"Yes," Rob said. "She's in America. I told you."

"And he's sleeping with Vita. Doesn't his wife mind?"

Rob rolled his eyes at this. "And your point is?"

"Well..."

"Well what?"

"You know. You must know. Its – "

"Immoral? Is that what you think? I don't believe you."

Rob got out of the bed and stood over him, a dressing gown wrapped around him.

"It's not that simple," Louis said, "I'm not condemning her. It's just that, well, I would have thought it might be rather hurtful to his wife, don't you agree?"

Rob laughed at this. "Anyone who gets married to a man like Willi knows what they've got coming to them."

Louis found this difficult to accept. It was all very well to follow your appetites, but there was a reason for the marriage vows.

"I suppose I was taught to believe sex and marriage go together," he said. "Old fashioned, I know."

"What do you imagine you've been doing with me?" Rob was laughing again. "We're not married."

Louis laughed back as the absurdity of his position dawned on him. He persuaded Rob to get back into bed with him. But he was still uneasy about Willi and Vita; what they were doing wasn't right. Rob's comparison wasn't a fair one: neither of them was married to someone else. But it was better not to say this because he'd only get laughed at again.

Later that morning he set off home, leaving Rob, Vita and Willi still in bed. There was one revision day left before he sat the Cambridge exams.

CHAPTER 5

Cambridge always felt colder than London, a freezing wind blowing in from the North Sea, across the fens and flat countryside to penetrate his clothes and chill his skin. He faced the interview panel with apprehension, three grey men in brown and beige.

They asked him about school, the cadets, his sporting achievements. He was glad they failed to ask him why he wasn't following the family tradition and applying for medicine. He could only have said he didn't want to be like his father.

Instead, they grilled him on his knowledge of Latin. He'd taken a written test earlier in the day, translating passages into and out of the dead language. Now the one called Professor MacDonald spoke to him in Latin, leaning his leather-patched elbows on the table, his fingertips together, asking him questions about the Punic Wars. As MacDonald spoke, Louis noticed a smile passing across the lips of the man on the left, a long-faced lecturer in German.

He answered as best he could. The night before, awake in the narrow bed in the halls where the candidates were billeted, he'd imagined himself giving the wrong answers, spoiling his chances of admission, stepping into the adventure of a new and different life. He thought of Rob and the sense of freedom he gave him. Then he looked at the cold walls of the room in the moonlight, the curtain flapping as the chill draught entered through the gaps around the window.

As Louis rambled on in his best schoolboy Latin, Professor MacDonald held up his hand to silence him. Louis had done enough. The panel smiled on him, a weak, collective smile, like a flickering candle lighting the way in a dark tunnel.

That same evening, as he was returning to his room, a young man's tall, bony frame emerged naked and wet from a communal bathroom, a tiny towel held in front of him as he prepared to run along the freezing corridor. Louis recognised him.

"Peter!"

The young man paused, recognising Louis.

"Haven't you got a proper towel?" Louis asked.

"It's all I've bloody well got. Hang on a minute will you. Which room is yours?"

He ran as Louis shouted out the number of his room. Peter Dashwood had been impossibly tall as a child, six feet at the age of thirteen. Louis had noticed popular boys were often tall, but at school neither he nor Dashwood had been part of the magic circle of youths who excelled at sport, became prefects, boasted of female conquests in the holidays. Dashwood's height was of the wrong sort, gangly, an angular and awkward towering above others, mildly freakish.

A few minutes later a clothed Dashwood appeared at the door to Louis' room, his hair still damp, a bottle of whisky in his hand.

"Got a glass?" he said with a smile.

Louis fetched one from the sink in the corner. They sat

opposite each other on the wooden, institutional chairs.

"It's good to see you," Louis said, sipping the liquid which made him want to retch, "What are you here for?"

"You don't have to drink it."

"No, it's all right. I like it." Louis took another sip, forcing himself to smile.

"I'm going for modern languages," Dashwood said. "Clare College. Spent the last couple of years in Father's firm. Hated it. The old man. Under his watchful gaze and all that. Time for a change I said to him. Took it in his stride."

"Clare? That's where I'm going, modern languages too. We'll be together."

"Jolly good. Nicholson minor and poor old Peter Dashwood, holed up in this windy tomb for three years. What a prospect." He knocked back the rest of his drink and poured himself another.

"Been interviewed then?" he asked.

"Yes, it was -"

"Me too. Thought I'd look around tomorrow. Never been here before," he said, waving his drink so it spilled on the carpet. "What do you think of it?"

Louis shrugged. "Old. Everything's old."

"Haven't you got a family connection going on here," Dashwood asked with a grin. "I remember you saying…"

"Oh, yes. My father, his brother, my brother - they all went to Clare."

"That should see you sorted out then," Dashwood said. "I've got nothing like that. Just a yokel from the sticks." He paused, then added, "I forgot to say. Sorry to hear about Chris. He was a fine fellow and a great friend."

Louis nodded and shifted uncomfortably on the hard seat. Dashwood had been an unlikely member of Christopher's circle at school, after they'd been put in a shared study. Dashwood's star had then risen by association. Despite himself, Louis felt intimidated by this memory.

He broke the silence: "How did it go for you today?"

"Not bad. I've got the gift of the gab. Two bluestockings and some ancient cove running the show. I reckon the ladies fell for me."

"I didn't know there were women on the staff."

"Oh, languages: they get people in from Girton to cover the teaching. It's not a high priority."

Louis recalled the smell of pipe smoke that had permeated his interview room that afternoon. He'd thought university would be an entirely masculine affair, like school.

"I went for languages to give me the best chance," Dashwood explained. "My parents will be cock-a-hoop if I get in."

He poured himself another drink while Louis sipped cautiously at his, noticing the round scar on the back of Dashwood's hand. He'd seen how this had happened. Dashwood was two years older than him, but had invited him into the study he shared with Christopher, a great honour for a younger boy. They'd been drinking and Dashwood had taken a cigarette and stubbed it out on the back of his hand, staring at Louis all the time. He must have been demonstrating how he could withstand pain. Louis had been both scared and impressed.

Louis had a second drink while watching his friend finish the bottle and stagger off to bed. Another memory from his early school days came back to him. He and Dashwood had been play fighting on the grass circle in front of the school. Dashwood, taller and stronger, pretended he knew judo, got him onto the ground and fell on him to pin him down with his hard, heavy body. But he'd jumped on Dashwood's back, where he held on tight despite the older boy's energetic attempts to shake him off. Then, to Louis' great surprise, Dashwood had collapsed and started crying. Louis let go and tried to ask what the matter was, but was brushed off. Red in the face with the tears running down his cheeks, Dashwood had run off, leaving Louis wondering what had happened. Even now Louis couldn't explain it.

The next morning the two of them, after a hearty breakfast of a greasy quality that appeared not to offend Dashwood, despite an evident hangover, went to see what was in the FitzWilliam. "Ought to get ourselves some culture while we're up here," Dashwood muttered through a bleary haze.

They wandered around the top floor of the museum, shifting their gaze from murky pictures of ancient battles to dull portraits of grandees from the past, looking out at them from heavy frames.

Then, downstairs to a ceramics exhibition where a somewhat larger crowd shuffled around peering into the glass cases. There was a temporary exhibition by a modern ceramicist in one long room, which Louis found to be a welcome change after the heavily decorated vases, goblets and plates in other rooms. Here, there were white vases and plates projecting a delicate beauty. Nearby were labels with long explanations written by the artist.

"Bloody pansy," Dashwood said on reading one of these. "Pretentious rubbish."

A middle-aged couple nearby overheard this, the man wincing and glancing at the two young men. He wore a dark hat and heavy black overcoat in spite of the heat coming from the iron radiators around the walls. His wife bent over under her coat, a shopping bag hanging from her hand.

"I can't stand it when artists go on about their own work, 'specially this sort of nonsense," Dashwood said in a loud voice, pointing at the label which Louis bent to examine.

Before he could read it the middle-aged man said something in German to his wife, to which Dashwood instantly responded, taking a step towards him, much to the man's surprise. More words in German were exchanged, but these only further inflamed Dashwood who grabbed the man's collar.

Louis rushed forward to take his friend's shoulder. "Hey, come on Peter, let's calm it down shall we?"

But Dashwood shrugged him off, spinning round, and in doing so knocked violently against a cabinet, so that a tall vase teetered, fell and, to Louis' horror, broke apart.

Dashwood must still have been drunk from the night before. A museum attendant in uniform jumped up from his seat and ran across the room. The German couple slipped away as other staff gathered at the scene, one of them holding Dashwood by the arm to escort him to the front of the building, Louis following behind with more attendants keeping an eye on him.

A grey-haired woman emerged from a back office to deal with the miscreants. She sent an attendant to fetch the broken exhibit, which he brought to the desk wrapped in cloth, laying the pieces out on the counter.

"Do you realise there was only one of those? A unique piece?" the woman said, picking up a fragment and shaking it at them. "What did you think you were doing, brawling in the gallery?"

"It was an accident," Louis said.

"George here says you were arguing, fighting. What did you think you were doing?" She wanted their names and addresses, which they gave. When she saw they were not from Cambridge, she demanded an explanation for their presence in the town, which they also gave.

"I should call the police. There's a case of criminal damage here. You know that, don't you?"

Louis nodded. Dashwood looked ready to object but Louis signalled to him to keep his mouth shut. They needed to take the pain.

"I could tell your parents. Tell the college authorities."

Dashwood stayed quiet, apparently chastened, leaving Louis to do the talking. Louis sensed the woman was bluffing about the police. This wasn't a Ming vase. The potter could make another one. But her threat to tell the colleges worried him. That could sabotage their chances.

"Look," he said, "we can pay for this I'm sure. I promise you, it was an accident. Please."

"Yes," Dashwood said, finally. "It was my fault. How much do you suppose this artist chappie wants for it?" He stretched out for a fragment of vase. An attendant pulled his arm back before he could touch it.

"I must ask Mr Burns what he'd wish to charge. But that's not the point. The museum has suffered too. You cannot just replace exhibits like this at the drop of a hat."

At this, Dashwood gave further reassurances that he was sure they'd be able to compensate the museum for any loss. Louis knew Dashwood's father was wealthy. In due course the woman, using her social antennae to pick up the necessary messages about Dashwood's family tree, sensed this too, and allowed herself to be persuaded that it was just an unfortunate accident. After giving their names and addresses, they left and went to a nearby tea shop on King's Parade to recover. Their trains left that afternoon.

"What did that fellow say to you, the German I mean?" Louis asked as they went over the events, which had shaken him up far more than his companion, who tucked into his slice of lemon cake with gusto.

"Oh, he was a bloody Jew. Aesthete type."

"But what did he say?"

"I don't know." Dashwood's face was growing redder in the heat of the small tea room. "He annoyed me, that's all. Those people, they think they know everything. Get's my goat up."

"A Jew?"

"Yes, skulking around in the warmth I expect. A lot of them over here, clogging up the galleries!" Dashwood laughed at what he clearly felt was a joke.

Only a month or two ago Chamberlain had signed the agreement with Germany in Munich. Louis and Rob had debated this hotly, Rob accusing him of changing his tune. Why was he so against the agreement, which would bring peace, when he'd wanted the International Brigades out of Spain? How could he want to fight Fascism now, and get his country into another war? They'd argued late into the night, sitting in Vita's conservatory after she'd gone to bed. Then the perfume of the flowers and warm wet earth, the night stars above them through the glass, had cast their magic spell and they went up to Rob's bedroom to make love and fall asleep in each others' arms.

Peter Dashwood finished his cake.

"I've had enough of this place," he announced. "There's an early train. Need to have a word with the old man. I'm sure he'll stump up."

"How is he these days?" Louis remembered Dashwood's father - a large man with a flamboyant moustache, dressed in country tweeds.

"All right. Looking forward to the next war. Hoping his only son will follow in the family tradition. Charge headlong into the guns and so on."

"I don't think it'll come to that."

"That's what I said to him. He harrumphed and whacked the table with a stick. I tell you, he's looking forward to it. But it won't be him doing the bloody fighting this time, it'll be me, damn it all."

With that, he wished Louis luck, slapped a ten shilling note onto the table and strode off.

Two weeks later Louis received a letter from Clare offering him a place to read modern languages, starting in October 1939. His parents were delighted. Then Dashwood wrote to say he'd got a place too

.

CHAPTER 6

Louis had a spell in the Royal Free last week. I got a call from Age UK to say he'd pressed his alarm button. This happens sometimes - he presses it by mistake when he's out in the garden. He can't hear the phone, so he can't tell them it's a false alarm.

But this time I found him on the kitchen floor. He'd been trying to lift a kettle full of boiling water. He didn't know what had thrown him off balance but he couldn't get up - his shoulder hurt, he said, so the ambulance came and they kept him in for the night. Nothing was broken, but he's frail and they wanted to keep an eye on him. There will come a day when worse things happen.

Last night I discussed the situation with Karen and suggested Louis could come and live with us. I knew what her reaction would be, but felt it worth a try. We were in the kitchen and I'd just finished clearing up after the meal. Time for a glass of wine was her first reaction and she went over to the fridge, but then she turned around and faced me. She said Louis wouldn't like it. He'd been born in the Hampstead house and she was sure he'd not want to leave it. In our place his bed would be in the living room. He'd hate that. We'd hate it. Karen stopped herself from saying we'd end up hating him too.

I know how she feels about Louis, however much she claims otherwise. When Rob was alive it wasn't so obvious because she and Rob got along so well, so she'd be over there, both of them talking nineteen to the dozen, Louis hanging around in the background with one of those Sunday afternoon smiles on his face. It made him seem part of it even when he was miles away. With Rob gone, Karen has hardly set foot in the place. I'm Louis' main supporter now, glad to repay him for the love he gave me when I was small.

Still, Karen chips away at me. Says I ought to get to the bottom of things, lance the boil. God knows, Karen's had to put up with a lot from me over the years, and she knows the cause lies in my childhood. Where else would it be? I can't argue the case like Karen does. She's a therapist and she's got all the language and ideas to back her up.

I should stay over with Louis more often. Really, I should.

Don't get me wrong. Karen's a wonderful person and I love her dearly. She's been right about so many things. She says I need to ask Louis about Ellie. Her name's the only thing I know, and that's only because I caught Rob in an unguarded moment. They never wanted to talk about her, so there's still that barrier now: a no-no topic. An affair, I've always imagined. I must have been a product of an affair between her and Louis. But I don't really know and Karen says it's my last chance to find out more. What happened to her? Did she ever try to see me? Is she still alive?

I've got to get over this idea that I'm still a child when I'm with Louis, too scared to ask in case it upsets him. Karen's right, I really must grasp the nettle.

When the hospital discharged Louis he refused my offer of a wheelchair to get him home, saying he could walk perfectly well. This turned out to be true as long as he leaned on me and moved at a snail's pace. Luckily the house is only a couple of hundred yards from the hospital. I've no idea why they sent an ambulance to fetch him when he'd fallen. It must be standard procedure.

We creaked along the road to the house, with him on my arm, and I sat him down in the living room with a cup of tea. We don't always sit there. Often we're in the kitchen or upstairs in his bedroom, but that day it felt like the right place. I pulled the curtains open. It's always been too dark in that house.

"I want to tell you," he said, his breath coming in gasps, "keep telling you. After Cambridge. Everything. It was so difficult after that, so hard. Not so much time left now."

He was making a huge effort, even to get those words out.

"Stop. Please stop. You don't have to - "

"This hospital thing has brought it home, made me realise. You've got to know. Everything..."

He gripped his mug so tight that tea spilled over the tartan blanket I'd put over his knees.

"No need to launch into that now Dad. You've just got out. You need a rest."

He grunted, a reluctant assent, and put his mug on the little table, exhaling as he leaned back.

I found that table in a charity shop. It has a picture on it, a Lichtenstein pop-art image of a drowning woman printed on the wood. 'I don't care! I'd rather sink than call Rob for help!' she says, disappearing beneath the waves, a tear in her eye. Louis saw it in my flat and laughed his head off, said it was wonderful, so I gave it to him. His mug now covers her face.

"You can tell me about your work if you want," I said. "Those foreign trips. Where did you go?"

A frozen look came over him, his eyelids lowered and he looked sideways at me.

"Can't discuss that," he said. I hardly caught the words.

I can see I was being disingenuous, raising that as if it was a neutral topic.

"I suppose I thought, well, you know - you might be able to talk now. Finally I mean…"

"Before I die?"

I gave up.

"Yes, Dad. Before you die. I want to know. All those years, all the times you were away."

"Can't." His voice was a whisper. "Official Secrets Act. Once you sign it, you just can't. Not even supposed to tell you I signed it. Sorry."

"How can it still matter?"

He picked up his mug and stared into his tea for a long time, his breathing calmer. Finally, he spoke.

"It matters."

Children usually leave it too late to ask their parents about important things. It's easier to rub along day by day, without confronting the uncomfortable issues. Louis had always liked to control the flow of information about his work, even when Rob was alive. If you asked him, he spoke in generalities. You were supposed to pick up on the meaning behind the words. He'd deflect the issue by saying, with a touch of humour in his voice, that he was paid to swap stories with other people. If I wanted to learn more - about his work, about the things Karen wanted me to raise with him - I'd have to go at his pace, listen hard and not press him until he was ready.

"I can help you make sense of things."

He was speaking again, his voice stronger now.

"What things?"

"Your upbringing. It wasn't perfect. I know it's caused you, well -"

"Nobody's -"

He held up his hand to stop me. "Nobody's perfect, you're going to say. Nobody's childhood is perfect. Is that it? I couldn't agree more. But you can try to understand

45

the imperfection. You can try to see it from our point of view."

"Yours?"

"Me and Rob. You were our darling boy. We loved you so much, you know that don't you?"

I did know. I leaned forward, put my arm around him and kissed his cheek.

He continued. "With my own mother and father I never had that chance. She died too soon, and my father wasn't much of a talker. I'm sure I held back too. There was so much I could have asked them."

He pointed to the cupboard. "Get the photos. I want us to look at them."

I brought him the blue album.

"That's Christopher." He was pointing to the image of a laughing young man, a wide brimmed hat on his head. Uncle Christopher looks happy in photos, smiling, confident. Louis always said he was popular at school. Then later, when he was home from Cambridge, he was out a lot and there were women friends.

We turned to the earlier photographs, tiny black and white images taken on beaches, or on Hampstead Heath, or in the garden. There was one with Christopher astride a tricycle, aged three or four, a big grin on his face. Another showed the two of them holding hands, Louis with his big brother. They were in dungarees, Christopher with a stick that had something dark at its tip.

"He used to get mud and squeeze it in a ball onto the end of the stick," Louis said, chuckling. "He'd whip the stick so the mud whizzed through the air."

This is one of my father's stories, endlessly repeated. The boys would hide behind a wall and use the sticks to lob their projectiles at the flats on the edge of the park, trying to hit the windows. Not to break them, just to get a mud splat stuck onto them, then run for it, laughing.

"I was jealous of him," Louis said.

I looked up at him. His eyes were far away in his

wrinkled face.

"He was so successful, so popular, and I…" He stopped.

The pictures of Louis differ from Christopher's. In the early days, both have the sunny, happy look of little boys together, but while Christopher kept that throughout his life, photographs of Louis show a more anxious child with a worried expression. His rare smiles are tentative, a boy pleading to be liked.

"He was ashamed of me," Louis said.

"No Dad, I'm sure…"

I knew Christopher's asthma had kept him at home, at day school, until he was twelve and was finally fit enough to join Louis at boarding school. By then, Louis had been there three years.

"You need to listen to this," he said, gripping the arms of the chair. "It's true. He was ashamed of me. I'm quite sure about that." He paused, his shoulders tensing, "And I hated him for it."

"How could you know?"

"That's easy. I was seven when they first sent me away. Can you imagine that? Seven. The homesickness was terrible. I used to hear these little boys crying in bed in the dormitory, denying it in the morning, trying to become men. Except I didn't. I wouldn't. I just refused."

"What?"

"Trying to be a little man. Something in me rebelled against it. I missed home and I didn't see why I should fucking well shut up about it. And they sensed it, they all sensed it."

"The other boys you mean?"

"Yes, them. And the masters. The matrons. Everyone. They could all see Louis bloody Nicholson was different. They heard his angry bawling and decided he was an unhappy little weed, so they all thought they'd kick him in. Saw it as a sign of weakness."

"Boys can be so cruel," I said, my hand on his arm.

"They were wrong. It was strength of will that made me different, not weakness. I've had time to think about it and I realise now. I could see through all that rubbish about being a man, even at that age. But there's only so much kicking you can take."

He'd clenched his fists, his face twisted in pain. It was terrible to see an old man, a lifetime of experience and authority behind him, my protector when I was a child, my father who I loved and respected above all other men, so gripped by these excruciating memories.

"And I wasn't strong, you see. Physically that is. So games and all that. Fucking hopeless. Your reputation sticks to you like glue."

"But Christopher joined you there didn't he? That's what you always told me. When his asthma got better. It must have been nice for you - to have your brother there."

Louis snorted and an ugly sneer came across his face. I'd never seen him so gripped by such harsh, angular emotions.

"Christopher? Yes, Christopher arrived all right, and instantly saw what was going on. Not that it was much of a secret at home. That first year I used to beg my mother not to send me back. I told you didn't I? He must have heard those scenes I had with her. Snotty nosed crying, all that blubbing. So when he appeared he knew exactly what to do."

"Didn't he support you?"

Louis looked into my face and laughed.

"Support? You're joking. He ran a mile, cut me dead, passed me in the corridor with his friends around him without a glance of recognition. There was no chance of him getting involved with Nicholson Minor. He regarded our brotherhood as strictly a home affair. He had his own agenda in that place and he pursued it ruthlessly."

I'd attended a day school on Haverstock Hill. Like any child, I understood the cruelty children mete out to one another. But I'd had my home as a refuge, Rob's studio, the warm kitchen, Louis' study and my bedroom.

"Naturally, in the holidays school got forgotten," Louis continued. "I was ashamed of myself. Can you believe it? Ashamed. Thought it was all my fault. So he knew I wouldn't dare to bare my soul to him and make him feel guilty. We'd go out on the Heath together, just us two boys, the way we'd always done. Those were the times when I loved him and I believe he loved me. But school was another world, a nasty dream."

"You've always said Christopher was popular, had a lot of friends."

"Yes, he did. And later it was girls. He was out all the time then. Once, I must have been fourteen or so, I came across him on a bench on the Heath. He was, oh, about seventeen years old. A girl had her arms wrapped around him and he was kissing her. They didn't see me. I was consumed with envy."

"Was that Ruth Crossland?"

"Ah, you remember me telling you about her. Yes, it was. It was her brother you know - "

"Alec Crossland."

"That's right, the poet. He was at Cambridge with Christopher - introduced him to the Communist party."

This part of the story I'd heard before. How my uncle Christopher came to join the International Brigades and die a hero's death. The good Christopher story, not this bad one.

"He came to supper one day. Announced to our parents: 'Crossland says I should go. He's a poet. Poets have a special connection with the truth.' My parents, bless them, couldn't think of a response to that. Such pretentious rubbish he spouted."

"But people don't go to war just because a poet -"

"He joined up for a mixture of reasons. It was one in the eye for our father, who didn't approve of socialism. Then there was the adventure. But his ideals were only skin deep. He thought the war would be like an exciting rugger match, but with guns."

Louis looked up at me, a bitter look on his face that was unlike him.

"Christopher wanted to be admired," he spat out.

CHAPTER 7

Louis sensed that Vita was distracted. Her thumbs dug into his back in awkward places, producing little sparks of pain. He was used to discomfort during their sessions, but normally got a rush of pleasurable release as she found a knot of muscle and loosened it. This was different, her fingers stabbing into his neck now. He must try to relax to let Vita explore his muscles, but she was making it hard. And he was thinking of the coming war.

It was inevitable. Everyone said so, the younger people hot with excitement and fear. In the older generation there was much hand wringing about repeating the horrors of the last war.

Vita turned him over and began on his chest and arms, her hands uncomfortable on his skin. Usually she spoke as she worked on him, but now she was silent, lips pursed with the effort, air hissing through her nose. He smelled alcohol on her breath.

He'd no idea what would happen about Cambridge. The government had published a list of reserved occupations earlier in the year and it didn't include modern language students. His father, somewhat pointedly, observed that medical students were exempt from military service. No doubt the thought of Louis going to war, after Christopher's death, was too much to contemplate. Typically, though, this was never stated in so many words.

Vita's hand slid downwards, beyond his stomach, and she gave out a strange breathy sound as she moved it around beneath his underpants.

"Hey, no!" he said, sitting up and grabbing her wrist.

Vita started back, lifting her hands away in a sudden apologetic movement.

"What did you think you were doing?"

Vita said nothing, closing her eyes and holding her arms up as if surrendering. Then she shook her head from side to side and, to Louis' surprise, started sobbing.

"I'm sorry," she said through the tears. "I don't know how that happened, why I -"

"Christ, Vita. You can't do that kind of thing with me."

Before more was said she exited the room, leaving him to put on his clothes. His face was flushed and hands shook trying to button up his shirt, so he gave up and ran out in search of Rob.

He found him in the conservatory, sitting in the wicker chair on which his mother had been when Louis first came to the house, reading a letter. Louis stood in front of Rob, demanding his attention, until he looked up. He couldn't bring himself to describe what had happened.

"I don't want any more massage from her," he said, reliving the touch of Vita's alien hand on his private parts. "What's the matter with her?"

"That's my mother for you," Rob said, apparently unmoved.

Louis was furious. Couldn't Rob have asked what Vita had done to upset him?

"What kind of explanation is that?"

Rob gave him a serene smile. "I don't have to explain her."

Then he handed Louis the letter he'd been reading.

"It arrived this morning and upset her."

It was hard for Louis to focus, but Rob continued to hold out the letter without saying any more. He buttoned up his shirt, tucked it in and, though still thoroughly unhappy, managed to read the letter.

It had been sent from Vienna the week before and was written in perfect English. It was from Rob's aunt, Wilhelm's sister Esther, concerning her plans to leave the city for America. The situation was desperate, she wrote. The family had only just obtained visas, had been subjected to humiliations and delays. They'd arrive in New York with nothing.

"This is terrible," Louis said, reading an account of brown shirt thugs who invaded their apartment in April, smashing furniture and terrifying the younger children.

"They have money. It's awful, but they'll get out. Read the bit there. That's what upset Vita."

It concerned Kurt, Vita's son, now twenty-one years old. The boy had always been difficult, Esther wrote.

"Difficult?" Louis said. "Why does she say that?"

"How would I know? I've never met them."

"But you know about them, don't you? Vita must have -"

"Oh yes, she's talked about it. She regrets giving him to Esther, that's what she's always said. Willi forced the issue though."

"How could he force her to give up her own son?"

Rob took the letter back. He seemed annoyed at Louis' questions.

"You don't know my father. He can be very persuasive. And she had no money in those days."

Rob seemed to believe anything his blessed mother did was all right.

"That's no reason," Louis said. "If people don't look after their own children you wonder why they have them in the first place. Didn't she love her son? Children should -"

"For god's sake calm down. Why don't you ask her yourself? She doesn't tell me everything."

Louis still couldn't understand Rob's attitude but took the letter roughly out of his hands.

Esther wrote that Kurt counted as a mischling, the son of a Jewish father and a British, non-Jewish mother, putting him in a different racial category. Now he was refusing to come with them, asking why he should share their fate if he wasn't one of them. How could he say such a cruel thing, Esther wrote? She suspected him of Nazi sympathies. He was young, rebellious, angry, but it was a crazy decision. They had a visa for him. He'd have a new life in America. Didn't he realise what was in store for people like him? Did he imagine they'd go easy on him because of an Aryan mother? Esther wrote that he rebuffed these arguments with the simple statement "I'm not a Jew."

The letter gave a brutal account of the family's troubles and Louis realised how insulated from the real world he had been over the last few months, living in a beautiful erotic dream, featuring only him and Rob, as if the troubled world outside lay behind a screen.

Rob spoke. "She wants Vita to persuade him, but it's hopeless. She hasn't seen him since he was a baby. Why would he listen to her?"

"Why's he so bolshy with them?"

"I suppose he's angry. I don't know why, but he takes it out on Esther. Vita's written him a letter offering him a place in England if he wants."

Louis recalled the tense atmosphere with which Vita had begun the massage session.

"I don't see how that excuses her," he said. "She touched me. What was she thinking about?"

"What do you mean, touched you?"

"I mean she touched me. Put her hand on..." he was pointing.

At this moment Rob actually laughed and Louis was

again furious.

"She's going through a troubled time," Rob said, trying to control his laughter. "She's upset about Willi leaving, she's stopped painting and spends all her time crying instead. She's jealous too."

"Jealous of who?"

"Of us, of course, you idiot." Rob paused, watching his expression. "Oh, don't ask me to explain my mother. Ask her."

But Louis made no approach to Vita. Something was going on there that he didn't understand and, if he was honest, he didn't really want to understand. There'd be no more massage sessions that was for sure. It was Rob he needed, not this strange, troubled mother of his. And Rob, he then believed, was a much more straightforward character.

CHAPTER 8

"I couldn't have been more wrong," Louis said.

I was sitting on his bed at home, holding a cup of tea for him. He was too weak to hold it himself - it burned his fingers - so I was giving him sips, bringing it to his mouth while his hands closed around mine to help me.

I can't tell you how important this was to me afterwards, this feeling of having been with him in this way, helping him with the simple physical actions that we all usually take for granted. Just being with him, really. I wonder if Karen would see the value in this, and in leaving things open, unresolved. Therapy is all about carving out a singular story about the people you love, putting that into words, getting it out there. That way you exorcise any demons. The singular story that makes sense of everything, satisfies the urge to explain, pins you down to the truth.

Karen exercised more gentle pressure last night, wondering when I was going to get the answers I need. I'm ashamed to say I snapped at her, said I hadn't even put the questions to him yet, didn't know if I ever would, in fact. I'd go at his pace and we'd see what came up. She backed off, said Louis was my father; it was up to me.

The tea was finished and I put the cup down. Louis was too tired to say any more. He lay back and I drew a blanket over him.

There was an old leather trunk, bound with wooden bands, that he kept against the wall opposite his bed. It was the sort on which owners used to put labels from passenger ships and airlines, carriage companies and hotels, advertising their travels to exotic destinations. There was one label from Panama, another from Cuba. He and Rob had gone there after the war, before the revolution.

"Look inside that while I have a doze," he said.

As Louis slept I obeyed, opening the trunk to find a mass of photographs, papers, ring binder files and notebooks of various sorts. There was no order to them. The photographs were of all stages of my life with Rob and Louis, blurry Instamatic snaps in the '60s, later on replaced with larger formats, pictures of us in restaurants, on holiday, swimming, with family friends. The older ones showed earlier generations, ladies in long dresses in the garden, stiff portraits of unsmiling children in Edwardian costume, holding still for the camera.

I saw a picture of a dark haired woman sitting against a whitewashed wall, next to four young children, smiling in the sunshine. On the back was a scrawl: Me and my brats! Ellie. The image was indistinct - taken with a cheap camera - and the faces were far away. So there were more children after me. My brothers and sisters. I didn't even know their names. For a long time I looked at the image, trying to extract something more, yearning to know these children.

Then I decided I didn't feel anything. I put it in my jacket pocket. I'd show it to Karen later.

There was a studio photograph of Christopher, taken in profile. He had fairer hair than Louis, his face handsome, his eyes burning bright as they gazed into the distance. It was a romantic portrait, like that of a Hollywood film star.

Then I noticed a typescript of four or five pages bound with a treasury tag, a carbon copy in blue, and read its title, 'A Lazarus beside Me', the author's name being typed in capital letters: 'by VITA GILL.' It was dated 1946 and began 'One evening in the Spring of 1937...'

This looked interesting. I glanced over at Louis who was snoring gently in bed, closed the trunk quietly and left the room. Downstairs I poured myself tea and settled down to read.

It was an extraordinary document. The author wrote that she had gone to an open meeting of the Sex Education Society, an offshoot of the World League for Sexual Reform at the Grafton Galleries in London. She announced, early in the article that she was 'attached to' the world famous Wilhelm Reich, whose writings and clinical work in sexology and psycho-analysis would no doubt be known to readers.

Vita described the room as being full of 'extraordinary', 'distinguished' and 'famous' people who were 'progressively minded' and keen to hear the star speaker, a Dr Harry Benjamin from New York, introduced by Dr Norman Haire, the well-known sexologist with a thriving practice in Harley Street.

Initially wrapped up in thoughts about Haire and the speaker, she had then noticed a presence a few seats behind her: a distinguished, tall man with untidy white hair and a large ring on the little finger of his left hand. As the lecture started he caught her eye and smiled.

Benjamin spoke of his work as an endocrinologist in New York, focusing on the rationale for a surgical operation designed to 'rejuvenate' both men and women. As I read on I realised this was a euphemistic term for restoration of sexual potency. In men it involved a partial vasectomy which Benjamin claimed increased the flow of hormones controlling the sex drive.

For Vita and the assembled company, sexuality was something much grander than the desire for physical release, so 'rejuvenation' was no euphemism. They equated the sex drive with youthfulness and the energetic, vigorous pursuit of life in all its richness, releasing the wellsprings of creativity. It was a philosophy of life, and Benjamin and Dr Haire were offering to unlock urges whose expression Vita ardently desired.

Benjamin expounded his critical views on the marriage vows.

"Sex," he said, "is natural and pleasurable. It is an animal appetite, no different from the desire for food. Certainly," he continued, "I will not deny that in humans it is the basis for many long-standing attachments, but there are occasions when it is perfectly reasonable to treat it as a temporary personal refreshment."

There were gasps and titters from the audience, suppressed by the disapproving glances of more sophisticated listeners.

"Masturbation, while harmless, is a poor substitute for sexual encounters between consenting parties from which both may expect considerable benefit. This fact requires greater recognition. All available scientific evidence indicates that the human animal, unlike gibbons, wolves, beavers, barn owls, bald eagles and, as I am sure you will be aware, schistosoma mansoni worms, is naturally polygamous."

A ripple of laughter passed though the audience.

"And why not admit, no celebrate, the fact that many people are attracted to the idea of congress with members of their own sex? You will know of the great unhappiness caused by keeping men and women ignorant of this fact of life and the many neurotic problems which arise from this sexual repression. In this modern world, people deserve better."

Benjamin then provided further details of his work in New York, rejuvenating the more enlightened members of the population of that city.

Haire had invited Vita and several other guests to a

party after the lecture at his rooms in Harley Street, to which she intended to drive. Her car was one of the last to leave after a variety of more luxurious and chauffeur-driven vehicles had whisked the rest of the guests away. Vita had an old Singer whose battery often went flat, obliging her now to crank the starting handle to get it going, while dressed incongruously in an evening gown. As she did so, the distinguished gentleman who had sat nearby came up to her and wondered if she could give him a lift, to which she agreed.

When he revealed his identity as they drove along Regent Street, she was bowled over: the famous poet, William Butler Yeats. She wrote:

If he had said his name was Michael and declared himself to be an archangel it could not have had a more catastrophic effect on me. 'What?' I exclaimed, 'Yeats! The Irish poet! My God - well, my God... well... Yeats... well...'

She was so flustered, she lost her sense of direction and they got to the party late. Buttonholed by an artist acquaintance as soon as she stepped across the threshold of the crowded flat, she was separated from Yeats. Haire had laid on what he described as 'experimental cocktails', alcohol free mixtures of vegetable juice in a variety of colours. They were not popular. Fortunately, a more conventional punch bowl was available and Vita scooped a glassful before it all went. Her artist friend monopolised her, pressing Vita so that her back was against a wall, the friend excited about the new exhibition of Henry Moore's work at the Warren Gallery. Vita was distracted, her eyes searching for Yeats, who was nowhere to be seen.

Later, the crowd thinned out and she saw him again, standing with Haire at the mantelpiece, apparently saying his farewells. She went to offer him another lift in her car. This time it was to the Athenaeum, where he was staying. After a drive through dark, rainy streets, they parked outside the club and talked.

He asked her about herself and she explained she was an artist, though not very distinguished. She'd always wanted to write, but lacked the courage to do so. He told her she must try. This typescript must have been one of her attempts. She wrote that his interest in her was both flattering and overwhelming.

Sitting in the passenger seat, the ring on his hand flashed in the light of the street lamp as his hands moved to animate his words. He was speaking enthusiastically of Haire and Benjamin's work, its importance in transforming the present-day moral stranglehold over sexuality. Then he revealed that he'd had the rejuvenation operation himself. It had been one of the most profound experiences of his life, he said, and had led to a renewal of his energies as a poet. The implication, of course, was that the great man had also renewed his more animal passions and wished to express them with help from Vita.

She filled her writing with superlatives. Yeats' greatness lay in his simplicity, she wrote, there was no trace of patronage in his attitude towards her. 'Fame had left him unspoilt' she pointed out. He exuded directness, bold sincerity and friendliness to her, Vita, a mere mortal and a woman. It was this last 'and a woman' that I found particularly shocking. How could she imagine that a woman had less right to his attention than a man? Vita was recording her abasement to Yeats, dazzled by his reputation, subjugating herself. It contradicted my image of her as confident, bohemian and liberated.

At any rate, they didn't sleep together. She made the error of talking about Willi and that instantly cooled Yeats' ardour. He announced the Athenaeum did not allow women on the premises after midnight. He promised to write to her when he next came to London but, she records, he never did. Later, she went to another of Haire's parties where he remonstrated with her for 'turning down the greatest literary man of the age.'

This telling-off must have mortified her as she then

makes a number of disparaging remarks about Haire. It seems Vita's espousal of free love and her dismissal of marriage as a bourgeois institution, required that she be available for sex with charismatic men who asked her for it. Yet something had held her back when she met Yeats. Her attachment to Willi - who showed no such loyalty to her and exploited her sexual availability (a pattern he repeated with many women, as the biographical accounts of him show) - was profound, and placed her in a hopeless position.

I put the typescript back in the trunk and went over to the window, looking down at the garden. For a long time I stood there, Louis' steady breathing behind me the only sound in the room. I suppose Vita would have been a grandmother to me. And Kurt, her son, was my uncle. She'd been forced to leave him behind in Vienna, to give him to another family. It must have been terrible for her.

Then I wondered what she would have felt about Rob and Louis' long life together, whether she had known about me, what she knew about my mother.

That evening I returned home filled with determination. The photograph of Ellie was burning a hole in my pocket. I wanted Karen's advice on how to steer Louis towards the subject. Why did this fear grip me whenever I thought of confronting him? I could say: 'Tell me more about Ellie.' How easy that sounded. But I'd had the same feelings before, about other things hard to face. Karen would help. She'd know.

I found her in the living room of our flat, a book in her lap. It was Melanie Klein's Love, Guilt and Reparation, a book she never tires of re-reading. Pools of light came from the lamps standing on the floor. I like that effect - shadows cast around the room as the evening gathers. She frowned from the concentrated effort she was putting into her reading.

"You can surface now," I said.

She gave me a lovely smile and put the book face down next to her on the sofa.

"You look like you need a glass of wine."

She nodded, yawned and stretched. "I've done enough for the evening. Wine's in the fridge."

I came back with the glasses filled and sat opposite her. We sipped and looked silently at each other until, finally, she laughed.

"Oh, come on then. Tell me what happened with Louis today."

Karen isn't my therapist, you realise. But sometimes it's hard to know where the boundaries are. I joke about it with friends, saying I've been in therapy with her for ages, but I'm still hoping for a cure.

"He was tired this afternoon. He slept, and I dug around in an old trunk. All kinds of papers, photographs I hadn't seen."

I told her about Vita's document, her meeting with Yeats, my shock at realising how much she was in thrall to the men in her life.

Karen listened, waiting for more.

"And I found this," I said, showing her the photograph.

She stared at it for a while then turned it over to read the inscription.

"Your mother."

"Yes."

"And her children."

I nodded.

"About whom you didn't know."

I nodded again.

"You need to find out about the children."

"I had no idea. They never told me a thing about her. The children. They'd be my, my…"

"Brothers and sisters."

Karen came over, sat next to me and held my hand in hers.

"Are you going to ask him?"

I released her hand and leaned forward, holding my head as I looked at the carpet.

"What is it that stops you, my darling?" Karen stroked the back of my head. "There has to be something."

It was pure dread, irrational, a blockage. I've had some dreams where snapping monsters have chased me, signs that deeper things are trying to emerge. I could feel those monsters now.

But I shook my head. I couldn't express it.

We both looked at the photograph. There were four small children, sitting on the grass next to Ellie. One was a thin girl serious and glum, another a little boy with a happy smile and eyes screwed up against the sunlight.

"I bet nobody ever took them away," I said.

"What do you mean?"

"When they took me away. I've told you."

"I don't know, have you?"

It was when I was tiny. I was sure I'd told Karen, but then again, perhaps not. The episode felt like a dream. Was that all it was?

I'm not sure how long I was away. Rob had brought me to hospital, worried about something wrong with me. I remember the smiling nurses, the brightness of the white walls.

But then I can't recall any more. Only that someone took me away from Louis and Rob, my two fathers who loved me, and that it was too long before I was given back.

CHAPTER 9

Frank Lemaire turned up in Louis' life shortly after the incident with Vita's massage. He and Rob were walking on the Heath when they saw a wavy-haired young man coming up the path from Parliament Hill. Rob bounded forwards and shook his hand enthusiastically.

"Frankie!" he exclaimed, pulling him towards Louis. "This is Frank Lemaire. Frank, this is Louis Nicholson."

They shook hands, eyeing each other suspiciously. Frank wore a flat cap and looked older than Louis. He'd rolled up his shirt sleeves to show muscular arms and a large bag hung over his shoulder.

"Nice to meet you," Louis said, receiving nothing but a sly smile in reply.

"What're you doing here Frankie?" Rob asked.

The newcomer shrugged to indicate his bag. "Selling these down the tube station. If you ask me, it's a mug's game, but you gotta do yer bit I s'pose."

"What's that?" Louis asked.

Rob fished a copy of the Daily Worker out of Frank's bag and offered it to him. "Here, you can buy one."

Louis looked at the headline: JAPAN PROVOKES NEW CRISIS IN FAR EAST.

"Are you still in Stepney?" Rob asked.

Frank hesitated and before he could answer Rob turned to Louis, "I met up with Frank again at a Party meeting."

"I'm two days a week with the mineworkers now," Frank said. "Stepney wasn't my cup of tea and they reckoned I'd be more useful to them."

"Oh, what are you doing for them?" Rob asked.

"Research mostly." He didn't expand.

They were walking down the hill together now, Rob in the middle, his hands on the shoulders of each of them as they walked beside him. Rob was animated, cheerful, said they must have tea at the café ("A cuppa" Frank said, "just the ticket") and fired questions at Frank about his work at the mineworkers' federation. It seemed to involve writing a lot of dull reports.

"Frank was at Cable Street," Rob said.

Louis imagined Frank running through the narrow streets of Whitechapel in the midst of the battle, the shouting, curses, blows and danger. Police, Blackshirts, cobblestones flying. Louis had been a school boy. Christopher had heard about it from his Party friends and told Louis stories about the heroic anti-fascist demonstrators and their clashes with police and Mosley's thugs.

"Yep," Frank said with a shrug, "our famous victory."

"So what were you doing in Stepney?" Louis asked.

"Organiser I was," Frank said, again declining to expand. "What about you mate, what're you up to?"

Louis said he wasn't doing much that summer, just waiting for his Cambridge course to start. He felt embarrassed to have so little to report and Frank didn't make it any easier. He had a way of both smiling and sneering when Louis spoke.

At the café they sat outside and Rob got them poppy seed cake and a pot of tea. Frank gobbled down his cake and slurped his tea, making loud sighing noises ("Bin on me feet all day"). He dragged another chair over to rest his legs, looking round suspiciously at the other customers - nannies with prams and middle-aged ladies.

Inevitably, talk turned to politics. They agreed the Pope's welcome for Spanish fascists disgusted them. The Japanese aggression in China was appalling though far away. The League of Nations was hopeless. The King and Queen, who'd been touring Canada and the USA, were robots; popular adulation for them was almost as bad as the worship of the Germans for Hitler, or the Italians for Mussolini. They found common ground in these subjects.

Bombs had been exploding in post offices earlier that week and people had been injured. The action, as he called it, was welcomed by Frank, who said the Irish had a lot to be pissed off about. He said anyone who thought different was just a sentimental bourgeois.

That word again, Louis thought, bourgeois this, bourgeois that.

Then Rob told Frank about Louis having a brother who'd fought with the International Brigades. Louis felt uncomfortable as Christopher was mentioned. Even worse, he realised it made him feel like crying.

Frank listened with no expression, then turned to Louis. "What's the matter mate? Cat got your tongue?"

Louis pushed his plate away and sat back. He couldn't believe how hostile Frank was towards him. Any more and he'd crack up and look a fool, a weakling. He made a supreme effort at self-control and asked at random, "So where did you go to school?"

Even as the words emerged, he realised it sounded stupid, what maiden aunts said to youngsters. But it was all he could think of. To his surprise, Frank was taken aback, blushing and stammering.

"With Robbie here. I went to school with Robbie."

Rob put his hand on Frank's arm.

"He was at Monkton Hill with me. Weren't you Frank?"

"You must have been a bit older then," Louis said.

"Two or three years, yes."

Rob intervened. "Age didn't make much difference at school. We didn't worry about it. Not like the place you went to."

"It did, and it didn't," Frank said.

"How do you mean?" Louis asked.

"We had meetings, discussed everything, made rules together, together with the teachers, old ones and little ones, all of us. No-one cared how old you were."

"Democracy in action!" Louis said, laughing. "Not like the Party."

"No, I s'pose not. Actually, I'm leaving the Party."

Frank said he'd had enough. He'd been a member for years now, ever since school. Stepney had made him realise he wasn't cut out to be an organiser. He was sick of selling the paper at tube stations, pointless hours standing around as commuters brushed past him. His sales figures were hopeless. The research job was okay, but it made him realise it was time for him to get an education, a real academic education, he said, one that could make him useful to people who had power. Social policy, they taught it at the LSE. He'd go there.

As he spoke, Louis noticed he'd lost his Cockney accent.

"And I've joined the Peace Pledge lot," Frank said. "I'm a pacifist. No more wars, I say."

"Oh, I tried them out too," Louis said.

That led them into another argument. Why had he left the Peace Pledge, Frank wanted to know, weren't they good enough for him? Louis defended himself as well as he could, said he too was sick of standing at the tube station trying to dish out Peace News, but Frank wouldn't let it go. He was clearly someone who moved from one fanatical attachment to another. He declaimed there was no way he'd ever fight in an imperialist war. It was an argument Louis knew came straight out of the pages of the Daily Worker and he pointed this out, saying the

Comintern was hardly the best place to look for arguments justifying world peace. Frank asked Louis if he was a fucking warmonger then? Who did he think betrayed Austria? Who had sold Czechoslovakia out? Why fight for that bloodsucking bastard Chamberlain?

Rob fell silent. The foul language prompted the ladies at other tables to cast looks of disapproval at them and Rob said it was time to go. Frank headed for Kentish Town, leaving them to climb back up the hill towards Vita's house.

"What do you see in an annoying fellow like that?" Louis asked, still smarting from the skirmishes at the café.

"Oh don't say that. He was a good friend at school, and after - "

"He doesn't know what the hell he thinks. First, he's crazy for the Communists, then its peace at all costs. Doesn't he realise what's happening in the world? And why the fake accent and that stupid rolled-up shirt business?"

Louis had taken off his jacket as he walked up the hill, but his shirt sleeves were firmly buttoned down around his wrists.

Rob conceded the point, explaining that Frank, whose real name was Francois, because his mother was French, had had a tough time in Stepney. He'd come out of Monkton Hill and immediately got involved in the Party. But he was unsuited to the job, so put on the flat cap, called himself Frank and the rest of it because he wanted to fit in.

"Then there was Cable Street," he added.

"How do you mean? Surely that boosted his ruddy credentials?"

"No, he made a mess of it. Not his fault, but he took the blame. The District Committee told him they should go to Trafalgar Square for something else. It was Frank's job to get them there. But the Stepney lot refused and went to Cable Street instead and you know what happened there."

"Why's that his fault?"

"Cable Street's been the best thing for the Party since… I don't know what. They doubled their numbers within a month. And Frank was labelled as the man who wanted to stop them going there. He never got over it."

"Poor bloody Frankie."

Rob ignored the sarcasm in Louis' voice. "The Committee didn't back him up and then the members wouldn't do anything he said. No wonder he's disappointed."

When they got to Vita's house, they found her sitting on the lawn surrounded by a huge pile of garden litter, broken branches, hedge cuttings and tangled stems of honeysuckle she'd been cutting back when they left for their walk. The disordered mess had overwhelmed her, and she'd been crying. Vita had been doing this more since the letter arrived, saying she'd never forgive herself for abandoned Kurt. If only she'd brought him back with her to England instead of giving him up. Why had she listened to Willi?

Rob went to her, put his arms around his mother's shoulders. Things had been awkward with Vita since the massage incident and Rob was going to have his hands full. Louis said he'd go back to his parents' place. But as he walked away it was his bruising encounter with Frank which played on his mind.

CHAPTER 10

On the day war was declared everything went wrong for Louis.

Dashwood was staying with him. He'd come to London from 'the sticks,' as he put it, a small town in Lincolnshire, where he rattled about in his parents' house with nothing to do. A trip to the city was more than welcome.

Technically, they were still waiting to go up to Cambridge but the uncertainties of the preceding months, and the fact that last spring many of their friends were obliged to complete military training, made them doubtful about what the future held.

That morning, like the rest of the nation, they'd listened to the prime minister's radio announcement. Louis' mother brought a handkerchief to her eyes when the broadcast had finished and looked over to her husband, but his father had left the room. The atmosphere was tense and unhappy.

"Well, that's blown it for Cambridge then," Dashwood said, leaning back with a sigh, ignoring the tearful woman on the sofa.

Before Louis could reply a siren started up, the air raid warning.

"Good god, they haven't wasted much time!" Louis' father said, coming into the room and urging them to go to the shelter they'd built in the garden.

It was a false alarm. As they crossed the lawn the all clear sounded and they returned to the house through the French windows. It was the first of many such scares that autumn.

Back in the house, Louis saw his father put his arm around his wife and whisper a few words into her ear. His mother, handkerchief still pressed to her lips, moved closer to him. They were shaken by the announcement of war, despite having expected it since Poland.

Louis said he ought to see how Rob and Vita were.

"Do you think you should?" his mother asked, "what about aeroplanes? It could be dangerous."

Christopher had been killed by German planes bombing the republican positions at Jarama. Louis imagined the explosion, blowing bodies into the air. Parts of bodies.

"Don't worry," he said. "It was a false alarm. Nothing will happen this soon. I'll give you a ring when I get there."

His mother reluctantly let him go and Louis left with Dashwood, heading for the Heath. Before they climbed the path to Vita's house they went over to Parliament Hill to get a view of London, barrage balloons floating like silver fish over the city, gleaming in the sunshine against a blue sky. Bulldozers had thrown up earthworks in the past few weeks as the prospect of war grew closer. An anti-aircraft gun was planned for the hill.

As they looked out, Louis did something that he later came to regret. Part of him wanted to impress Dashwood, no doubt because he'd been a friend of his brother's so had acquired something of Christopher's aura. But at a deeper level, he knew that he longed to talk about the great transformation he'd been through as a result of meeting Rob.

"I've been seeing Ruth," he blurted out, and then there was no going back.

"Ruth?"

"Ruth Crossland? Not the Ruth Crossland who - "

"Yes, the girl Chris was seeing. She got in touch and, well, we've been seeing each other."

Dashwood shook his head and clapped Louis on the back. "You old devil."

Louis experienced something close to panic, but couldn't stop himself from saying more.

"I think she loves me and, well, I think -"

Dashwood laughed, not allowing Louis to finish. They turned away from the view and began the climb up to the Vale of Health. Then Dashwood started his questions

"So, what's she like?"

"What do you mean, what's she like?"

"Come on Lulu," his companion said, using Louis' school nickname, which he hated, "give us the low down on your floozy won't you? You wouldn't deny that to an old pal who's only got your best interests at heart?"

"She's a nice girl. You'd like her. And she's not a floozy."

But Dashwood wouldn't let up. "You always were a sensitive soul weren't you?" he said, smiling as he shoved at Louis' shoulder, sending him off the path. "But come on, don't leave me in suspense. What's she like?"

"What do you mean?" Louis asked again, feeling increasingly uncomfortable with the lies he was spinning.

"You know. Is she a peach? Is she tasty? I bet she is."

Dashwood's flushed, grinning face turned to look at Louis, who stopped and faced him.

"She's a nice girl. I said so didn't I?"

"That doesn't sound like much fun. Poor old you." Dashwood made a face of pretended disappointment. "Haven't you, you know, done it yet?"

"Don't be such a bloody schoolboy Peter."

There were boys at school eager to boast of their fledgling sexual experiences. The young women they'd bragged about were usually other boys' sisters who guarded their virginity with moral padlocks and thick layers of underwear. One boy boasted of a successful visit to a prostitute, but no-one had been sure whether to believe him. Chris's relationship with Ruth Crossland had started just after he left school but he'd made sure most of his school friends heard about it. Louis calculated Dashwood, though older than Louis, was probably still a virgin.

Louis looked over at the woods surrounding the women's bathing pond, remembering his first time there with Rob.

"You don't understand Peter. I love her," he said, and then again, "I really do love her."

As he said this, he experienced a surge of emotion, realising the truth of it: he was in love. This is what it was like.

"Yes," Dashwood said, "but what form does this adoration take, that's what I want to know. These arty girls can be, you know…"

Louis' regret for his lie overcame him.

"Come on, let's go," he said. "We don't want to get caught in another aerial bombardment do we?"

Dashwood laughed at this, and they strode on.

There was a bonfire in the garden and Vita was in her gardening clothes, throwing branches and sticks onto the blaze as the two of them approached. She turned to greet them as they came through the gate, her shining face peppered with ash from the fire, dark curls of hair loosened by her efforts and blowing into her face.

"Hello Louis. Got to get this burned before it's dark. Come and help!"

Louis started towards a pile of brushwood.

"Who's your friend?" she said, looking Dashwood up and down.

Dashwood stood firm at this inspection, was introduced and then got to work helping with the fire. They dragged branches over from a far corner of the garden and threw them onto the burning pile. It was mid-afternoon, still light. The blackout meant the fire would have to burn down by the evening or they could get into trouble.

"Important to get it done now," Vita said, panting as she heaved a branch into the flames. The fire was hot.

"Where's Rob?" Louis called above the crackling flames.

"Inside somewhere," came the reply, just as Rob emerged smiling with a tray of glasses and a jug of lemonade.

"I thought you might want a drink," he said, setting it down on a white ironwork table.

As they each took a glass, Louis saw behind Rob the unwelcome figure of Frank Lemaire, who came out of the house with a drink in his hand.

"Helping wreck the garden are we?" Frank said, sauntering down the steps. "The Germans'll be 'appy."

"Where's your shelter?" Dashwood asked Rob.

"We haven't got one. Vita didn't think it necessary. Who'd drop bombs on Hampstead Heath?"

"I'm not sure their aim's that good; I'd be worried if I was you." It was Frank, continuing with his cockney display.

They sat on the grass watching the blaze, Vita behind them in a chair. Rob was between Dashwood and Frank Lemaire, with Louis out to one side. He'd shied away when Rob had put his arm around him with Dashwood watching.

They talked of the war, Chamberlain's announcement, the false alarm.

"What are you boys going to do now?" Vita asked, light

from the flames showing her with a solemn look.

"I'll be joining up," Dashwood said. "My father was in the last one and he'll expect it. Can't get out of it, anyway. With luck it'll be over by Christmas."

"You're a fool," Frank said. "Why fight for the capitalists?"

"Ruddy hell," Dashwood said. "Are you a Red?"

"It's an imperialist war. I'm not going near it."

"Well that's an original point of view, I'll say that for you," Dashwood replied, standing up and swigging the rest of his drink.

"It's obvious," Frank said, "bloody obvious to anyone who's got any sense."

Louis expected Dashwood to go on the attack. His friend came from a military family, his father having been an artillery captain in the last war, returning from the Western Front with a row of medals. But Dashwood reached over to the lemonade jug, poured himself another drink and said nothing.

Louis looked at Frank. "What are you going to do then? They'll call you up anyway,"

"They did. And I refused to go."

"But they'll stick you in jail!" Louis said, reflecting that he actually wouldn't much care if Frank got put away. "What happened when you refused?"

"Oh, it was all right. There's a lot of us now. The bloke at the recruitment office wasn't very impressed, but I stuck to my guns. You've got to show the bullies you're ready to stand up to them."

Dashwood spluttered into his drink. "Why not stand up to Hitler? He's a bully."

Frank ignored this.

Rob spoke: "No, come on Frankie, what happened?"

"He gave me a lecture on the usual rubbish, fighting for King and Country, white feather, lily livered, all that. A real sergeant major type. But I told him I knew my rights: you don't have to fight if you don't want to."

"You'll be shot," Louis said, although he had no real knowledge of what happened in such cases.

"You've got a lot to learn," Frank replied. "What are you going to do?"

"I haven't heard anything. I was hoping to go up to Cambridge next month."

"Well that's no good now," Dashwood said. "We'll be sent off to kill the Hun!" and he gave a bloodthirsty laugh.

Vita got up and went into the house. Rob gave Louis a worried look, mouthed "Kurt" silently to him and followed his mother. Louis realised Kurt might be on the opposite side: one of the Huns.

Further talk between the young men seemed pointless, so they knocked back their drinks and went to clear up scraps of leaf litter and smouldering pieces of wood strewn around the bonfire, throwing them into the centre where the heap of glowing ashes sparked them into brief flame. Dusk was drawing in and Louis remembered he said he'd call his mother, so he went indoors, passing Rob and Vita who were talking quietly in the living room, Rob's hand on his mother's knee.

Later, they all sat round the embers of the fire eating cheese sandwiches and drinking wine Vita had brought up from the cellar. Vita talked about Kurt, saying she didn't know what would happen to him, or what the future held for them all. They hadn't lived through the last war like she had. She'd seen Vienna in the 1920s, old soldiers begging on the streets, the children in rags.

Dashwood was more subdued now, listening carefully to Vita, asking her questions about her time there. This sensitivity was something Louis hadn't seen in his friend before and he felt suddenly very fond of him. If only he could be that way more often.

After a while, Louis noticed Rob and Frank Lemaire were no longer by the fire. He experienced a pang of anxiety and irritation and went to discover where they were. Going through the conservatory he made his way through the downstairs rooms and found them in the kitchen. Rob was leaning back on the kitchen table with Frank pressing against him, Frank's hand between Rob's legs. They were kissing each other passionately.

"What are you doing?" Louis shouted, striding over to Frank and pulling him by the shoulder, away from Rob.

Frank turned.

"What do you think you're fucking doing!"

"What do you think I'm doing? Get off me." Frank shoved Louis, so he staggered backwards and banged up against a chair.

Rob said nothing, but stood to pull his clothing straight. Louis felt a surge of anger and he pushed Frank back, at which Frank advanced on him and tried to punch him, striking the edge of his shoulder. They locked arms, Frank gripping Louis' wrist, Louis's other arm desperately trying to fend off another blow. Frank was much stronger than him, but he heaved hard to push him back.

Suddenly he felt an immense pain in the centre of his face and he fell onto the floor, blood streaming down his chin and onto his shirt. Frank had brought his forehead onto the bridge of his nose with force.

"There," Frank said, panting, "didn't expect that did yer, you little shit."

By this time, the others were inside. Vita went to Rob who stood cowering and crying. Dashwood helped Louis to his feet. The pain from his nose increased as he got up and he gave out a moan.

Dashwood shouted at Frank although he did not try to attack him. Frank listened to the tirade for a moment, silent, white faced, fists clenched by his side, and then walked out. At that point Vita brought a cloth over to stem the flow of blood and they sat Louis on a chair. His mind focused again on the image of Rob on the kitchen table with Frank's hands all over him. He felt overwhelming despair, rage and confusion.

"Why did you do it?" he blurted out, the blood still

dripping through his teeth.

Rob looked at him in shock, but then glanced over at Dashwood who had entered the room too late to see the embrace. "You need to see a doctor."

Louis continued to look at Rob with furious, accusing eyes and Rob's gaze dropped.

"I can't explain it now," he said quietly.

"We need to get this looked at," Vita said. "I'll take him to the hospital."

From then on it was a miserable sequence of getting into Vita's car with Dashwood, driving through the dark streets to the hospital where a tired looking doctor examined him. By that time the bleeding had stopped and after a very painful manipulation of the injured nose the doctor pronounced there was nothing broken. He said they got a lot of this, what with people bashing into lampposts in the blackout. Then there was another dreary ride with Vita who delivered Louis and Dashwood back to Louis' house.

Dashwood had been silent up until then, but now, alone on the porch in the dark, asked Louis to tell him what the fight was about.

"Politics," Louis said, monitoring Dashwood's face. Then he added, "and I hate the little fucker."

Dashwood grinned back. "I think I can see why. Shame you didn't get yours in first. I 'spect he'd be a right little bleeder."

"I'll know next time," Louis said, with all the manly reserves he could muster. It seemed to work and Dashwood asked no more.

In his room that night the image of what he had seen in the kitchen filled Louis' head, Frank's groping hands and Rob pressing their mouths together. How could Rob do this to him? And with a pretentious creep like Frank Lemaire.

Louis had a dismal night with these thoughts and in the morning had to put up with his mother fussing around him during breakfast. A large blue bruise had spread out from his nose. He told her he'd banged into a lamppost on the way back and Dashwood backed him up. But the boys must have looked wrong as they told this lie since Louis' father raised his eyebrows in disbelief. But he kept his counsel and said nothing.

Dashwood had to catch a train back to Lincolnshire that morning, so they said their goodbyes, promising to get in touch if either of them heard anything about Cambridge, joining up, or the future. Dashwood avoided the subject of last night's fracas, but then as he left he cast a backwards glance at Louis, saying, "Cheer up old man. There's always the Crossman girl to give you comfort and joy."

Louis had no time to reply as his friend walked away, leaving him alone with his angry suffering.

At lunchtime he told his mother he wasn't hungry and stayed in his room to try and sleep. His face hurt but his feelings hurt more. He kept thinking he should go over to Rob and insist he explain himself, demand something, force him to make the hurt go away, anything that might cure the pain he was feeling. But then his anger and pride took over, and he refused to give in to his desire to see him. Rob ought to come to him.

And he did. At four o'clock that afternoon the doorbell rang and shortly afterwards he heard a cautious knock on the bedroom door. His mother told him he had a visitor. He came downstairs and Rob was standing in the hallway. His mother sensed the tension in the air and made her excuses. They went into the living room and closed the door.

At first, Rob asked about his face. He moved towards Louis and he could see Rob wanted a closer look, wanted to touch him, but he backed off.

"Nothing broken," he said.

They sat facing each other. The room was dark, clouds obscuring the sun, the heavy curtains half drawn.

"I take it you want to know about last night," Rob said, his lips tightening as he spoke.

"I saw what you were doing." Louis held up a hand to fend off the explanation.

"I can see you're upset, but you don't need to be, I promise."

"Bloody hell, that's quite a statement. What do you think you were doing with him?"

Rob looked away.

"I was kissing him. That's what."

"And you expect me not to mind?"

"No, not when you put it like that. But I did know him before I met you."

"What do you mean, before you met me? Have you got any idea how much you've hurt me? I love you Rob. Well, loved you I suppose. I really don't see how we can carry on after what's happened."

Louis had screwed himself up to say these words, going over them in his mind beforehand as he lay in his bed. He really couldn't see how they could carry on after what had happened, he'd said it again and again, repeating it to himself, he really couldn't see... But even as he spoke the words he was rebelling against them. He wanted nothing more than to carry on with Rob, but he was bitterly angry at what had happened and he would not offer him a way out.

"Nothing happened," Rob said. "He kissed me, that's all."

"Don't give me that," Louis hissed, mindful that his mother could be behind the door. "I saw you. I know what he was doing."

"I was fending him off. He was getting too keen."

Louis knew what he'd seen, Rob's hands on Frank, grasping at his back, the other man's hand between his legs. It disgusted him. He clasped his head in despair, tears beginning to well up.

Then Rob came over to him and put his arms around

him. He found he couldn't resist. He melted. Rob held him for some time until eventually Louis responded, lifting his head up to Rob's. But when they tried to kiss, it hurt him too much. He wanted to believe him, to accept that Frank had forced himself on him. He couldn't bear the thought of losing him.

"I love you Rob," he said. "I want to be with you for good."

Rob pulled away.

"Love me?"

"Yes, why not?"

"That's ridiculous. We hardly know one another."

Louis couldn't understand this. He'd slept with him. How could Rob say they didn't know each other?

"And what makes you think we need to be together for good, as you put it?"

Louis realised in a panic that he'd said the wrong thing, but couldn't see why.

"Well I didn't mean…"

"Yes, you did," Rob said. He seemed angry. "Look Louis, I like you. I want to see you. But I don't want to marry you. It's not like that between men. You realise that, don't you?"

Louis must have looked unhappy because Rob softened.

"Look, I'm sorry, all right. I didn't mean to hurt you with that, that business in the kitchen, Frank and everything. And, well, it's nice that you say you love me. I like it actually. I like you too, a lot, very much. More than anyone else in fact."

They managed to kiss then, navigating delicately around his bruised face. A warm feeling came over Louis, but then he considered what Rob had just said.

"Anyone else?" he said. "What does that mean?"

"Well, there are other men. You must have known that. Surely you realised," and Rob tailed off, breaking away from Louis and staring at the floor.

But Louis hadn't realised. Or at least, he hadn't wanted to think about it. He felt utterly naïve, ashamed even, to be so stupid. What had he been thinking?

"Who?" he asked. "How many?"

"That's not important. But, I suppose, well, Frank. He was one. At school."

"Frank?" Louis' anger surged up again and he spoke loudly, forgetting the need for caution.

"Yes, but don't worry. We're not, not any longer."

"Do you mean at that place, Monkton Hill?"

"Yes, at school. That's when we first got together. But I'm over him now. Last night was just -"

"Did Vita know?"

"Yes of course, Vita knows all about me. We do talk you know. And you know what she's like - sex is health-giving and all that. She's keen for me to have as much as I like."

"That's, that's - simply astonishing."

Rob was smiling now, making Louis feel even more small. Rob had turned everything upside down. In salacious books that circulated at school he'd read of confident, sexually experienced men 'deflowering' virgins. There'd been no books, of course, where both parties were men, but somehow, he'd always seen himself taking charge. Yet it was he who'd been deflowered. He found this incredibly embarrassing.

"You must think I'm such a fool," he said.

Rob smiled at him and put his hand around the back of his neck.

"But I have such feelings for you Rob. I'm very, well, keen on you. You haven't felt that before, have you?"

Rob didn't respond to that, and they heard movements outside the door that made them cautious about standing so close, but they continued talking as the shadows gathered.

Rob made a point of laughing at the way men and women thought about marriage. He agreed with Vita who said marriage was a bourgeois institution, a set of chains, immoral really, the source of far too much unhappiness. For two men, thank goodness, it was a different thing altogether; they were free from all that.

Louis didn't object to this discourse, though he sensed that it was aimed at lowering his expectations, and he didn't press Rob to tell him about his other lovers, only happy that the feelings they had for each other had been restored, so he might once again bask in Rob's warmth.

When Louis' father came home from work, they all had supper together. His parents were careful in their conversation around the dinner table, aware that something was going on, but doing what they always did when something difficult came up, engaging in small talk. After supper, Rob stayed on and a calmer, happier mood spread between them so that when they parted, Rob heading out to walk home in the night, armed with a torch to find his way, Louis believed there was hope for them yet.

CHAPTER 11

“If I'd known then what I know now, I doubt Rob and I would have stayed the course.”

Louis was in bed again, sipping orange-brown liquid from the Teasmade.

“How do you mean Dad?”

“It wasn't just Frank Lemaire. There'd been lots of others, and there were more to come.”

Louis laughed, his drink spilling onto his pyjamas. “He was very busy on that front.”

I leaned over to mop up some of the tea snaking down his chest.

“I can see you're twitchy about my talking like this dearest boy.”

“Oh no, not really. I want to know -”

“Oh, but you are. Embarrassed aren't you? Me talking about this? But you realise none of it matters now. It certainly doesn't matter to me any longer. We've all got the same nature, however much we suppress it. And it releases a lot of tension when it all comes out.”

I recognised this theme from the psychobabble Rob used to prattle on about when I was a teenager and things were first troubling me. I'd been complaining to them about the lies I had to tell my school friends to keep their big secret safe. The casual abuse of queers and poofters at school bothered me a lot. I knew if I spoke up, defended men who went with men, the other kids would say I must be one. I'd never live it down. I resented having to carry this burden. It wasn't my fault.

Rob listened, sympathised and then persuaded me to go to a Reichian massage therapist who he thought might help. There were plenty of those about in the 1960s. Some dive in Camden Town reeking of joints and joss sticks, a man with a huge amount of facial hair kneading my back. I went once and never again, just squirmed inside when other boys talked about poofters and fairies.

"Go on," I said. "What happened after you made up with Rob?"

"Oh, I'll get to that," he replied. "First, I'll tell you how I got involved in the intelligence services. You'd like to know about that, wouldn't you?"

My father had a manipulative side, something I know he found useful in the service. He was drip feeding me with snippets, things he knew I was curious about, leading me down a pre-arranged path.

Nothing came through to him when his age group was called up, so Louis hoped all would be fine when it was time to start his undergraduate life. But he didn't want to get into trouble, or appear unwilling to do his duty, so he visited the recruitment office. He was no pacifist, so wouldn't be taking the conscientious objector route Frank Lemaire was planning. But nor was he an automatic militarist like Peter Dashwood. He just wanted to do the right thing.

At the recruitment office he ran into a War Office official who overheard Louis explaining his situation to the desk sergeant and took him to one side.

"We'll need linguists," the man said.

"I wouldn't say I'm one yet," Louis said. "I was hoping -"

"Yes, I heard. Cambridge. Hoping to go. Well perhaps you can."

Louis felt a surge of hope. He'd be studying for his degree after all.

"Deferred embodiment," the man said.

"Deferred what?"

"Embodiment. Deferred embodiment. It means we wait for you. No point in sending you off to square bash if you can be useful elsewhere."

If he avoided the call-up Louis didn't care what it meant.

"We'd be keeping you on ice. You can go up to Cambridge. An accelerated degree of course, and in the holidays more language courses. We're planning that now. What do you say?"

"Well, I -"

"We'll also need Arabic and German speakers. I don't suppose..."

"No, I'm afraid I applied for Romance languages. French, Italian, Spanish, that sort of thing."

"Doesn't matter. Some chaps have got a flair for language. Later, we'll take you into the army. If anyone asks why you're not in uniform, you can tell people you're not shirking your duty. D'you know of any other men?"

"Other men?"

"For the Cambridge course. Anyone else?"

Louis mentioned Peter Dashwood and the Whitehall man took a note of his address. But for this encounter he'd have been signed up then and there; his life would have taken a different course. Things were shambolic in the early days of the war, and people like this Whitehall man were making it up as they went along, seizing any opportunity to strengthen the war effort as they saw fit.

So both Dashwood and Louis got to Cambridge. It wasn't much of a time to be a student there. Intellectual life had almost shut down. Most of the healthy young men were in the forces, leaving the medical students to maintain the ethos of the rugger and rowing set, although their degree, too, was 'accelerated' so there was little time left over from study for athletic pleasures. Some dons who'd fought in the first war made no secret of their disdain for the language students' apparent avoidance of armed services. Others found in the diminished war intake a new reason to lament the decline of academic standards.

Yet Louis and Dashwood got through their degrees, Dashwood specialising in German and Slavic languages, including Russian, Louis in Italian and French. In the holidays they were obliged to attend Arabic classes at SOAS and Louis tried to pick up some German by taking evening classes in Russell Square nearby. Dashwood took to Arabic easily, but Louis struggled with the language.

Louis' difficulties on the SOAS course were exacerbated (quite apart from the bombing Londoners experienced after the fall of France) by worries about his mother's health. Since Christopher's death she'd been depressed, had eaten less and less, stayed in bed for days on end and hardly left the house. Now she complained of stomach pains. Louis' father was very concerned.

Once in a while Dashwood would ask about Ruth Crossland. Louis thought it best to pretend the relationship continued, but never again invited Dashwood to visit Rob. It was too dangerous. In fact, he had less and less contact with Dashwood while he was at Cambridge as they made different friends, with Dashwood gravitating to the more robust characters who liked to row and play rugby.

The distractions Rob provided were another problem.

In the early days of the war Rob attended a first aid post in Heath Street with Vita, where they learned how to treat casualties. When the bombing started, Hampstead experienced only a few hits and the first aid post wasn't called upon, but when the Blitz got going they were busier.

Rob sometimes did night duties, bandaging people up who'd been hit by falling bits of shrapnel from the guns on the Heath or on Primrose Hill, or those who'd tripped or banged into things in the darkness.

But then Rob had decided he wanted to be an artist and began life-drawing classes at the Hornsey School of Art. This brought him into contact with students from Highbury and Islington and often he'd tell Louis he couldn't see him as he was spending the night at someone's place. When he met some of these characters Louis was unimpressed. They were a pretentious, over-privileged lot whose paintings and sculptures were unoriginal. They liked to exhibit their disdain for convention by talking ostentatiously about sex and mocking anyone who took the war seriously. Several of the men, in Louis' view, were terrified of being called up and were thinking of becoming conscientious objectors, justifying their choice with abstract talk about spiritual ideals and art.

Yet Rob enjoyed their company, so Louis put up with them as far as he could and when in London did his best to see him at Vita's house.

During this time his feelings for Rob never waned, although it sometimes felt as though Rob pushed him away. He would lead Louis eagerly to his bed when he visited, but at the same time insisted that he was a fool to get so attached to the first man he'd slept with. Louis ought to experience other men, women too, because a varied sex life was good, healthy and so on. Rob said he'd been with women himself and liked it, though he knew he was mostly queer. Louis should try it - he might find something out about himself.

Louis tried to take these lectures seriously. He was getting worried about his future life if he stayed this way. From time to time the newspapers carried stories of men being prosecuted for going with other men, adding to his fear. This thing with Rob might be something he just had to get out of his system. But although he found some women attractive, they were insipid beside Rob.

Rob took him to Piccadilly to look at the painted boys beneath the fire office arches. There were catcalls, repartee, which Rob responded to with sharp wit. This was enough of a shock, but then they went on to the Criterion, where rouged men, some with lipstick and waved hair, were drinking and dancing. Scent wafted across to them as they sat at the bar and Louis' bourgeois sentiments were horrified when two of the dancers kissed openly, groping each other's arses, while others whistled and laughed at the pair. Louis panicked and dragged Rob away from the place.

He knew Rob was having affairs on his trips to Highbury and suffered agonies of jealousy. But he tried his best to conceal this, for fear it would drive him away.

It was sometimes pure torture. Once, he was in a bakery in Heath Street buying bread for his mother and glanced out of the window. Rob was walking by with another man. Louis followed the pair at a discreet distance as they went up the hill, laughing and chatting, absorbed in each other. At Whitestone Pond they turned to enter a part of the Heath that had plentiful cover from bushes and low trees and Louis knew instantly what they were going to do. That evening he was supposed to be seeing Rob, but Louis couldn't bring himself to go. He was humiliated when Rob didn't even ask him why he hadn't kept to their arrangement. But a week later they were in bed together at Vita's place, Louis having suppressed his misery at the betrayal.

Sometimes he wondered what Rob saw in him. He didn't have the courage to ask and was afraid to let his thoughts about it go too far. He sensed he was different from Rob's other boyfriends, but he wasn't sure how. It was usually enough that Rob still wanted to see him when he turned up at Vita's house.

From time to time he couldn't resist asking about

Frank Lemaire. Frank had made a successful application to the tribunal that considered conscientious objectors and was now in a non-combatant unit somewhere near Bath, doing quarry work. Although Rob always said he'd finished with Frank, he suspected they still saw each other when Frank was in London and didn't trust Rob's protestations of innocence.

In June 1941 he was once again living at home, having graduated, waiting for his call-up. The worst of the bombing raids were now behind them as Hitler turned his attention to Russia. He was having an evening meal with his parents, who had stayed in London during the blitz, descending to the cellar when the sirens went and setting themselves up in bedding beneath the Anderson shelter in the basement. Celebrations of his graduation had been extremely muted. His mother was by now very weak, eating poorly and apparently suffering from a variety of ailments, the cause of which were, his father had confided to him, psycho-emotional in their origin. She could not stop the gnawing anxiety and sadness about Christopher from eating into her. The meal was a silent, gloomy affair in the dining room, and the noise of dishes being placed on the table, of cutlery against the plate, of chewing, even breathing sounded unnaturally loud against the silence.

The doorbell rang and Louis jumped up to get it, pleased to have a reason to escape the atmosphere. To his surprise, it was Frank, wearing the blue uniform of an auxiliary in the fire service. He looked hot and out of breath.

"It's Robbie," he said. "He's in the hospital. He's asked for you."

"Is he all right?" Louis asked.

"Of course he isn't fucking all right, he's in hospital. Come on, get your jacket on. It's not far."

They hurried through the streets in the light of the summer evening, Louis' anxiety growing with every step. He'd had this feeling before, when the policemen had come about Christopher.

He tried again: "What's the matter with him?"

This time Frank was less aggressive, turning back and meeting his eye. "I dunno mate. An overdose I think."

"What is it? What did he take?"

But Frank claimed not to know. Perhaps the doctors would tell them.

They got to the hospital and Frank led him up the stairs. Looking at Frank's thick legs powering up the stairs ahead of him, his revulsion for him increased. What was he doing there? Why was Rob involved with a man of this sort?

Vita was standing outside a cubicle, looking worried, the door shut.

"We can't go in," she said when Louis reached to open the door. "They're doing something in there."

Louis tried to peer through the glass, but a screen was in the way.

"What happened?" he asked.

"Early this morning. He came in with Frank and just collapsed," Vita said. "Then he couldn't get up. After an hour he still couldn't get up. When he tried, he fell down and I couldn't get anything out of him."

"We brought him down here," Frank said. "They said it's an overdose."

"Of what? What's he been taking?"

"They don't know yet," Vita said. Her hands picked nervously at wisps of greying hair escaping from her scarf. "I need a seat."

They each took an arm and walked her over to a bench.

"They pumped him out," Frank said. "Got rid of whatever it was."

"How could he have done it?" Vita held her head in her hands.

Louis put his arm around the tall woman, whose hunched shoulders diminished her usually imposing presence. Then a white-uniformed nurse came out of the cubicle.

"He will be all right Mrs Gill."

Louis stood up. "What happened to him?"

The nurse looked him up and down. "And you are…?"

"Oh, just a, just a friend."

"You must ask Mrs Gill, I'm afraid I cannot…"

Louis held his palms up to show he understood. Who was he to Rob after all? A friend, just like any of his other friends. Just like Frank was a friend. What the hell was Rob up to with Frank, anyway?

When the nurse had departed, heels clacking across the linoleum, Vita knocked on the cubicle door. It opened, and she slipped in, giving a backwards glance at the two men.

"You'd better fucking tell me what happened," Louis said.

"Keep your cool mate. He'll be all right."

How do you know?"

"I've seen this before. Bennies and booze. Bad combination. He'll get over it."

"Benzedrine?" Louis said. "How long's he been taking that?"

Frank just laughed at this and didn't respond. Louis realised he wasn't going to get any more out of the other man.

"What's this then?" Louis said, pointing at Frank's fire service uniform.

"I got sick of breaking rocks with the conchies," Frank replied. "I dropped in on Robbie and we went out for the night. My day off. Bin doing fires for a month now. It's not bad. You see some things though."

Frank's jacket smelled of smoke and Louis imagined him pulling people out of the ruins of bombed buildings.

"You?" Frank asked.

Louis explained his situation, then fell silent. They sat, uncomfortable with each other, but neither of them willing to give way and depart.

After a while, Vita came out with a doctor, who said his patient was on the way to recovery but should spend a night in hospital. They could see him tomorrow, but he needed to rest for now.

When Vita said Rob wanted to see him, Louis felt a sense of triumph over Frank. The doctor said a brief visit was acceptable and Frank shrugged, turned away and said he'd better be off to his shift.

Rob looked pale and tired, his eyes red. He smiled weakly as he saw Louis and lifted a hand to grasp his. To his visitor's questions and expressions of concern, he made little answer, just whispering he was glad that Louis had come, before the doctor returned and ushered Louis out of the room.

The following day he was allowed to visit in the afternoon for an hour. Vita was there at first but then announced she was going to get a cup of tea, leaving them alone. Rob was much better, sitting up in bed. He told him the doctors thought he'd be fine to go home tomorrow.

"I'm such an idiot," he said, his head down, "causing all this trouble."

"What happened? What did you take? You can tell me."

Rob rolled his eyes up and pursed his lips. "Benzedrine and booze. I got the balance wrong."

"What on earth did you do that for?"

"Oh. I thought you'd know. Silly me."

"Sorry, but I don't."

"It keeps you high. Parties, that sort of thing."

The penny finally dropped.

"So you were out at a party?" Louis asked.

"A club." Rob paused, looking at Louis. "Yes, with Frank. I was with Frank."

Then, without warning, Rob started sobbing. "I can't shake him off. He's inside my mind somehow. I keep going back to him. I'm so sorry."

Then he really cried, his shoulders shaking so Louis, in

spite of the feelings of rage that battled within him, moved round to his side and held him.

In a while his sobbing stopped, and he explained that he'd gone out for the evening with Frank, who had given him the stuff. You could extract it from inhalers, or even get pills. With alcohol, Louis knew, it was famous for pepping up a flagging sex life, or making one that wasn't flagging even more sensational.

"Did he give them to you? The pills," Louis asked.

"Yes."

"How many did you take."

"I'm not sure. I lost count. Frank told me it was safe, he'd done it hundreds of times. I must have had a bad reaction."

Again and again this happened with Rob. Why did he keep coming back to him? Why was he here now? Louis got up to leave.

"Oh no, don't go." Rob was quivering again. "You don't understand."

"What is there to understand? I tell you that I love you, that we could be together, just us, but you still go with other people. I've seen you. You say it's a good thing to have sex with lots of people and you won't stop. Very well, that much is clear. I must be such a fool, an idiot, to keep on hanging around you. What's the point of all this, what is the bloody point?"

"Sex and love aren't the same thing," Rob said, though without much conviction. "I've told you that."

Indeed he had, Louis reflected, and at length. Rob now expected him, as he'd done so often before, to say, pathetically, "So does that mean you really do love me?" and then Rob would skirt around the topic, avoiding the word, but patching things up enough so he carried on with him, leaving him feeling as uncertain as ever. But this time he glared at Rob.

"I can't have this conversation again right now Louis, I just can't…"

Rob was crying again. Louis couldn't resist a last dig.

"And when are you going to join the army?"

Rob stared at him blankly. Louis continued. "Got your conscription papers yet? Isn't it about time you did your bit? Or is that all you are, a fairy who won't fight?"

At that moment Vita entered the room and went to her son's bedside.

"I'm going now," Louis said, and he left without embracing Rob, ignoring the look of desperation and hurt in his eyes, striding back to his parents' house in a dark cloud of anger and misery.

The next day he received a letter telling him to report at Victory House the following week for a medical. His army service was about to start.

CHAPTER 12

Basic training was a shock. Three months of endless marching, naming of rifle parts, saluting in the freezing cold of a Northern Irish winter. Then a transfer to Winchester, in theory to learn intelligence work, in practice, for more of the same. Plus cutting the lawns with a dinner knife. Plus the motorcycles.

The motorcycle course lasted three weeks. They were thrust onto old Matchless, BSA or Norton bikes and sent hurtling across the countryside, through forest, over streams and fields and then, one day, to the top of a steep hill outside town.

"Right. Lie them down," the sergeant major ordered. "Yes, I mean it. On the fucking floor!"

The bikes were heavy. They'd have a hell of a business getting them upright again.

They were told to disconnect the brakes and pick the bike up again. It was a struggle but Louis managed, noticing with satisfaction that a couple the others needed help. Now he had to turn the bike round, so it pointed back down the hill, another massive effort in the mud. The idea was to learn to use the engine for braking.

"Remount!"

He looked down the hill. There was an ambulance waiting at the bottom.

Later, in Winchester Hospital with a broken rib, his senior officer, Ken Gillett, came to see him.

"Hello Nicholson. I heard you had a prang."

"Yes, sir." The effort of speaking made him wince.

"What's the matter with you?"

"It bloody hurts, doesn't it?"

"I'll thank you to mind your ruddy language when you address me."

Gillett was a broad-faced man with a permanently blank expression on his face, even when issuing threats.

"Sorry, sir."

"Thought I'd better come and tell you the news."

"What news, sir?"

"Your posting. Liverpool. It's been decided you're to go there. Port security. Best to tell you in person."

This was hard to take. The others had all been given overseas postings.

"Why's that, sir?"

"You're not really suited to field service. Disappointing news, I know."

There was no point in objecting. Once the army decided something, it was immovable. It was good of Gillett to tell him in person, unusual in fact. Perhaps it was Gillett who'd made the recommendation and felt guilty. But this was unlikely: the captain was a distant figure, not much given to introspection or doubt.

After Gillett had left, Louis' sense of disappointment grew. He'd failed. Going overseas wasn't the point - they'd cast him out. 'Not suited to field service.' The words stayed with him, ringing in his ears. He guessed what they meant. Physically he could keep up with the others, but he knew he wasn't the same as them. Although one or two had girlfriends back home, it didn't stop them going for what was available in the local dance halls. He said he had a fiancée, trying to make this the reason for him not chasing after girls. Perhaps the others sensed something different about him, he didn't know. But this was the result.

"I served more than a year at Ellesmere Port," Louis said, chuckling to himself. "One of the dullest times of my entire life."

He was in bed again. The Teasmade hadn't worked that morning, and he wasn't up to struggling down to the kitchen, so he'd waited for me to turn up and make him a cup.

"I was bloody upset. Hit me hard. But now I wonder if they'd discovered my brother was a communist. They worried about that sort of thing. So having trained me up in intelligence work they put me on port duties with a bunch of duffers. I thought I'd be there for the duration. But it gave me time to think over things with Rob. Did I really want that sort of life? It would have been so much easier to have taken up with a girl."

He gestured with his hand for me to take his tea away.

"Look, I can't talk any more now," he said, "I need a sleep. Read that if you want to know what he was doing." He pointed to a brown notebook on the bedside table. "I got it out for you. It's his journal."

Rob had always kept a journal. The notebooks sat in a row on the top shelf of the book case, well out of my reach when I was a child. I was sometimes tempted to look at them, particularly after he died, but something held me back. I never saw him writing entries so he must have done it late at night, or at other times when I wasn't around, but the journal's existence hadn't been a secret. When he filled one book, he'd buy another one from Rymans in Great Portland Street - always the same brown cover, lined pages. The company had been making them for decades although the later ones were a lighter colour.

The one on the bedside table had "May 1940 - July 1943" on a label stuck on the front.

Inside was Rob's familiar handwriting. The loops and swirls of his script scudded across the page, like clouds racing along in a wind. Rob's writing was breathless, his letters to me dashing off great gouts of prose, filled with exclamation and question marks, underlining and the occasional word in capitals for emphasis. Every now and again, he'd pop a drawing on the margin - a rabbit sniffing the air, a funny face. The contrast with Louis' more controlled, measured script couldn't have been greater. They were so different from each other. Yet they had a deep bond which gave their life together a solid core of stability, care and mutual support that exceeded their differences.

I leafed through to the end of the book and saw that Rob had written entries at irregular intervals - presumably whenever he had something of interest to record. The last entry was dated July 4th 1943 and said, simply, "Louis has gone." There were several blank pages after that, which Rob could have used, but at that point he must have started another book.

In May 1940 when Louis was in his first year at Cambridge, Rob lived with his mother in the Vale of Health serving occasional shifts at the first aid post, sometimes sleeping there overnight, and attending art and drawing classes in the day at the Hornsey School. It remained open throughout the war, despite the Blitz, while other art schools closed or decamped to the country. Hornsey wasn't exactly a prime target for the Germans, so the bombing there was less intense.

The first entry concerned Frank Lemaire, who had shown up in London and came over to visit him. He was tired of living at the camp in Melksham where the non-combatants had been working in the quarry. Not that he minded hard physical labour (Rob wrote, "Frankie showed me his biceps, and I gave them a squeeze!") but he'd decided it was pointless work for an intelligent chap like him. Privately, Rob thought Frank was finally suffering from guilt and wanted to do his bit for the war effort. He wouldn't admit to these feelings though.

The diary soon moved on to document Rob's perambulations around London during the spring of that year. He liked to walk from Vita's to Hornsey in the mornings, carrying art equipment in a canvas bag, going across the Heath, through Waterlow Park and over the bridge they call 'suicide bridge' at Archway. I remember him saying he once saw a man jump from there. He wobbled for ages on the brink, Rob and other onlookers watching in horror, before he plucked up the courage to leap. Now, on the way to art classes, he'd stand there looking out over London, where sometimes aeroplanes flew overhead during daytime raids, or made their way to the aerial battlefields of Kent.

Anthony Coxon was the drawing teacher at Hornsey. Years ago I saw his pictures in an exhibition of British twentieth century painters at the Tate. His stuff looked like a cross between Stanley Spencer and Paul Nash. Iron girders in abandoned warehouse yards, workmen with shortened bodies, cranes, a graveyard in the middle distance. Not the most prominent painter of his time, but he certainly knew how to draw, and Rob and his fellow students were pleased he was teaching them. Rob wrote a lot about the life drawing classes, recording what Coxon said about his work, and how he was improving.

Life drawing wasn't just confined to the Hornsey School. Some students from wealthier families rented studios around Holloway where the taller buildings meant the upper storeys had plenty of light. These towers became their playgrounds, places where they pretended to be real painters and sculptors, and tried out being adults. Prudey was the leader of one pack of these young hopefuls. Prudey was short for Prudence, but she liked to say she did her level best to live down her unfortunate name. Slightly older, she took up Rob as her special friend, using the weekly money she got from her indulgent parents to fund excursions around the bars, dance halls, cafés and restaurants around London. For Prudey and Rob, and the circle they mixed with, the Blitz provided an extra urgency to their lives. When the sirens sounded, it was an excuse to dive under a table with their partner of the evening, the noise of explosions adding a thrill to the proceedings.

Prudey soon worked out that paying a model to pose in the nude made no sense. She took the lead in exposing herself, much to the delectation of the floppy-haired young men who rolled up at her studio, and Rob soon followed her example. Then they persuaded boys and girls to take their clothes off in a rota system of their own design that allowed for a detailed inspection. The diary containing numerous instances of hilarity shared between them as they discussed the parade of flesh. Although Rob and Prudey treated this as a meat market, Rob also wrote about life drawing in more high-flown terms, describing the difficulties of shading with charcoal, the spiritual beauty of the human form, all of it language he was taking from Coxon.

When these extra-curricular drawing sessions were over, Prudey and Rob would each pick a target and invite them to stay on. They'd cook a stew on the oil stove and crack open a bottle of Chianti. Prudey would retire to a back room with her chosen one. Rob used a divan in the studio, choosing a woman at times if a man could not be persuaded.

Rob and Prudey hunted together, discussing their strategies and reviewing their conquests and the diary hinted at things between them that perhaps went deeper than mere friendship, a lot of hugging, kissing and cuddling, even sleeping in the same bed, but nothing more explicit was written.

At any rate, towards the end of this time, Prudey struck up an unambiguously sexual relationship with a French girl with the extraordinary name of Fifi. Her entry on the scene meant Prudey grew tired of the meat market and wanted to be alone with her girlfriend. So Rob spread his wings and visited other friends in Highbury, found other divans.

At this time, Louis was writing letters to Rob from Cambridge and seeing him when he returned to London. I skimmed over a lot of entries, looking for ones mentioning Louis. Rob was clearly very fond of him, recording how much he looked forward to his visits. He thought of him even when he was with other people.

I found this hard to understand. It was as if Rob had two lives, two personalities, pursuing pure pleasure with his art student friends, but a more complex relationship with Louis. Other things suggested a dual life too: his art school friends scoffed at his service at the first aid post with Vita, which he took very seriously. It gave him stability, duty and obligation. Perhaps Louis signified those things for Rob too, who clung to him like a swimmer clings to a life raft on a tumultuous ocean.

His moods with his various lovers at Prudey's place swung wildly. He experienced brief passions at his conquests and intense disappointments when he couldn't have who he wanted, each of these feelings subsiding as rapidly as they arose. The friendship with Prudey meant he had someone to talk to about his adventures, so he could regain a more strategic mentality for the next campaign of seduction.

And in a few entries Rob documented explicitly some sexual practices which I found difficult to read. Ones where he played out a submissive, even masochistic role, the men standing over him...

You've got to realise, I loved Rob, almost as much as I loved Louis. He was a father to me too. And by the time I knew him, there was none of this behaviour in his life. He was devoted to his sculpture and to Louis and to me, in that order. Those were his horizons. The men that Rob was involved with in those days - arrogant and narcissistic, taking a perverted pleasure in playing out theatrical scenes of sexual humiliation - were a million miles away from what he had with Louis.

Not all of these people who spun around in Rob's orbit were as invulnerable as they made out. If they became too attached to Rob, the ball was in the other court. Both he and Prudey were adept at dismissing people who got too serious. Why, I wondered, did he not dismiss Louis in similar fashion? He was so different with him, accepting and enjoying his devotion. Once again, he appeared to live in two separate worlds.

The life he was leading unbalanced him in the end. I expect the continuing use of drugs contributed. One of the diary entries, written in January 1941 after an alcoholic, Benzedrine and sex-fuelled party the night before, contained this:

> We just heard the news from Tobruk. I had no reaction. It ought to please me, but I can't feel anything about the war. Nothing is real any more. My drawings aren't real drawings and nor are any of the stupid sculptures and paintings that the others do. They all talk filth and they make me talk it too. Everyone tries to fuck me, even the women. Prudey is a tart and we all sponge off her. I'm awake at night and sleep all day and can't tell the difference. It's as if we're living in a dream, with bombs falling all round us. I feel desperate.

Around that time, during a similar episode of unreality, he described digging the nib of a pen into his hand, the pain of it helping him regain a sense of being in the world.

Things took a turn for the worse in the spring of 1941 when he revealed in his journal that on one of the rare occasions on which he had slept with a woman, he had made her pregnant. She had come to him, asking for help. The girl, whose name was Virginia, had missed her period two months in succession and Prudey advised her to get an abortion. But the girl had mixed feelings about this, wavering between wanting to have the baby - if baby there was - but fearing the consequences of keeping it.

She decided to confront Rob about what she saw as his responsibilities and came to his house one evening when Frank Lemaire was there.

I put the journal down and looked at Louis. He was sleeping in his bed, a tranquil expression on his face. Had he read the diary? He must have done. I couldn't believe he'd been ignorant of Rob and his sexual adventures. Surely he'd realised Rob and Frank were carrying on, despite Rob's denials. How much had he known about the life he'd led with the Hornsey students?

Louis stirred in his sleep, wheezing a little, but didn't open his eyes, so I continued reading.

Rob, Frank and the girl Virginia were in the conservatory at Vita's house. Virginia was convinced the baby was Rob's, and she was determined to keep it. Becoming a mother would help her lead a better life, she was sure. Rob's diary entry records that he felt sympathetic towards her plight and was racking his brains as to what to do about it all, when Frank made a brutal intervention that changed the girl's mind. Rob wrote:

Virginia told us she now hadn't had the curse for three months and Frank started shouting at her. He told her she was being selfish and anyway, didn't she know what kind of man I was? What did she expect me to do for her? I tried to shut him up, but he shoved me aside and went on about how she should have an abortion and why hadn't she told us sooner. Then he got sly and said how did she know it was mine, and that was even worse. He was horrible to the poor girl who was crying by then. I wish Prudey had been there. Frank got so worked up and said no-one would ever marry Virginia, how people hated illegitimate children. I begged him to stop, and he calmed down, started joking about how he'd have to throw her down the stairs to get rid of the child. Frankie can be a bastard. So I told her, as kindly as I could, that I could get her some quinine pills from Prudey, if she wanted and she could see if they worked. She seemed to accept that and went away, still in tears though. I told Frank he didn't have to be so hard on her, but he just shrugged it off like he does with everything, said you've got to get tough when people behave like wet rags. Then he had to get off to his fire service thingy. God knows what will happen. I don't like what Frank did, but the alternative is marrying her and that would hardly be a kindness to the poor girl. Fingers crossed the pills work.

I'd discovered more than I ever wanted to know. As my second father, Rob had given me no real hint of this wild period of his life. I had believed he was settled in his relationship with Louis, even though he had odd ideas compared with the fathers of other boys. On the other hand, in the 1960s people with odd ideas flourished, so perhaps he didn't stand out so much.

Louis was awake. I saw him watching me from the corner of his eye.

"Have you read this?" I asked.

He shook his head. "Bits of it. I can guess what's in the rest. Hope you found it interesting."

"To say the least. Did you know about him and Pru -"

Louis held up his hand to stop me. "I don't need to hear about Prudence Cartwright. It was a mad time, and he went wild with the rest of them."

"And Frank Lemaire? Did you know about him?"

Louis shook his head. "It wasn't Rob's fault. He caused me a lot of heartache, but it really wasn't his fault. I could see under the surface of all the madness. At some level

Rob knew that, and that's why he kept on wanting me."

"Sounds like he did his best to avoid letting you know."

"Yes, he didn't give me many clues. I almost left him. It wasn't just his behaviour; it was thinking about my future if I stayed with him. In those days, the newspapers - filled with the most vituperative filth. You've no idea. It was starting to terrify me. I was hanging on by a thread."

He reached for his tea and I handed it to him. It was lukewarm so I offered to make a new cup, but he waved me away.

"It was that school that started it off. Monkton Hill. That's where he got his first experiences and he was too young. He was just a child."

"How do you mean?"

"I mean his sexual experiences. At Monkton Hill. The teachers, or one of them, anyway. All that bloody body massage stuff. There was a chap there who used the opportunity - "

"You mean…"

"Yes, that's right. They'd call it child abuse now." Louis gave out a bitter laugh. "Abuse. Yes, I suppose it was that. Ill treatment, exploitation, whatever you want to say. That's not what this fellow called it though. He'd get them into a darkened room, soft lighting, put his hands on them and see how far each one would let him go. A little further each time. And always under the cover of therapy."

"That's disgusting." I recalled the hairy hands of the man in Camden Town.

"And it affected them, the children, teenagers you'd call them. The entire place was charged with sexuality. Don't believe that guff you hear sometimes from people who were there. The brothers and sisters thing, 'they were like my brothers and sisters', they say, 'I can't imagine doing it with one of them.' Load of rubbish."

Louis spat out with his lips as he said this.

"A load of rubbish. They were at it like rabbits and the school authorities turned a blind eye. That's where Rob got lost. It was incredibly harmful. He spent most of his life getting over it."

"Did Vita know?"

"Oh, Vita: she was as mixed up as that bloody headmaster, that fellow Lorenz. You've got to realise, she was Reich's lover, and Reich and Lorenz were as thick as thieves in Vienna when she was there with them. Reich was a genuine nutcase, but he fascinated Lorenz, who took up his ideas and put them into practice at Monkton Hill. Lorenz thought he was freeing children from the same repression he'd suffered himself as a child. He didn't realise he was presiding over a moral cesspit. It was like Lord of the Flies, but with added sex."

"Do you think Vita knew?"

"Vita? Ha! She was so confused about right and wrong by the time she left Vienna she hadn't got the capacity to be a decent mother to Rob. She thought sex was like health food, like taking vitamins or, or, doing calisthenics. Vita needed someone to be devoted to her. Unfortunately she chose that madman Reich. He was a complete bastard, he really was. He went properly crazy later on, too. But I'm sure Rob wouldn't have told her everything about his Hornsey friends. People don't do that with their parents, do they? Even ones like Vita."

I thought about the two lives Rob had led. I realised that I'd always sensed a mental hardness in him, a liking for feral things. His art was proof of that.

"So how did you hang on," I asked my father, "by that thread?"

CHAPTER 13

In the summer of 1943 Louis was in London on leave. His mother had died the year before. The doctors said it was a cancerous growth that killed her, something in her stomach. His father was convinced it was her grief about Christopher, gnawing away inside her, which had caused the cancer. His father dealt with his loneliness by grimly carrying on with his medical practice, seeing patients in the surgery near the main entrance to the house every day, sharing a night rota with colleagues.

One morning Louis went for a walk. As he climbed up Parliament Hill, he glanced at the path leading up to the Vale of Health and thought of Rob. He'd written to Louis in Ellesmere Port, but Louis hadn't replied. In London for his mother's funeral, he'd seen Rob at the ceremony, which he attended with Vita. Rob had taken Louis aside, begged him to come and see him, claiming his life was on a more even keel, but Louis shook himself away and didn't visit before returning to his posting.

He looked out over the city, still strung with lines of barrage balloons, although air raids were now a rare occurrence. Things were calmer now, a sense of purpose imbuing people with a determination to finish the job they'd started. Events in North Africa and the German defeat at Stalingrad had made people realise an end was in sight. Children were returning to London from the countryside.

He was frustrated to be playing such a small part. For over a year now he'd been carrying out his port duties, patrolling the docks, searching ships for contraband, chasing people trying to filch from the cargoes. He lived in a Nissan hut with others of his unit, stunned with boredom most of the time. When off duty he spent far too much time in local pubs, having overcome his earlier distaste for them. There were dances too, and women to meet. He tried it on with one or two, wondering what it might be like with a woman. They were Northern girls doing war work, out for a good time, but Louis' sense of fun didn't run in the same direction as theirs.

Still, he did a good, conscientious job and was duly promoted to sergeant. And then, the news came that he was to join the men of his original training unit in North Africa. Someone had decided he'd done his time, kept his nose clean, had somehow proved himself. Or perhaps they just needed a replacement and thought of him. At any rate, it lifted his spirits.

He was just turning away from the view to go home when he felt a light touch on his shoulder and a voice saying his name. It was Rob, his dark hair shorter than he remembered. He wore a blue cotton shirt which blew a little in the breeze.

"Yes, it's me. Long time no see. Out for a walk?"

Louis opened his mouth but nothing came out.

"What are you doing in London?" Rob asked.

Somehow Louis managed to say he was on leave, visiting his father. In the grey drizzle of the Merseyside he'd forced himself to forget Rob, censored his mental images of his face, his touch, his body.

Like him, Rob was out for a stroll. He said he'd been working in his studio and suggested they walk to the café nearby.

The poppy seed cake was still being served, just as before. The matrons were there too, thinner now, sipping tea and making quiet conversation.

He asked about Vita, who Rob said was well. Rob asked about Louis' father.

"And you?" Rob said, "How've you been? You didn't answer my letters."

The letters were in a pile, unopened at home. Louis mumbled an apology.

Rob placed his hand over Louis', ignoring the fact they might be seen.

"I understand. I treated you terribly."

Louis shrugged his shoulders, saying nothing, but looked around him and drew his hand away. Then he asked what Rob was doing with himself.

Rob laughed. "Trying to avoid conscription. They're calling up men my age. I can't leave London. My work's too important."

"Your work?"

"Yes, I'm using Vita's studio now."

"So you're still going to Hornsey? Seeing all those, those people still…"

Some of Louis' old resentment was coming back.

"Still at Hornsey, yes. But those people, they've all gone, that whole thing in Highbury, finished. Prudey's a WAAF now. She volunteered, believe it or not. Said it would get her out of London. I haven't been there for months."

"I'm glad to hear it."

"I'm still doing shifts at the first aid place you know, with Vita." Rob spoke as if he had something to prove. "But there's less call for it now."

There was a silence and Rob continued. "What are you doing now? Come with me and see Vita. She'd love to catch up with you and I can show you some of my stuff."

Louis had nothing else to do, but he hesitated.

"Come on Louis. No strings attached, promise."

He gave in and they left the café, walking in the sunshine past the boating pond and up the narrow passage between trees leading to Kenwood. As Rob strode along beside him he found it hard not to keep looking over at him. At one point Rob stumbled and held on to his arm for a while. Then they were going past the turning to the women's bathing pond.

"Do you remember this place?" he asked, his smiling face turned towards Louis. Against his will Louis found himself smiling back. He tried to fight his feelings as his hand brushed against Rob's when they climbed the slope to the beautiful white façade of Kenwood House which shone in the sunlight.

"The Germans missed it," Rob said.

"It's heavenly. I'd forgotten."

"They moved the paintings out. There are soldiers staying there now."

"What on earth for? They'll ruin it."

"Don't ask me. I'm sick of the war. Nothing to do with me."

They walked on through a forested area and came out near the highest point of the Heath where a flag post flew a Union Jack, then began a short descent to the Vale of Health. Louis saw a huge crater in the ground, just above the clutch of houses. A tree had fallen across it, crushing a wooden fence.

"We were in the cellar when that one went off. Broke a few windows."

"Why didn't you leave London? You could have found somewhere in the country."

"I told you, the war's got nothing to do with me. I hate it, and I won't have anything to do with it."

In that case leaving London would have made sense, Louis thought. Rob and Vita could have gone to some wilderness, a Scottish island or something, and ignored the rest of the world. It was typical of Rob to talk like this.

Vita was in when they got to the house, sitting in the conservatory, smoking a cigarette in a long holder, a cat on her lap. The familiarity of the scene jolted Louis. It was as if he'd been there only yesterday.

Vita stood up, a look of surprise and pleasure on her face, and the cat leapt to the floor.

"Louis!" she exclaimed. "I can't believe it. Home from the wars!"

"Not exactly," he said, putting his arms round her. She felt thinner, smaller.

"Well look at you," she said, indicating his uniform trousers, which he hadn't bothered to change. "A soldier."

Louis grinned. "I don't feel like one."

He looked around, memories flooding back. The green growth pressed against the glass as before, the smell of wet earth filling the warm air.

Rob was pulling him away. "Come on, I want to show you."

He took Louis through the house and into Vita's studio. Where before there had been paintings, oils, mosaic tiles, the smell of turpentine, now there was the paraphernalia of a sculptor's workshop. On one side of the room was a wooden stand with an untouched block of stone on it, a mallet and several chisels nearby. On the other were brown forms on a long bench, one covered with a wet cloth. Moulds lay on a shelf below the bench. The air smelled of clay.

"This is new. I thought you were going in for painting after Coxon."

"So did I."

Then Louis turned and saw shelves holding an extraordinary collection of objects. He was drawn to a dark bronze figure of a bird, except it was only half a bird. It had the legs of a man and its head jutted out like a gun. Next to it was another piece - two animals of some indeterminate species, their limbs entwined in a brutal embrace, one with its mouth open, teeth bared, in a howl of agony, or ecstasy - he couldn't be sure. The shelf had five or six of these figures, all of them half way between animal and human, like nothing on earth. They were wildly disturbing, speaking at once of shattering agony, fury, intense beauty.

"What are these?" he said. "What are they?"

"They're sculptures Louis," Rob said quietly, next to him. "Bronze. I made them."

"They're, they're, incredible."

Rob gave a little smile. "I can't make any more, not now. Can't get the materials, so I draw and make models." He gestured over to the block of stone. "One of these days I'll have a go at that. If I have to, I'll chop down the trees on the Heath and carve them if I can't get any other stuff to work with."

"How did you get into all this?"

"Henry Moore. They closed down Chelsea Poly because of the bombs so now he's teaching at Hornsey. He's wonderful."

"They're wonderful Rob. Terrible too. I can't believe it."

Louis was still shaken by the writhing forms on the shelves. They looked as if they could move at any moment.

"It's how I see things, what I feel. I can't explain it."

Louis looked at the other man in wonder. Rob turned away from his gaze.

"Come on," he said. "You should talk to Vita. She's got some booze in her cupboard."

Louis followed him out, noticing Vita's paintings on the walls as they passed through the house and out again to the conservatory. Vita was in the wicker chair again, the cat on her lap purring as she stroked it with her long fingers. Louis remembered their sessions together when Vita's fingers had explored his own body.

"I've been looking at Rob's things," he said as he sat down on a bench. Rob poured them each a drink and held up his glass in a toast.

"Here's to finding Louis again."

"And do you like them?" Vita asked, clinking his glass.

"Like? Well, yes, they're amazing. Disturbing. I can't quite believe it. He's, he's really got something."

Vita smiled and her bangles rattled on her arm as she took a drink. "He's got my studio, that's what he's got. More or less kicked me out of there."

"Oh come on Ma," Rob said. "You weren't doing anything in there anymore."

"True," Vita replied, "too true. Trust the young to put their finger on it. I've run out of inspiration, Louis. Never had much in the first place if the truth be told."

Rob protested, but only half-heartedly. Louis knew what Vita meant. Her efforts at painting, what he'd seen of them, had nothing of the raw originality of Rob's art.

"Perhaps if you -"

"No, leave it alone Louis," Vita said. "Sometimes we have to face facts. I'm Rob's assistant now, aren't I darling?"

"And a very wonderful assistant you are too," Rob said. "And an inspiration for me."

Vita smiled and took another sip of her drink.

Rob put his empty glass down heavily.

"The bloody war's going to stop me though. I'll get a call-up any minute and have to fuck off to some ghastly barracks with a bunch of roughs running the show. I'll die!"

Louis laughed. "So, you don't want to do your bit then?"

"Not bloody likely. I told you, the war's got nothing to do with me."

"So you're a pacifist after all then?"

"What do you think?"

He thought of the twisted, angry figures in the studio.

"No, perhaps not."

They hung on, around the bottle, until it was empty. The evening was coming on and Vita got up and said she'd get them something to eat, so they were alone.

"So what are you going to do?" Louis asked.

Rob bit his thumb, pausing. "I'm going to tell them I'm queer."

"That's not going to work."

"How do you know? Depends how you do it. Worked for a friend of mine."

Louis felt uncomfortable. He'd been careful with the other men on his posting at Ellesmere Port. The story about Ruth Crossland helped, and his occasional dates with the Northern girls. If Rob let the cat out of the bag at a recruitment office, might it somehow get back to him?

"Who was that?" he asked.

"Quentin he's called. Told them he was homosexual and they referred him to the medical board. They decided he was suffering from sexual perversion. Dismissed him on medical grounds."

"That must have taken a bit of nerve," Louis said.

"Quentin's got that in spades. Walks around Soho in women's clothes. Doesn't care."

The thought of this appalled Louis. "But we, I mean us, we've never been like that."

"No," said Frank thoughtfully. "So I'll have to screw up my courage, won't I?"

Louis couldn't think of anything to say, his mind racing with the thoughts of what might happen. The recruiting people could sign up Frank anyway and throw him to the lions, his status known about.

"Expect Vita'll lend me a bit of lipstick," Rob said, and they both laughed.

There was a gathering at Louis' house one Sunday evening before Louis was due to go overseas. His father and an army friend were there, and Vita and Rob came over. They had a subdued afternoon sipping tea and eating cake together. His father was miserable about the overseas posting, fearing he could lose his only remaining son. At the same time, he tried to put a brave face on it, drawing Louis aside at one point, saying "It will be the making of you, my boy," following this with an awkward slap on the shoulder that wasn't quite an embrace.

Vita tried to talk to Louis' soldier friend across a gulf separating them. Louis and Rob behaved as though they hardly knew each other.

Rob's idea for avoiding the call-up seemed to be working. Apparently, the sergeant in the recruiting office had taken one look at the lipstick and sighed, "Another one," signing the form that would refer Rob to the medical board. They'd see him the following week, by which time Louis would be gone. Louis was uncomfortable about Rob's attitude to war service. Certainly, what he'd seen of Rob's art had been impressive. But didn't he feel any sense of patriotism, of common cause with the other young men who were going off to risk their lives in the fight against fascism? Clearly not.

But most of all he wanted Rob to stay in his life now, to be there when he returned from the war.

CHAPTER 14

"I told them I was married," Louis said.

There was an exhibition of Paul Nash's war paintings at the Tate Britain and Louis had asked me to take him. I stopped the wheelchair in front of a large canvas showing a blasted wood, shattered tree stumps black and brown, thrusting upwards from a sea of mud below a dramatic sky.

"Who was the lucky girl?" I asked.

"Ruth Crossland. Poor thing. I had no idea what she was up to or where she was - hadn't seen her since my brother died. But I told the army and I told the other fellows I'd married her before I left. Very handy with the other chaps."

"In North Africa you mean?"

"Yes, that's right. It's where I linked up with Peter Dashwood again too."

I'd known that. Louis had sometimes spoken of this friend from school, with whom he'd spent his time overseas.

"Why was being married such a good thing?"

Louis looked away from the painting.

"It made me seem more grown up, I suppose. More of

118

a man. At least in their eyes, the other men. It meant I
didn't have to go off to any brothels."

I smiled. "I can see that might have been handy."

"They didn't mind that I wasn't one of the boys. You
know how that one works don't you? That much hasn't
changed has it? A fellow has to show he's red blooded but
then, if he's married, he can be different. At least that's
how I played it and it seemed to work."

"Tell me about Peter Dashwood."

I rested on a bench. In the corner, an attendant in blue
uniform sat in a chair, snoozing.

"He was a friendly face," Louis said. "I hadn't expected
to see him there, but I felt happy when he appeared in the
mess room. He'd transferred from another unit, making up
the numbers, like me I suppose. Replacing those who fell
by the wayside."

"Casualties?"

"No, not in that sense. We weren't a fighting unit,
thank God."

I looked over at the Nash painting. Apparently Nash
survived the trenches because he fell and broke a rib.
While he was hospitalised, most of the rest of his unit were
killed assaulting a hill.

"I'm glad you weren't," I said.

"So am I, believe me. Only idiots say they're longing to
go into combat. Still, there was a lot to do and Peter
showed me the ropes. He'd been out there a year. My
Arabic was hopeless. He was a better linguist than me.
And I suppose…"

"What?"

Louis looked at his lap, lost in thought.

"What were you going to say Dad?"

"I was going to say. Well, that I was a bit in awe of
him."

"Of Peter Dashwood?"

"Yes. He was older you see, and he'd been a friend of
my brother. And, oh, this will sound foolish."

"Go on."

"He was a lot taller than me."

I laughed. "Taller than you?"

"Yes." Louis was grinning too. "It makes a difference at that age. And in the army too."

"I suppose it does." I laughed again.

"He took me under his wing. I was very green."

I remembered how Louis had described his schooldays, how Christopher had ignored him.

"Must have been nice, an older boy, looking after you."

"Yes it was," Louis said. "And I was grateful."

I got up and wheeled Louis over to the main entrance hall where a lift took us down to the restaurant. It's a gloomy underground room, though they've done their best with lighting and the murals are worth seeing.

Louis insisted on leaving the chair outside the restaurant and took my arm to help him walk in, weaving between the white table cloths to the place they'd reserved for us. He didn't want much to eat, but had a glass of wine with his sandwich and then poured another one. It was unlike him to drink so much but I was happy to see him enjoying himself.

"Like the pictures?" he asked. A landscape of mountains and lakes ran along one wall.

"Beautiful. Who did them?"

"Rex Whistler. In the '20s. Rob knew him."

I knew about Whistler. He'd not been as lucky as Paul Nash. In 1944, mortar fire in Normandy got him.

"They were a pretty casual bunch in North Africa," Louis said. "Gillett had relaxed his grip. No saluting and everyone used first names. Uniform code went to pot - the souks sold belts, scarves. We all decorated ourselves with the stuff. Wish I'd got a picture to show you."

"So discipline went to pot as well?"

"No, no. I've given you the wrong impression. We were just more informal. 93 FSS were a very competent lot."

"FSS?"

"Field Security Section. The clue's in the name. We provided field security. Meant we looked after the bits the military police didn't cover. Intelligence, civilians, that sort of thing."

I knew not to ask more, although there can't have been much secret work at that stage.

"I was only a few weeks in North Africa. The calm before the storm. Did I ever tell you about Lofty Elliott?"

I shook my head.

"My abiding memory of him was on the quayside in Oran, waiting to embark. One of the bikes was sputtering so he took the cylinder head off, cleaned something out, got the lid back on, all in fifteen minutes. Incredibly skilled mechanic."

Louis poured more wine. The sandwich wasn't getting eaten.

"Then there was Norman. Norman Gray. Interesting fellow. An older chap. Well, older than the rest of us. Spoke Arabic like a native. Wrote a lot of books after the war."

"What about?"

"Well, he wrote one about Naples. You should read it one day - I've got a copy he signed back at the house. Gives a good sense of what was going on there, what we were doing. Wrote others too. A travel writer I think you'd call him. I liked his company very much."

"Did he come to Naples with you?"

"Oh yes. Same unit. We all ended up there."

I sat back and looked at the half-eaten dinner on the plate. Louis took another sip of wine and I noticed the bottle was nearly empty.

"How's Karen?" Louis asked.

"Fine," I said. "Worried about you."

"So why doesn't she come and see me?"

I had no answer to that. I felt guilty that I hadn't pressed Louis hard enough, allowed him to avoid my needs. Louis was putting it off, stringing me along.

"I'll suggest it to her," I said.

Louis shrugged.

"It wiped the slate clean," he said.

"What did?"

"Going overseas. Going to war if you like. It wiped things clean. I could get enough distance from him, from Rob. I could try new things, new people. I thought I could try for a normal life, one with a woman in it. That I could grow out of him."

CHAPTER 15

In the late afternoon of 9th September 1943, Louis was in a landing craft approaching a beach near Paestum, Italy. He and the nine other men in his unit were standing with their packs between the rows of motorbikes lowered into the craft from the American troop ship. Shelling from the invasion fleet, which had been going on since early morning, had ceased, with only columns of smoke in the distance providing evidence of the conflict.

He fingered the stone in his pocket and thought of its other half, sitting in a glass jar on the mantelpiece at home; and he thought of his brother, what it must have been like for him to approach the battlefield at Jarama.

As the ramp lowered, Louis saw the beach ahead of him, rising to a low line of trees. Men were on the shore, unloading equipment onto wire mesh placed on the sand. To his left he saw dark shapes, laid out in a row, empty stretchers stacked nearby. With a jolt, he realised these must be soldiers killed earlier in the day, men he'd seen embarking at Oran only yesterday, some laughing and jostling each other, others grim faced, cigarettes hanging out of their mouths.

They spent half an hour getting themselves and the

bikes onto dry land. Between them and the row of bodies American soldiers were unloading desks, chairs and filing cabinets.

"What the fuck…" Elliott said, staring in disbelief at the office things.

A GI heard him. "HQ," he said. "They gotta have this stuff."

"Jesus wept," Elliott muttered, then added "Better get on with it. We can head for those woods and shelter there for the night."

Louis wondered where the Germans were. The dead men on the beach showed they existed, somewhere. He fingered the pistol he'd been given. It wasn't enough.

They drove the motorbikes over to the edge of the trees, dragged some of the wire mats behind a screen of shrubs and parked the bikes on them. Going along a narrow path they found a place to set up a temporary camp, settled in, brewed up tea, opened the ration packs and chewed on biscuits and canned meat. It was quiet, the sun sinking over the sea behind them, bird song in the trees dying with the evening light.

"Fancy a stroll old man?"

It was Peter Dashwood. It felt good to have his friendly presence. He made it sound like they were boy scouts on a camping trip.

He and Louis set off, moving inland with the leaf litter crackling under foot and the sound of birds overhead, until they reached the edge of the woods. Crouching, they peered out across the fields through gaps in the bushes.

Several hundred yards away were three ancient temples, two close together, the other away to the left. Rows of huge columns supported the remains of a roof structure on each. It was an astonishing sight; here was the grandeur of a two thousand year-old civilisation, the stones oblivious to the human conflict raging nearby. Without thinking, Louis stepped towards the monuments, leaving the shelter of the trees.

"Hold on," Dashwood said. He pointed to the cows in a field between them and the temples, lying lifeless on their backs, legs pointing up at the sky. "I wouldn't."

Louis saw what he meant and hurried back. They looked for a while and then turned to retrace their steps, keeping as quiet as they could. Louis was glad Peter was with him.

When they arrived at their bivouac Louis felt in his pocket again and, to his horror, realised his stone was gone. Frantic, he started searching through his things. It must have fallen into the leaf litter. He'd never find it there.

"Looking for this?"

It was Norman Gray, holding the stone.

Louis was embarrassed, but took the precious object from the older man. Gray smiled.

"Saw it drop out of your pocket before you left. Don't worry, lots of people have them. Want to see mine?"

He showed Louis a small wooden pig, no more than an inch long.

"This is Roger. Been with me since Tobruk. Got me out of a lot of scrapes."

The pig had black spots for eyes.

"Where d'you get it?"

"Fellow gave it to me. Both his legs got blown off by a mine. Afraid he'd lost faith in Roger so I said I'd look after him."

Gray put it back in his pocket, grinned at Louis and turned away.

During the night, lying in the undergrowth, Louis awoke and heard bushes rustling with the movement of men, their low voices speaking. After a while, he heard no more and fell asleep. Then he woke up again and wondered about the voices. Had they been German? The thought kept him awake until dawn.

That morning they broke camp and headed back towards the beach. As they approached the place where they'd left the motorbikes, a young American soldier leapt out from behind a bush, his rifle pointing straight at Norman who was in the lead.

"Password!" shouted the soldier, gripping his rifle tight, shaking with nerves.

"Careful or that'll go off," Gray said.

"Who in hell's name are you guys?" the soldier asked, relaxing his grip.

"Afraid no-one gave us a password. We're British."

The sentry, if that's what he was, looked puzzled but lowered his weapon. He must have known enough about the army to realise this was plausible. A couple more GIs sauntered over.

"Nice bikes," commented one of them as Louis and his friends took the machines off their stands. "Where you headed?"

"Where's HQ?" Norman asked. "We're attached. Need to get over there."

The soldier replied: "Up at the ruins."

Louis realised this must mean the temples. It might have been safe to go there last night after all.

"They figured the planes wouldn't get 'em there."

"We'd better find them then," Norman said, kicking his bike into life.

There were only six bikes so Louis joined men trudging on foot towards the temples. With them were streams of American soldiers lugging typewriters, filing cabinets, folding tables and chairs from the pile of office equipment on the beach.

Norman Gray was on the temple steps by the time he arrived. He had their orders, he announced. They were to stick close to HQ and await further orders.

Jimmy Harris, the unit's clerk, issued his verdict. "They've got no bleeding idea what to do with us."

Then they heard a lone engine in the sky, approaching them. The men moved towards the stone columns, looking up. It was a German plane, flying low and fast.

There was a brief burst of machine gun fire as it passed over them.

"On its way to the beach," someone said.

Something knocked against Louis' pack and he turned round. On the ground was a large bullet, warm to the touch. There was no damage to his pack as the bullet was spent when it reached him. He picked it up, felt its weight and put it in his pocket, a souvenir.

They spent the next few days following the American HQ as it relocated, first a few miles north, then further along the road to Battipaglia near a bridge over the Sele river. This was about sixty miles south of Naples. The Germans had blown the bridge but only weakened it, and British engineers were repairing it to allow tanks to cross.

They camped for two days in an abandoned farmhouse. In the distance there were columns of smoke rising into the blue sky, evidence of fighting further north. American soldiers hung around in groups, smoking or playing cards, or raided the orchards for apples. An enterprising group chased down a cow, butchered it and shared the resulting meat which they cooked over a fire. There were still no further orders. Gillett had embarked from Oran separately from the rest of his men and was believed to be in Salerno, so Norman Gray had taken temporary command. The HQ staff must have sensed that he had no real authority and avoided answering him whenever he approached them. Louis found the absence of meaningful activity unsettling, but the others were clearly used to it.

Then, groups of Italian soldiers appeared, disarmed and plodding southwards. Their government had switched sides in July and they were happy to have given up the fight. Louis handed them sweets from his rations and practised his Italian. It looked as if Louis and his friends were in for an easy time, mooching around all day, lining up at the chow wagon in the evenings and finishing the days with bottles of wine from the cellar.

But on the morning of the third day everything changed. Sitting outside the farmhouse in the sun, expecting another lazy day foraging for food and drink, Louis heard vehicles coming towards them from the bridge. Two field ambulances swerved round the corner followed by a jeep with a man on a stretcher slung across the back.

Minutes later, American soldiers came running, some without helmets or limping as they ran. A shell whistled overhead and exploded where the ambulances had been a moment earlier. The soldier at the head of the fleeing group was blown over by the shock waves, but then stood up, at first wobbly on his feet, and resumed his flight.

Louis stopped one of the men. "What's happening?" he shouted, but the man just looked at him with fear crazed eyes, shook himself free and headed on down the road.

"I suppose we'd better start packing," Norman said.

Hastily, they stuffed what they could into their packs and started up the motorbikes. Elliott had obtained a van from somewhere and Louis was in the back as the convoy roared off past the fleeing soldiers.

A half mile later they were stopped. The Americans were regrouping. German tanks had penetrated the lines between the Sele and Calore rivers, hoping to roll the Americans back into the sea at Paestum. They were to hold the new line against the German advance, defend the HQ. Louis and the others were told to dig slit trenches in the olive groves alongside GIs. They hacked into the stony earth all morning, until they could dig no deeper, and waited.

That afternoon and throughout the night there was an almighty din as the battleships anchored off shore opened up on the German advance. Massive explosions vibrated the ground and sent winds that shook the olive trees and blew across their faces, orange-red flashes in the distance.

Then, around midnight, rifle fire started up. Louis

crouched down in his trench. Were they being attacked? A pistol and a few rounds of ammunition were all he had. His heart was racing and his chest moved with short gasps of breath. He wasn't sure if he should look out over the top of the trench until he saw someone else curled up in his own dugout, arms over his head. Louis followed suit, terrified but also horrified at his own terror.

Men were screaming with pain as bullets hit them. During a lull in the noise from the offshore guns, an American officer shouted at the top of his voice "Stop shooting! Cease firing!" The GIs had been shooting at each other, spooked by the idea they'd been infiltrated by Germans.

Apparently the naval bombardment was enough to persuade the Germans to withdraw. The next day, the Americans emerged from their trenches and Louis and the others found their vehicles and drove back past the positions they'd abandoned. Then they advanced up to the river. The bridge had collapsed under the weight of a tank, stuck nose down in the water. The British engineers had done an inadequate job of strengthening the structure, and that had saved the day.

The work of re-establishing Headquarters proceeded, and it seemed things would return to normal, the farm house once more being occupied by the FSS men, when Norman Gray announced he needed volunteers to go to Salerno to see if Gillett, their CO, had arrived yet.

Louis said he'd go and Dashwood said he'd better come too. They set off in a jeep. The ruined tank had been detached from the bridge by then and a temporary structure allowed them to cross. On the other side, they drove along the road to Battaglia. There were two German tanks, one on its side, the tracks blown off, a dead man still hanging out of the turret, the other at the bottom of a huge crater, blackened by smoke. These were the armaments that had nearly overrun them, halted by the naval gunfire.

They stopped. One of the dead man's arms was twisted round his head, as if he were wrenching it off. His other arm had been torn off at the shoulder. He was black with smoke.

"It's hard to believe we're here, in the middle of this," Louis said.

"Better get used to it old son," Dashwood said. "Want to take a closer look?"

Louis shook his head. Dashwood descended from the jeep and walked over to the tank, approached the body and poked it with a stick. Louis, watching him, could see that there was a pool of translucent liquid beneath the tracks.

"What's that?" he called out, then in more alarm, "it could be petrol. Don't get too close Peter."

"Not petrol," Dashwood called back, turning toward the jeep

"What is it? That liquid?"

"You really don't want to know."

"What is it?"

"Fat. Human fat," replied Dashwood starting up the engine again. "Melted. There were other men inside that tank. Like an oven in there."

Louis wanted to retch and leaned over the side of the jeep. The only bodies he had seen so far in this war were sanitised: the rows of body bags on the beach when they landed. The Germans had died a dreadful death, one that might happen to any of them.

Further down the road they were stopped at a village by an American, who held his rifle to their faces, ordered them out of the jeep, and asked, once again, for the password. This had been amusing the first time, but now was just irritating.

"We haven't got the fucking password," Louis said. "No-one's bothered to tell us."

Once again, the soldier had no idea what to do. They explained to him they were British, attached to HQ, on the way to Salerno to find their commanding officer who'd landed with the forces further north. The GI, mesmerised by their British accents, relented, directing them off the Battaglia road. If they wanted to get to Salerno, they'd have to take the smaller roads nearer the coast. The route to Battaglia wasn't cleared of Germans yet.

"So what is the password then?" Louis asked.

The man hesitated.

"In case we get stopped again."

The GI nodded, understanding. "Oh, okay fellers. It's Thunderflash. That should work, mostly. They keep changing it though."

They followed a narrow side road and wended their way through a network of small lanes in a direction they judged to be roughly parallel with the shore.

"What a shambles," Louis said. "No-one knows what's going on."

"Fog of war old son, fog of war. You'll get used to it."

"Did you see that paratrooper the other day, the one who got back from Avellino? He was crystal clear about what happened to him."

The paratrooper had been furious, cursing his superior officers for dropping six hundred of them miles to the north in a failed attempt to breach the enemy line from the rear. They'd been so widely dispersed at the drop site they were split into isolated groups, which the Germans had picked off at their leisure. He'd somehow got back with a few other survivors.

"I reckon the Yanks are winning though," Dashwood said, bumping the jeep over potholes. "We'll see Rome, eh?"

"Or die," Louis added.

Dashwood grunted and drove on.

As they approached the outskirts of Salerno, they realised fighting was still going on. Near Security

Headquarters there was the sound of mortar bomb explosions. Next to a fountain an officer was hitting a man around the head. The man was in a chair, his hands held behind him by a large, muscular sergeant. The man's head was bloody, and he took the beating without uttering a sound, too dazed to feel the blows. As Louis watched, the officer pulled out his pistol and put it to the man's head, then called out to them.

"Hey you, soldier. Do either of you speak his lingo? Tell him I'll shoot him if he doesn't tell me what I want."

Louis was repelled by the scene. Blood dripped from the man's chin onto the ground between his feet.

"Get on with it, or I'll do him anyway," the man with the gun said, breathing heavily.

Louis found the Italian words to express the threat. There was no reaction from the prisoner.

"I think he's -"

"Bloody wops," the officer said, holstering his pistol. "Hold him will you," he said to the sergeant behind the chair who increased his grip. The prisoner gave out a low groan as the officer raised his hand again, ready to strike.

Then Louis felt Dashwood shove him in the back, pushing him away from the scene and into the building. As he crossed the threshold into the coolness of a dark interior, Louis waited for the sound of a shot outside, but none came.

They went up a stone staircase. It was the town hall. Ken Gillett was in a room, behind a desk strewn with papers. He was thinner, looked tired, his skin shaded yellow.

"Did you see what's happening out there?" Louis said as Gillett nodded a hello to them.

The FSS captain stared at Louis, then walked over to the window to look at the square below.

"Nothing going on down there," he said, returning to his desk. "Good to see you," he said, sitting again and waving them to do the same. He offered each of them a cigarette from a silver case.

"How is everyone?" he asked.

It was as if they were paying a social visit to an older relative, an uncle perhaps, who'd been out of touch for a while.

"We're all fine thanks," Dashwood said. "Thought we'd come and see how you're getting along."

Outside, a pistol shot rang out. Louis started out of his chair and went over to the window. The prisoner was on his feet, staggering across the square, held up by the burly sergeant. Dashwood came over and put a hand on his arm, guiding him back to his seat.

"He wouldn't have done it you know," he whispered into Louis' ear. "Just putting the wind up him."

Louis noticed that the mortar fire had stopped.

"It's been busy here," Gillett said, waving his hand to indicate the town. "I could use you fellows for a few days."

"That's a relief," Dashwood said. "There's nothing going on at Paestum. They don't know what to do with us."

"Well that's par for the course," Gillett said. Then he explained what he needed them for. Lights had been seen at night in Piezzo, about two miles inland. The villagers could be signalling to Germans in the nearby hills. They had to put a stop to it. They'd go with a detachment of men from the Hampshires that night and question whoever they caught.

"You can show off your Italian," he said to Louis.

Louis' mind was still filled with the image of the man in the square outside. Is that how he was supposed to treat prisoners? He wasn't sure he could do it.

"There's food downstairs," Gillett told them. "Get some rest and be ready for your little outing at nine o'clock, sharp."

Louis turned to go. As he reached the door, Gillett spoke again.

"And do stop worrying about that Italian cunt out in the yard won't you? Spoil your appetite."

That evening, after nightfall, they went through the dark streets with five of the Hampshires. The town was quiet. Patrols stopped them three times with a whispered challenge, but they knew the password so they moved on without trouble. They turned out of the town along a narrow lane to Piezzo, the moon behind clouds most of the way. A sergeant shone a thin beam of light onto a map and directed Louis and two soldiers down a path between olive groves. The larger of the soldiers walked ahead until they found a position on a rise above the settlement where they lay on the soft earth and waited.

Three hours passed with no sign of life. Louis was stiff and cold. He turned to lie on his back. They'd take turns watching.

He thought about the dead German he'd seen that day, the man's body, twisted out of shape, blackened. Other images formed in his mind, the distorted shapes of the bronzes in Rob's studio, their cruelly deformed features, the torment they expressed. Then one of his companions grunted in surprise and Louis turned to look. He saw a light winking on and off in the valley. There was no doubt: it was a torch, swaying back and forth.

"Bastard," the larger soldier said. "Let's fetch him out of there. You stay there," he said to Louis, "we'll bring him to you."

Louis almost said "Don't hurt him," but bit his tongue. There must be Germans nearby if the torch was signalling to them. He stayed quiet, wondering again how he'd manage the interrogation.

Moments later, the men returned, half shoving, half carrying an old man who clutched a torch in his hand.

"It's the fucking village bog," the smaller soldier said, laughing, "but you'd better get it straight from him."

Louis spoke with the Italian, who was terrified. His trousers were coming apart at the waist and Louis let him tie them up with a piece of string serving as a belt. They'd found him in a wooden hut, sitting on a toilet.

Louis' ear was not yet attuned to the dialect spoken by the frightened man, so he only got part of the story. The hut was the only outside lavatory for the small settlement at Piezzo. At night, the villagers used a torch to light the way.

"False fucking alarm," said the smaller soldier. "The whole bloody show. Fucking wild goose chase."

The three of them grinned at the collective stupidity of their mission, of the situation they were in, of the whole army. Louis felt a momentary bond between the three of them as they laughed about it, and then they sent the relieved villager on his way.

CHAPTER 16

"Naples was bloody hard work," Louis said.

It had been a good day. He'd risen from his bed and announced he wanted to go out, so after dressing him, I helped him into a wheelchair and we emerged into the street, heading for the Heath.

"I want to go to the café," he said.

He was wrapped up in a tartan blanket, a hot water bottle on his lap, though the day was not that cold. In fact, the sun, together with pushing the wheelchair, made me warm, so I took off my coat as we passed the running track. Louis said he wanted to sit outside and pointed to a table.

"Over there. I want that one."

He sent me into the café with instructions to ask for poppy seed cake. But they had none, didn't seem to know what it was, so I got a couple of Danish pastries.

"Seventy years ago," he said when I returned, "I was here."

I had my own memories of being there; of me and Rob when I was small. We'd spend the afternoon at the playground, sometimes end it with a treat, Rob chatting with some of the mothers, most of whom seemed to find it amusing that he took me to the playground. I wonder, did they suspect anything? It was a time when the police were arresting men like Rob and Louis, though I knew nothing about that as a child. How did they get away with it? And with me, their son, living with them? It was unheard of in those days. But perhaps that was the very thing that protected them - it was simply too bizarre for people to believe.

Recently the park authorities had wanted to kick out the Italian family that had run the café for decades, to let a chain restaurant take over. Local people protested, signed a petition, and the strength of feeling led the chain to pull out. The link with the past was unbroken.

"Tell me about Naples," I said.

His abiding memories of the first few days were of the bombed houses, the ruined streets in which families lived their lives in full view of the passing public, the desperation of people who had been reduced to the level of starving animals, and the particular degradations experienced by women and children.

His introduction to the plight of Italian women came early, as the truck taking him towards Naples reached an open square and pulled in near a large public building, whose shattered windows spilled broken glass onto the street. Laughing soldiers were coming out, taking ration tins from a supply truck, then going back inside.

Louis, Elliott and Dashwood entered while the others stretched their legs. Inside there was a large meeting room. Forty or fifty GIs had packed into it, passing bottles around, joking and pushing each other, having a party. In a space at the far end three Italian women lay on mattresses, each with a pile of tins next to them. The soldiers had formed a semi-circle around them. There was no expression on the women's faces. One of them looked about eighteen. The other two were older than this, older in fact than most of the soldiers jostling around them, dark-haired, one with a dirty white coat unbuttoned, the other hard-faced in a dark blue dress. Catcalls and jeers started up when one GI walked along the line grabbing tins and dumped them angrily next to the women, then pushed his way out, shaking his head.

A group near the younger woman were egging on a soldier, encouraging him to drink from a wine bottle. The man seemed the same age as the girl, who looked away from him as he unbuttoned his trousers, swaying.

Dashwood and Elliott wanted to watch, but Louis shoved through the crowd and stumbled out into the open air, glass crunching under his boots. The older women could have been married housewives, the younger a sister to any one of those men.

Later, he got used to seeing queues of soldiers outside doors, going into basements where women made themselves available. In one house a father advertised his daughter as the only virgin left in Naples, charging men to inspect the young woman and see for themselves. In the Via Toledo painted women sat on steps, opening their legs as soldiers passed by, calling "Hi, Joe! Hi, Joe!" and disappearing with their catches down dark side streets.

And signs warning of the dangers of venereal disease were placed at strategic locations. One tried to play on the soldiers' consciences:

'EVERYONE is in this war. Your Mother Wife Sweetheart. They are LONESOME too. Give them a break. VENEREAL DISEASE can be prevented.'

The newspapers contained notices in both Italian and English for the troops to cut out, keep and use when needed:

'ATTENTION! I have no interest in your syphilitic friends, much less your sister. We are here to win the war and to make Italy free once again. Why don't you help?'

There were also aid stations where you could wash yourself after sex and obtain free condoms. But these, and the warnings had limited impact. VD was an enormous drain on fighting strength, and most of the infection came from Naples.

The unit set up shop in an old palazzo at the end of the seafront, a baroque fantasy of a place. On the fourth floor, Louis worked in an office with a view out to the Bay of Naples. At first he vetted Italians applying for jobs with the military authorities. But the battle for Monte Cassino held up the Allied advance and extended their stay from weeks to months. Increasingly he was given Italian women to interview, whose British soldier boyfriends had proposed marriage. He was supposed to discover the women were prostitutes, so the soldiers could be discouraged. But to Louis the liaisons made sense. The women would be able to feed themselves and their families; the men would find love. His sympathetic reports annoyed Gillett, so he was taken off this work.

"You're too soft on them," Dashwood commented when Louis received the news he'd been reassigned.

Now he had to examine the files the section had retrieved from the German consulate, cross-checking them against the denunciations flooding into their headquarters in the Piazza Vittoria. A lot of these were the product of vendettas, claiming someone was a fascist or a black marketeer. The work was demanding, but it got Louis out into the streets, meeting and questioning suspects.

He often felt exhausted, realising they'd never bring order to this devastated city, however hard they worked. Crime was everywhere and the Allied military government delivered rough justice. Those with connections got off; those with none were locked up, or were fined sums they had no hope of paying, so that they were driven to commit fresh crimes. It was a never-ending cycle.

While many Italians starved, restaurants providing meals for military personnel thrived. Dashwood and Elliott found a seafood restaurant and insisted he ate there. The owner threw live eels into a hot frying pan where they squirmed as they died. A cook nonchalantly sliced a tentacle off a writhing octopus, throwing the piece into a soup and returning the rest of the animal to its tank. Louis did not go back.

He preferred the café below his boarding house in Via Alabardieri where he and three of the others in his unit were billeted. The FSS men were popular with Gino, the owner, as their presence meant he could obtain kitchen supplies from the military. These he used to cook up gorgeous meals to feed both them and a series of better-off Italian clients, as if it were peace time in some well-heeled quarter of a European city.

Yet the café did not always insulate them from the sea of poverty and suffering that surrounded them. One evening they sat around a table eating lasagne when a group of little girls entered the restaurant, all dressed in black, led by a nun holding a tin. The girls looked eight or nine years old and were holding hands. The procession passed from table to table, asking for alms. This was unusual as Gino usually chased beggars away. Perhaps it was the presence of a nun.

When the girls got to their table, Louis realised the girls were all blind. He gave them the change in his pockets and his companions did the same. The little girls were silent, and in their silence processed out of the café. The talk around the tables had gone quiet, but gathered volume again as the image of the small dark figures faded, and normal service was resumed.

"It was the children that upset me most," Louis said, taking a bite out of his pastry. The sun came out from behind a cloud and cast a ray of warmth over us.

It wasn't just the blind girls in the café who distressed him. They were a sharp and stinging example, but they were only a symptom of what was going on as the delicate, complex economy of the city disintegrated. The children suffered worst of all.

Ragged, barefoot urchins ran round the streets, following army vehicles, calling out to the soldiers, scrabbling in the dirt for the sweets and food thrown to them. They dislodged limpets from the harbour rocks to boil up in repulsive stews. They approached soldiers on street corners, begging or offering to take the men to their 'sisters'. Louis wondered whether some were pimping for their mothers.

And the children died. Early in his time in Naples a vast booby trap bomb left by the Germans exploded in the Palazzo delle Poste, less than a mile away from his offices. He heard the explosion and the windows shook in their frames. He went to look. Rescuers had dug two small bodies out of the rubble, laying them side by side. Their heads hung backwards, mouths drawn open, their dark hair white with stone dust. In each one's arms, someone had placed a brand new doll.

Children could also be sold. The market for this was the Cappella Vecchia, where haggard women negotiated prices, their bony hands clutching smaller ones until money changed hands. Three dollars bought a small boy for an hour. The authorities periodically chased them away, but they came back. There were always customers. Anything, and anyone, was sold in the struggle for survival.

"It was a concentration camp for those children," Louis said, putting his pastry down uneaten. "There was no escape for them. They were treated like meat. It was the most appalling thing I ever saw as a soldier."

"Couldn't you have done something to stop it?"

"Yes, of course, we could have locked them up, opened up orphanages. As a matter of fact we did. But there were always fresh supplies, coming in from the countryside. You can't imagine what it was like. Cassino was going on up the road and the men who came back from there were often in a terrible state themselves. Their basest instincts were unleashed."

Most of my father's generation talked about World War Two, if at all, as an adventure, perhaps the greatest adventure of their lives. The trenches of World War One were the location chosen to illustrate the horrors of war. This sounded like a different kind of horror.

"Vesuvius blew its top while I was there," Louis said. "If you were religious, you might think it was the mountain rebelling against what was going on below. The Neapolitans certainly thought it was a sign from God. Gillett sent me up to San Sebastiano. Assess the situation he said, with Norman and Lofty. On the way there was this crowd of screaming women battering at the door of a brothel. They thought the eruption was a punishment for all that sin. Dragged the women out into the street and knocked them about. We tried to stop them but there weren't enough of us. Then we got to the village, ash still falling out of the sky and this great wall of heated rock crunching its way through the houses. Creaking, shuddering, then collapsing."

"Did it stop?"

"Yes. Eventually. And naturally they thought they'd done it."

"Who?"

"The Italians, the priests, the people with them, on their knees praying, shaking their crosses at the lava, some saintly statue nearby that they'd brought there to help. They thought that was what stopped the lava flow."

Louis was an atheist, Rob too. I looked at the playground where children slid down slides, laughed, pushed each other on swings. A toddler was sobbing while his mother tended to a graze on his knee.

"You must have grown up fast."

Louis smiled. "I suppose I did. Needed to, if the truth be told."

"Did you think about Rob?"

"I tried not to. And I succeeded for a while. I was incredibly busy in Naples, so intense I hardly had time to think about my emotional life. But then I got a letter from him."

"What did he say?"

"It was the handwriting that did it. You remember?"

I nodded.

"It brought him back to me, just seeing that wonderful script. But then the pain of it all came back too, if you must know, like an anaesthetic wearing off. Here, I brought his letter to show you. It made me very unhappy. You'll have to read between the lines; army censorship and all that. "

He handed me an envelope. The letter inside was dated March 1944, written in Rob's flowing, expressive hand.

Dear Louis,

Haven't heard from you in ages! You must write soon. Don't delay!

News from home (my contribution): I thought things were quiet, but it seems February is the season for bombing. Nothing near us, luckily and things have quietened down for now. Vita and I don't go to the first aid post any more - they don't need us - so I can work in the studio all the time if I like, except I don't like. Am missing your company. When will you be back? Don't they give you leave or something? I can only concentrate for an hour or two most days. Anyway, the modelling clay is running out too now, though I can't see why that's needed for the war effort.

I was with Vita at the Finchley allotments the other day. Peter next door has got one, and we helped him dig out the couch grass. He's got back trouble. He says he'll put a strawberry patch in. Imagine that! Strawberries! I hope the birds don't get them, or someone steals them. There's a lot of thieving up at the allotments. Talk about all pulling together. Pulling up each other's carrots is more like it.

Vita is well. I know you were worried about her last time you saw her. She's still thinking about Kurt but...

Speaking of which, I've just remembered. Vita says can you see if you can find Kurt? She's made me promise to ask. It sounds silly, the whole of Europe and everything, but she made me promise to say. She thinks he must be somewhere in Austria still. Might you be going there? I realise you're not allowed to say. She's going a bit mad about him.

Look, I have to tell you. Frankie was out of touch for ages, but now he's started turning up at the house again. You two didn't get on, but he's changed so much since he joined the fire service. I'm sure you'd see that if you got to know him better. He worked his socks off in the East End last month when the bombers came over again. He says he comes here for rest and recreation. That's what the Americans say, isn't it? Rest and recreation. There are so many Yanks in London now!

Message from Ruth: says she won't make a fuss if you stray. She's well aware of what men get up to when they're far from home. Says it's healthy and natural, and after all you put up with from her, understandable. Just come back safe that's all.

Off to Hornsey now. Moore's still teaching there. He's a brilliant man, and he takes a special interest in me, which is nice. I'll get this in the post if I hurry.

Eternal friendship, Robert.

"I can see why it upset you."

"Whenever Frank was around," Louis said, "Rob would go soft at the knees. He had a hold over Rob. I felt it when I first met him, in this café, right here!"

Louis thumped the table, a flimsy thing that rattled as his hand hit it, making the cups and saucers shake.

"Rob saw that letter as a contract." The memory of ancient hurt lined his forehead. "Except it was a contract I hadn't signed. I'll do what I want, he was saying, and you can do what you want. The problem was, I only wanted him. As he knew very well."

His fist was still on the table and I put my hand over it, gently moving it away to rest on his lap again. His fingers loosened as he relaxed.

"Do you want me to take you home?"

"No. It's nice here. It has some good memories too."

He leaned back in his chair, calmer now, and continued his story.

When the letter arrived, Louis was with Peter Dashwood. It was a Sunday, and they had a day off, so were sitting in battered armchairs in the entrance to the boarding house. Dashwood slumped in one, smoking a cigarette and recovering from a drinking session the night before. He'd been out on the town, the Galleria, at a bar.

It took Louis a while to realise what Rob was proposing, but when he did, he gave out a groan of pain that caught Dashwood's attention.

"What's that old man?"

"Letter from home. About Ruth. She's upset me again."

Louis felt the danger in saying this, but couldn't help himself. He'd told Peter he and Ruth had a quiet wedding in London, the day before he'd left for Oran. Once in a while the topic had come up, and he'd got used to telling Peter about his feelings for Rob through the smokescreen of his fictitious marriage to Ruth. It meant he could at least talk to someone, even if it was indirect, and Dashwood had shown no sign of suspecting.

"Let me read it," Dashwood said, sending a quiver of fear through Louis.

"It's private," he said, putting the letter into his jacket

pocket.

Dashwood shrugged. "Aren't you going to tell me what's upset you then?"

"She's taken up with another chap."

"Bit of a goer, that Ruth," Dashwood said, blowing smoke from his nose as he snorted out a laugh.

Dashwood could be disgusting. He knew how Louis felt. Again he threw caution to the winds.

"Don't you understand Peter? She's up to things with another man. Says I'm to do the same if I want. She wants it to look as if she's being generous, but -"

"What are you worried about?"

"We're married!"

"Strikes me that was a bit of a confidence trick."

"What do you mean?" Again, Louis felt terrified. Dashwood must have seen through the pretence. He'd better knock this conversation on the head. It was getting out of hand.

"I mean," Dashwood added, "It's not as if it's a real marriage is it? The night before you left. What's the point of that?"

Louis was unable to reply. His fear at being discovered rose up in him until he felt nauseous.

"You ought to take her advice," Dashwood said. "Help you get over her."

"But I don't want to get over her."

"Yes you do. You just don't know it. Come with me to Capri. Lofty's been sent to Sorrento so there's a girl going spare."

Louis relaxed. Dashwood suspected nothing. He'd heard about this trip, which Dashwood and Lofty Elliott had planned for the following weekend. But he'd have to keep up the pretence. "I'll think about it," he said and stomped up the stairs to his room.

CHAPTER 17

Louis leaned on the rail of the naval launch carrying supplies to Capri and looked back at Naples. There was a mist over the town and the powerful colours of the city had faded to a distant grey. Dashwood was right: it was good to get away. And he needed to take the idea of trying with a woman more seriously. Everything would be easier if he could just do that.

He ran his fingers over the stone his pocket. The smooth egg-like surface of the one side contrasted with the sharper parts where his brother had broken it in half before he went to Spain. Louis had a sudden urge to throw it into the sea, but withdrew his hand before he could act on the impulse.

Vesuvius was in the distance and he remembered the eruption, seeing the lava rolling along the main street of San Sebastiano, a giant invader. Now the mountain was quiet.

He turned to look at the girls Dashwood had invited: Susanna and Lola. He had no idea where Dashwood had found them and didn't much care. They were eating white bread, laughing as they threw crusts to the seagulls following the boat which was nearing the marina. A day in

Capri meant a day in a magical fantasy, under the illusion that the war did not exist, that Naples was clean and bathed in an airy lightness. Getting a pass for the trip would not have been easy. He should be grateful.

The two women had dressed for the occasion, ridiculously he thought, in furs and straw hats decorated with glass fruits. Dashwood looked awkward in his pressed uniform, a polka-dotted scarf around his neck pretending to a Desert Rat image he had little chance of carrying off. As the boat approached the harbour Louis found himself drawn to the sight of Susanna's generous breasts and buttocks as the women threw the last of the bread to the gulls and then teetered giggling on high heels across the swaying gangplank. Why not, he thought. He could do this. It was time.

They got off the boat and walked towards the funicular. On their way, they stopped to watch a pair of dogs stuck together after copulating. People were laughing and pointing at the animals. The girls giggled at the sight until Dashwood pulled them away.

The funicular elevated them to the main town and they strolled through the narrow streets. Louis wanted to see the cliffs on the other side of the island, but within fifty yards the girls complained they'd gone far enough in their heels, so they returned to the Piazzetta where there was a café. An American officer was at one table, his arms around two women, singing something from an opera. Dashwood ordered marsala for them. The girls took bread from their handbags they'd saved from the gulls, chewing it as they drank, laughing and chatting in rapid Italian.

Louis noticed a small, grey haired Italian man sitting at a table on the opposite side of the square who waved to him in cheery recognition. He realised this was someone he'd arrested for black market activities in December, which should have resulted in a long spell in jail. He must have had contacts who'd got him released. Louis didn't care either way. Cleaning up Naples was a hopeless cause.

Dashwood nudged his shoulder to point towards a middle aged woman, but Louis couldn't hear what he said as the municipal loudspeakers struck up with crackly dance music.

"Did they have to start that noise?" Dashwood said irritably, but then his red, sunburned face softened into a smile when he saw a woman from the American's table take her soldier friend by the hand and launch into a dance. Lola beckoned to Dashwood. "Suppose I ought to have a go," he said sheepishly, and shuffled around in front of the café tables with his arm around Lola's waist, she pressing her body into his.

Louis observed to Susanna in English, "She knows which side her bread is buttered."

She smiled happily at this, understanding nothing. It was enough for him. He'd agreed to this trip, but he still wasn't sure about him and Susanna. Dashwood could do what he liked with Lola.

"What's the fucking smirk for Nicko?" Dashwood said, returning to the table with Lola, his face hot with effort.

Louis pointed to the grey-haired Italian. "I was just looking at the fellow over there. He's a familiar face."

The girls noticed the man, whispered to each other and went into the café. Louis followed them, telling Dashwood to keep an eye on the Italian, who continued to stare. Inside, it was clear the women had left through the back entrance. Something was up and the men went in search of them.

The place was so small it wasn't hard to find them, sitting together on a stone bench in an alcove. Louis listened as the words tumbled out of Lola's mouth in rapid Italian to explain their departure.

"What's she saying? You understand the lingo better than me," Dashwood asked.

Lola claimed the man with grey hair was an old family friend who'd developed a crush on her. She'd told him a hundred times to leave her alone, but he followed her around like a dog, embarrassing her by turning up in odd places, though nothing had ever happened between them.

Dashwood offered to go back up the hill and confront the man, but Lola objected. She said he was a sorry fellow, she could manage him, she didn't want them to fight. But they should cut the trip short.

On the boat back to Naples, the girls sitting inside the cabin, Dashwood asked if he knew anything about the man.

"I heard what she was whispering to Susanna. She's making it up I'm afraid."

"Lola said she fancied me when we were dancing."

"And I'm sure she does. But Naples isn't a place for the weak hearted. How do you think they got those handbags and furs? Those things don't come without payment nowadays and Lola's only got one thing to sell. That chap back there - one of her clients."

"We must be in credit then. You should cash in tonight. Take your mind off things."

"And you?" Louis asked.

An awkward look crossed Dashwood's face. "Yes, me too." Then he brightened, adding, "Nothing like a bit of togetherness."

Later that evening after a meal and a couple of bottles of wine at the Alabardieri restaurant they proceeded upstairs with the two women to Dashwood's room. He had a gramophone, and they danced, getting through another bottle between records. It was a hot night, and the windows were open. The tinny sound of the music, the wine, the smell of sweat overlaid with a powerful perfume coming from Susanna as her thighs pressed against his, made his head spin. Lola lay on the sofa, arms and legs splayed out, snoring. Dashwood himself was nearly as comatose, holding on to a bottle from which he took occasional swigs, then lying back, eyes closed.

Louis kissed Susanna. Her tongue tasted of mint. To his surprise and pleasure, his desire surged and he pressed himself hard against her, his hand sliding inside her blouse.

She pushed him away a little so she could take the clothing out of his way and they fell onto Dashwood's bed, her hands parting his shirt to slide all over his chest. At her touch he remembered Rob's hands travelling over his body, but then put it out of his mind. It had been an age since he'd had this kind of contact with another human being.

He glanced over at Dashwood and Lola, who both seemed to be asleep. He was on his back. Susanna, in between undoing his buttons, was pressing her mouth to his and issuing little moans of pleasure which excited him. He got rid of his trousers and turned her over, lifting up her skirt. Looking again, he saw Dashwood watching them, now wide awake with eyes gleaming with excitement.

Louis stopped his movements, but Susanna drew his face back to hers, laughing and kissing him. She could see Dashwood too, but it didn't bother her. Her body moved under his insistently and he looked down at her, his excitement rising again as she whispered, running her hands over his back and onto his buttocks, pulling him into her. Her body arched under his as he came.

His desire subsiding, he rolled off and sat up, looking again at Dashwood who had turned his head away. All the way up his right arm, Louis could see a series of burn marks, just like the one he'd made at school when, showing Louis no hint of any pain, he had carefully stubbed out a cigarette.

"I'm ashamed of myself," Louis said. We were still at the café table. He'd told me about this episode with Susanna in a quiet voice, hushed so the people at other tables couldn't overhear us. It was getting cooler as clouds gathered overhead.

"It wasn't disloyalty to Rob," Louis continued. "All of that went by the wayside when I got that letter from him. I felt I needed a more normal life, and this was a way to find one. But I was taking advantage of Susanna. I could give her things she needed to survive, to have a reasonable life. And she gave me sex in exchange. I had no illusions that anything else was going on. But once I'd started I didn't want to stop. She was very lovely and I desperately wanted to make things work with a woman. I couldn't say no."

"We'd better get back," I said, gathering up his blanket and tucking it round his legs. I went into the café with the hot water bottle to ask for a refill.

I saw what he meant about Susanna, but didn't see why he should feel ashamed. He'd been dealt a pretty awkward hand himself as a gay man in the 1940s. It sounded like Louis was looking for a way out.

Was that what Ellie was too, a way out? Another escape attempt, with me as the end product?

I wrapped a blanket round his legs and offered him an umbrella to hold, but he shook his head. As I wheeled him past the running track a few spots of rain began to appear and I quickened the pace. Looking at his scalp, I saw patches of brown, mottled skin on the bald areas of his skull. His white hair flew about in the wind and his hands gripped the sides of the wheelchair.

Back at the house, he said he needed a sleep so we got him into the stair lift and up to bed. By the time I'd finished getting him settled I was tired. We should get one of those electric scooters. Louis would like that. He'd race about the Heath in it and I wouldn't need to push.

Downstairs I made myself a coffee. It had been a good day for Louis, out and about most of the morning, talking much of the time. Most of that week he'd not wanted to go out, had slept or sat at the window, staring out at people in the street below, apparently empty of thought. Is that what it's like to be very old, and to be dying?

We hadn't spoken about him dying. We talked about sex but not death, arguably a subject more relevant to his present circumstances. Death is the last taboo, some people say.

I wandered around the kitchen. A row of Rob's old recipe books was on the shelf above big cupboards containing bowls, none of which were used by Louis these days. Rob was quite a collector of cookery books and liked to tear out recipes from colour magazines too. He stored them in two files, one for savoury, the other for sweet. There were far more recipes than he needed; he didn't actually cook much. Often we ate 'meals ready to eat' as Louis used to call them; Fray Bentos pies, Vesta curries, beans on toast. Rob was too busy in his studio once his career took off and there was only me to worry about. I was pretty self-sufficient.

In the living room I drew the curtains aside to let in the early evening light. A shaft of sunlight struck the screen of the television in the corner. It was a monster. Louis bought it when colour TVs first came out in the 1970s, at huge expense. It had functioned, more or less, for decades, although there was a permanent white line across the picture.

As I took my cup back to the kitchen I stopped at the telephone table. The address book sat on the surface and a thought occurred to me. I didn't know her last name, but I knew Louis had been in touch with her, otherwise how did he get that photograph of her with her children?

The entries in Rob's hand were organised according to surname. Louis had entered his contacts by first name. I turned to E and found her. Ellie. It was just a word and a number against her name: Salisbury, 547359.

I got an answer machine. Richard and Ellie are away, it said, please leave a message after the tone. I said I was trying to get in touch with Ellie, left my number, then put the phone down. I don't know what I'd have done if someone had answered. Told them Louis was on his last legs? Said it was time I met her?

Then I heard Louis calling and went upstairs. Ellie could wait.

CHAPTER 18

It wasn't the last time he saw Susanna although now he made sure Dashwood wasn't around when they met. She'd come to him and he'd give her a good meal, a bottle of wine, presents from the NAAFI store, cigarettes, shoes and once, a penknife. Then they'd go upstairs. After sex, they played canasta, which she taught him. It was a shallow game of chance where skill could only get you so far, but he liked her excitement when she got a big score.

She spoke a dialect he still found hard to follow, but he was sure he didn't miss much. She was an uncomplicated person, and she enjoyed sex. No doubt she had other relationships but for him, he reflected, that was nothing new. He came away from these encounters physically sated but, at another level, dissatisfied. Too often Susanna made him think of his hunger for Rob. Sometimes he wondered whether celibacy wouldn't have been a better way of putting Rob out of his mind.

At that time he still turned to Peter Dashwood for advice. He made the mistake of confiding in him, hoping for guidance and sympathy for his dilemmas. One day, sitting in the café after an evening meal, he said he felt he was exploiting Susanna's poverty.

"How's that different from any woman?" asked Dashwood.

"Well, surely -"

"Don't be such an idiot. Women want a man who'll pay for their keep. It's how the world works."

Louis thought of Rob and how this couldn't apply to him.

"I know what's on your mind now. I can see it on your face."

Louis nodded. Dashwood could have no idea what was on his mind. The thought amused him.

"Ruth's the same, if you think about it. Tell me, has she ever done a day's work for pay? Why do you think she married you?"

Louis couldn't bring himself to answer.

"What about you Peter?"

"What about me?"

"You and women. Lola. Have you seen her?"

Dashwood's eyes glanced away, and he took a last swig of the wine that remained in his glass.

"Once in a while," he said. "When the need arises. Don't make a song and dance about it though."

Louis sensed that Dashwood had had enough and, once again, he had the familiar feeling of release at having discussed his feelings, mingled with frustration at being obliged to mask the truth about Rob.

"And there are a few others in the queue," Dashwood added, smirking.

Louis laughed in return, as he knew he was supposed to do.

He was curious know more of Susanna's life away from him. One day he thought he'd surprise her by visiting her place. She'd said she lived near the Piazza Olivella, so he went there and asked around. It turned out she lived in a basement room in an alley off the piazza, the houses close together, washing lines strung across the street. There was a thin wooden door which was open so he gave it a perfunctory knock, heard no response and entered, pushing aside a patched and grease-stained curtain. Inside the dark room Susanna was standing next to a child's cot holding a baby. She cooed at the child as it sucked on her breast.

She looked up, surprised and then worried, making Louis instantly regret coming unannounced to her home. Milk stained her blouse, and she wore an old brown skirt, her face free of the makeup she used when she saw him.

"Hello," he said. "I brought you this."

He gave her a collection of gifts he thought she'd like, tinned food, chocolate. She indicated a table in the corner where he could put the stuff, took the baby off her breast and laid it in the cot. While recovering her poise she adjusted her blouse and picked up a brush to get her hair into shape. He placed his hand on hers, gently pressing her to put down the brush. She didn't need to do this.

"Mio caro," she said softly, putting her arms around his neck. "So, you wanted to see how I live? Ecc' acca'."

The room was windowless. Apart from the table there was a bed against the wall, a dressing table and a chest of drawers. On the dressing table was a large glass bell with figures inside it: the Holy Family. A picture of Vesuvius was on the wall.

"Is he yours?" Louis asked.

Susanna smiled. "E' una femminuccia, a girl. Yes, mine. You want to hold her?"

Louis took the baby who was happy after her feed. At first he felt clumsy, unable to remember when he'd encountered a baby, or held one, or indeed if he ever had. Susanna showed him how to place the child's head on his shoulder and support her weight. It felt surprisingly comfortable and the little one was calm, gurgling into his ear, her tiny hand clutching at his arm. Susanna fussed around him as he moved around in the small space, feeling the warmth and softness of the little girl next to him.

"Nadia," Susanna said, "si chiamm' Nadia."

Nadia burped. He patted her back and looked around. Susanna had a life of her own, struggles she'd kept hidden until now.

"Where are your parents?" he asked.

Susanna looked away, saying nothing. Louis wanted to ask about the child's father, but sensed this would be another error. Then he realised Susanna was crying. She spoke in a soft voice.

"Ma che si venut' affa?" What was he doing here?

The affair was put aside when Gillett sent him into the countryside with Jimmy Harris, the unit clerk. They were allocated a company jeep and drove out to Benevento in the hills west of the city. The Naples palazzo had been a grand house with walls and ceilings dripping with decorative carvings, murals of saints and floating cherubs. Benevento had nothing like that. American bombs had flattened large areas of the town. The Hotel Vesuvio had a wall missing and several rooms uninhabitable but was functioning still, so they were billeted there, the two of them in one large room.

They met a man who introduced himself as Marshal Giovanni Muralto of the Italian police who told them he'd been put in charge by the authorities in Naples. Through him they met the town's notables, including the local brothel keeper. Muralto explained it had been necessary to keep this open under the occupation as there was great demand for its services when the Canadians were there. Of course, there'd been the Germans before them, and there were local patrons loyal to the girls whatever the occupying power. He shrugged and grinned. It was a well-run place, he explained, very clean.

Then it was the usual string of cases. Louis interviewed people while Harris kept records. Local boys had been beating up girls who'd been bought by soldiers; the boys were put in the cells for a week. A man arrived and showed them some paintings. Look what the Canadians did when they came to my house, he said. There are bullet holes in this one, a slashed canvas. He wanted compensation, of course. There was a stream of denunciations, stories designed to embroil the military authorities in local feuds. The tyres of their jeep were stolen one night but it seemed the police could do nothing.

Then a rumour spread that the whole town had been mined by the Germans and these were about to explode. This was plausible. Bombs buried under buildings in Naples had caused devastation. The people evacuated to the fields, the young carrying the old and the sick on carts or donkeys, and everyone waited through the day for the explosions to begin. By four o'clock nothing had happened and everyone trooped back.

The next day the police brought them a German boy for questioning. They'd caught him in an abandoned farm building where he'd been sheltering. He looked about seventeen. It was believed he'd spread the rumour and if so, Muralto wanted him shot.

When he met the boy, Louis was struck by how small and thin he was, a far cry from the classic Teuton. He even had dark hair, like an Italian. The boy was dressed in the clothes of an Italian peasant, had been beaten by the police and appeared to be starving. The first thing he said, in perfect English, after providing a decent imitation of a Nazi salute, was to ask for food, which was duly provided in the form of tinned meat and biscuits.

As he ate, the boy told them his name was Max Wertmann. He was a private. He'd volunteered to stay behind when the others left so he could make trouble for the Allied forces, knowing it was likely he'd be shot as a spy.

"I did it for my Führer" he stated. "I am willing to take the consequences."

Louis, listening to this, was appalled at his suicidal wish, which he knew the Italian authorities would carry out without compunction.

Harris agreed when he said the boy was deluded and had to be got out of Benevento. Louis went to Muralto and announced Max was now in their custody and they'd be taking him back to Naples to face a military tribunal. Muralto was furious but could do nothing. They departed the next morning, dropping the boy off at a POW cage on the outskirts of the city where he'd be absorbed into the system and his crimes forgotten. Then they drove to FSS headquarters in Piazza Vittoria and Louis reported to Gillett that the authorities in Benevento no longer needed their services.

Engrossed by his work and back at his usual billet in Via Alabardieri again, Louis waited for Susanna to reappear, but there was no sign of her. At Piazza Olivella he found her place occupied by a family who knew nothing about her. He asked the neighbours, but they were either unable or unwilling to help. She'd decided to leave no traces and, in fact, he never saw her again. His visit had violated a boundary.

That evening, Karen asked me about my day with Louis. She'd been seeing patients since early morning. She likes to tell me about them, while keeping their identities a secret, as she must. When I hear about their myriad personal troubles, I realise how many people hide their private lives from view. Now Louis' story has captured her interest, so she wants regular updates.

"So he never saw her again, this Italian woman?" she asked.

I pulled a cushion out from beneath me. I don't like them, cushions on sofas. They get in the way.

"Aren't you going to say?" Karen persisted. "What's the matter?"

"I don't like it. Makes me uncomfortable."

"Chuck it on the floor then."

"No, not the cushion. Louis and Susanna. I don't like hearing about it. Him with a woman. It doesn't feel right."

Karen laughed. "He was very explicit. Any child would - "

"No, it's not that. I think of him and Rob as a pair. It feels, well, like he betrayed them."

Karen nodded. She took off her glasses and polished them with a cloth. She's very precise, Karen, and she likes to see things clearly. The glasses went back on and she slid a printout of an article across the coffee table.

"Have you seen this? I found it yesterday."

It was from the British Medical Journal, about treatments given to homosexual patients during the 1950s and 1960s, based on interviews with both patients and the psychiatrists who'd treated them. Aversion therapy involving electric shocks, psycho-analysis for the wealthier ones. Men trying to change their natures. Fearful men suffering the humiliation and disgrace society heaped on them. Some were forced to attend as an alternative to prison. One doctor said he was ashamed of what he'd done. I read that and gave out a snort.

"Hmph. Good. He should be ashamed."

"It was the times," Karen said, as ever seeking to mollify. "They thought they were helping. They didn't know better."

"Well they should have done."

I went into the kitchen and stacked the dishwasher. Karen was right, but the article brought back memories of the subterfuges I'd used in my teenage years, deflecting other boys' questions about my home life, the fear of being discovered. It was so unfair; I actually fancied girls, not boys.

I returned. Karen closed her book and looked at me.

"I suppose that was the start," she said.

"The start of what?"

She gave a little laugh. "The start of you."

"Please, no riddles. What do you mean?"

"The baby. He described holding the baby, the pleasure of that. And he saved the German boy. And the other children he wanted to help. Louis loved children."

He did. On the rare occasions when he took me to the playground, something in him changed. He'd be miles away, his head wrapped up in god knows what, but the children warmed him, brought him back to earth, and then he'd be pushing me and others on the swings, spinning us on the roundabout, laughing at our joys and comforting our scraped knees.

"It was the start, don't you see?" Karen said. "When he held Susanna's baby in Naples it made him want a child of his own."

Karen has an uncanny ability to pick up psychological truths from the tiniest of hints.

We fell silent. I was thinking about our own struggle to conceive a child. It hadn't happened for us. I'm sure Karen was thinking about it too.

I broke the silence. "I remembered something last night, about the time they took me away."

"You said that was just a dream."

"No, I don't believe that anymore. It was real, and bits of it are coming back. I can remember their names."

"What names?"

"They were called Mr and Mrs Baker. She used to make me hot chocolate at night. Said it would help me sleep. Calm me down. I was crying a lot."

I don't know how long I was with them. It was after the hospital. This couple came to pick me up, the woman in horn-rimmed glasses I didn't like, but when she smiled it felt all right, just about. I can't remember the man. We went in their car, him driving, a long way. Perhaps it was out of London. It seemed far, to a four-year old. Yes, I remember that: I was four years old. A child knows how old he is.

And the hot chocolate, which I liked.

And the crying.

And wondering when I'd be going home, because no-one had told me.

CHAPTER 19

Dashwood was proposing another expedition.
"Come and see some fun," he said. While
Louis had been in Benevento Dashwood had
been assigned to weekend duties with patrols of military
police, something he clearly relished. Every time it was
different, an adventure, he said. It would do Louis good to
explore new places. He kept on about it, making it sound
like a holiday break, until Louis agreed.

Pretty soon it became clear there was a more serious
purpose to Dashwood's invitation. They'd be gathering
evidence. The MPs couldn't go undercover.

"It'll work better with the two of us," Dashwood said.

Louis had kept his distance since that night with Lola
and Susanna. He hadn't asked about the burn marks.
Dashwood gave the impression that nothing had changed
between them, keeping up his usual backslapping good
cheer.

The Galleria Umberto was a shopping arcade lined
with bars and cafés each of which was allowed to open for
three hours in the late afternoon, before the night curfew.
They strode past the beggars at the entrance, boys offering
shoe shines and who knows what else, men offering

cameos, watches, cameras, Italian and German military medals for sale, soldiers of all nationalities eating and drinking at café tables, the smell of food, drink, sweat and humanity. They made their way to a doorway marked by a beaded curtain in a recess at the far end of the place. The sign outside was smaller than those of other bars and said, simply, 'Momma's'.

Momma, a large woman in a flowery cotton dress, her full lips streaked with red, was installed behind the *cassa* and beamed at them as they entered. Dashwood lifted his hand in a friendly greeting and bought a couple of chits from her. He accompanied Louis to the bar, asked for gin without success, but instead got two white wines which they took to a table in the corner.

"We'll be able to see everything from here," he said, settling into his chair.

Mirrors covered the walls behind the bar, making the room appear larger. But there were darker alcoves lit by dim bulbs where there were no mirrors. In one were two men in American uniform, one of them black. Their heads leaned close together as they talked. A Desert Rat soldier stood at the bar, sipping wine and staring at nothing. He wore a necktie, had a waxed moustache and black hair. His legs were muscular and white.

Louis took a sip of his wine. "What are we doing here?"

"Just keep your eyes open and remember what you see."

A young woman in WAC uniform and dark-rimmed glasses came in, bought a chit, took her drink to a corner, opening a book. Soon the bar began was filling up with men, leaving the WAC to read. Louis approached the counter for a second glass and on his way back glanced over to the dark alcove. The black American had his mouth pressed against his companion's. Louis looked away.

"D'you get the picture now?" Dashwood asked as

Louis returned. Louis nodded, but still wondered what the point might be. Everyone knew these places existed. This one reminded him of Rob taking him to the clubs and dance halls in Piccadilly, trying to get him interested. In Naples he avoided such places like the plague.

Dashwood leaned over to whisper. "Fun's on its way."

Louis stood up to leave. "I've got better things to do with my time Peter."

"Take it easy old son, just messing about. Thought you'd want to see the place. Part of your, you know, education."

Education? What was he talking about? Part of him was tired of Dashwood's patronising attitude; another part was worried in case there was some underlying agenda to the visit. He'd finish the drink and go.

Two British sergeants entered, baggy shorts flapping around below their knees. They looked like a pair of old maids with pinched faces and spectacles.

"Oh my darlings, what have we got here?" exclaimed one of them on seeing the WAC reading in her corner.

"Mabel and I have been asking ourselves why you come here," continued the sergeant in a high-pitched voice, looking into a wall mirror and touching up his hair as he spoke. "You really shouldn't be alone you know. Why not bring one of your gruesome sisters with you?"

The WAC looked up from her book and in a surprisingly powerful voice said, "Get back to your knitting you old queen. I don't have to answer to you."

"Oh do leave her alone tonight," the other one said, giving his companion a glass, "Everyone else does."

"She's a tigress isn't she," the first one said. "We must have her round to our place, we really must."

The pair flounced off to the far end of the bar.

Then some Italians appeared, cautious as they entered, though with a look of determination on their faces. They draped their coats around their shoulders and wore shorts, all in different colours, and sandals. They got their drinks and stood in a circle, sipping them and looking around furtively, pretending to examine some photographs one of them brought out.

The Desert Rat spoke to one, a dark haired young man with blue eyes and tight shorts to match, and offered to buy him a drink. They retired to an alcove and Louis watched their hands intertwine as they leaned forward over the table.

Dashwood whispered in his ear again. "Bloody dilly boys."

Louis shrugged. It would be a dull evening, getting sozzled with Peter Dashwood again, putting up with his unpleasant remarks.

At that point, two military policemen came through the glass bead curtain. All eyes went to them as they approached the *cassa*.

"Our pals have arrived," Dashwood said.

The MPs were telling Momma she had to shut for the night, maybe for good. She'd allowed Italians into the place and that wasn't permitted, as she well knew. Momma started crying, making the flesh of her chin wobble, and the WAC left swiftly while some of the men edged nearer the MPs.

"Leave it out lads," the Desert Rat said, putting his hand on the shoulder of one of the MPs. "She's running a decent place here."

The MP whirled round, shouting "Get your hands off me" and shoved the British soldier away. "I'll have you -"

There was a crash as a chair flew at the two policemen and struck a mirror, smashing the glass so that Louis put his hand to his eyes in defence against flying splinters. It was the black American, who stood huge and heavy in the centre of the room, his face bristling with anger. The MPs, big men themselves, drew their sticks and rushed at him, some customers trying uselessly to hold them back, others scarpering out through the bead curtain. Then the man was struggling on the floor, the MPs trying to hold him down.

"Hey, that's enough," Louis shouted when one of the MPs cracked his stick hard on the soldier's forearm, prompting a howl of pain.

Then Dashwood came out of his chair, got on the floor and punched the man in the face, hard. Dashwood had big hands and there was a nasty sound as his fist came down. Then he struck again. And a third time. Before he could do more, one of the MPs grabbed him and pulled him off. The black man lay unconscious, blood welling up from his eye and shattered cheekbone.

The MPs stuck their sticks back in their belts and the larger one of them stood facing Dashwood, protecting the man on the floor. Momma was sobbing behind the *cassa* and the bar was empty, glass strewn about.

"Fucking pansies deserve what they get," Dashwood said, his breathing coming in gasps.

The other MP was on the floor now, his fingers prising open the unconscious man's eyes to look at the pupils.

"Better get an ambulance," he said. "This one's not walking out of here."

"You saw it all," Dashwood said to Louis. "He attacked them."

Louis said nothing. Dashwood had set this up, but what had he hoped to achieve? A witness? What was he meant to witness? He couldn't have planned his assault on the man, which was obviously something stemming from an uncontrollable rage.

"You'd better be out of here when the wagon arrives," one of the MPs said to them. "We'll sort this out."

Reluctantly, Louis left the bar, looking back at the man on the floor, who lay still, the pool of blood around his head now spreading. Dashwood was silent as they walked back to Piazza Vittoria, Louis by his side still shaken by the explosion of violence. A beggar boy came up to them but was thrust away with a curse. Louis felt it best to say nothing in case it provoked his companion.

At FSS headquarters Dashwood insisted they must write a report of the incident for the log of the day's activities. He made Louis sit and wait while he typed it out and Louis signed it without looking at what it said. He silently swore to himself it was the last time he'd follow Dashwood's lead. And there'd be no more veiled conversations about his love life.

CHAPTER 20

"He used me, you know," Louis said. "Knew I'd do what he wanted."

We were in the living room, sitting near the window. It was a breezy day, clouds scudding across the sky, the people outside wrapped up in coats. The tartan blanket was over his knees.

"How do you mean?"

"The paper I signed. It absolved him. He realised he'd gone too far. The man he attacked suffered severe brain damage, never recovered properly. Had to be sent home."

"That's terrible."

"And he was a war hero. A bloody hero. He'd done something at Cassino. Got a Silver Star for it."

"That must have made it worse," I said, thinking of the hue and cry that would have ensued.

Louis shook his head. "No, not really. He was black. And they knew about Momma's, its clientele and all that. They hushed it up. But signing that log for Dashwood - I should have reported him for what he did. The MPs knew what they were doing, but Dashwood just wanted to kill the man, I'm sure of it. His fists did the damage."

I've never been in a bad fight, let alone one involving

serious injury. I felt glad I'd not met this man Dashwood.

"There's another thing about my time in Naples," Louis said. "I got sick there. Again, not something I'm very proud of, but it did help me work out my priorities."

One morning, a few days after the incident at Momma's bar, he woke up feeling hot. He had a headache and his groin itched. When he examined himself, he saw nothing but during the morning he felt increasingly unwell, his hands shaking so much that he spilled his coffee at breakfast. He went in, but Gillett saw his flushed cheeks, asked him a few questions and sent him to the medical centre where they took blood and asked more questions.

He was hoping it was malaria, but the tests came back after three days: he had syphilis.

"I see you're married."

It was the medical officer who'd given him the result. They were in a cubicle and the doctor, a small man with a pencil moustache, had just shown him a pink slip. In red crayon it said:

Wasserman - pos
Kahn - pos

Louis had guessed the news was going to be bad. The itch had turned into sores on his penis and he had a white ulcer on his lip that stung when he ate anything with a sharp taste. This wasn't malaria. The growing realisation had filled him with terror. He'd seen the warning notices all over Naples. He'd been convinced Susanna was clean.

"So?"

It was the medical officer again.

"Yes, I'm married," Louis said. He didn't wear a ring. The MO must have seen his declaration in the records.

"Thank your lucky stars she's not out here," the doctor said. The white light in the cubicle was harsh.

"What will happen to me now?"

"That's up to the Americans. If you're lucky, they'll take you in. If not, you'll be shipped home."

The doctor explained that penicillin, a new thing, was being given to US troops with venereal disease. It would take eight days. There'd be no visitors, and he'd have to do as he was told. If he was clear after three months, he was cured.

"And the alternative?" Louis asked.

The officer ran his hands through his hair with the look of a man who'd explained this too many times before. "As I said, you'll be shipped home. You'll have to face your wife. No more relations with her for a very long time even if she's willing to entertain the idea. The treatment takes six months, at a minimum. We haven't got penicillin yet. You do know about this disease don't you? Why didn't you take precautions, wash yourself out at least?"

"But I did," Louis said, despairing. In fact, he'd only used a condom two or three times with Susanna, because he'd trusted her. Or maybe he just hadn't cared after the letter from Rob.

"Well whatever you did it wasn't enough. I'll try to get you into the American programme. You're not a fighting soldier I see, FSS isn't it?"

Louis hung his head further. No, not a fighting soldier. Most of the military men in Naples were there for brief periods before being sent back to the fighting. He knew their drinking, brawling and search for hurried moments of intimacy were responses to the brutal conditions at Cassino. He didn't have that excuse.

"You're not one of their priorities then. First they treat Americans, then the others. I'll try."

"Thank you," Louis said, getting up to leave. "When will I know?"

"Come back tomorrow."

He spent an anxious night imagining what a return home in that condition would entail - his father's reaction, what it could do to him and Rob, the humiliation.

But the next day brought better news. The MO had been successful and gave him an admission slip to the medical centre in Bagnoli. He got a ride in an American ambulance, sitting next to the driver.

"What's it for?" the ambulance driver asked. "VD? You ain't wounded that's for sure."

"No, it's nothing. Just a check up."

The ambulance driver shrugged. "Don't worry. I know the score."

Louis had told Dashwood about his problem the night before. His friend had been sympathetic, had agreed to tell Gillett that Louis was ill with a spell of malaria and wouldn't be in for a few days.

They rattled through the Bagnoli tunnel. The driver was smoking a cigar.

"Personally," the driver said, "I stick with one gal. That way, you don't pick up nothing nasty."

Louis smiled and shrugged his shoulders. He thought of Rob. He wondered if Rob had ever picked up anything. If he'd have told him. If he was clean. He realised he still felt angry about Frank Lemaire. What were they up to right now? Then his thoughts turned to his own miserable situation. He needed to keep the lid on this, get rid of this thing in his blood, get back to work, forget Susanna.

They came out of the tunnel, the sunlight blinding him for a moment. The driver shaded his eyes with one hand. They passed tenement buildings, washing hanging from balconies.

"It's up there," the driver said.

The Medical Centre was housed in a series of white buildings stretching out over a flat area with the hillside behind dotted with pine trees. The avenues between the buildings were wide, lined with gardens, trellises, arches and statues of naked men in heroic poses. Half way up the main avenue there was a huge swimming pool, empty of water and surrounded by barbed wire.

"The Eyeties built it," the driver continued. "Some kind of world fair. But they ain't got a lot to celebrate now, eh?"

They pulled up near a low building and the driver pointed up the hillside to a barbed wire enclosure surrounding tents laid out in rows. The place was like a POW cage.

"That's the one you want."

"It's a prison camp," Louis said, his heart pounding as he got out of the cab. The driver laughed as he started up again.

"Arrivederci," he shouted through the noise of the engine, "and good luck."

As the ambulance drove off, Louis mounted the steps to the compound. Moving around behind the wire were men, dressed in green overalls. 'VD' was painted in black letters on the back of each jacket. At the gate he presented his admission slip and went through, following arrows for new arrivals.

Entering a wooden hut, he showed the slip to an American army major.

"British, huh?"

"Yes sir."

"We don't see so many of you guys here."

"No sir," Louis replied, feeling he'd let the side down.

"Well, you do as you're told and you'll be out of here in no time."

"Eight days I understand, sir."

"That's right. But it's no picnic. When the bell goes, you jump, right?"

The major, a thin, languid man, spoke slowly as he explained the system. Injections every three hours when the bell rang. Sixty in all. If Louis missed one, it was back to the start.

"And you don't want to do that," the major warned,

"You really don't. The guys giving you the shots aren't the kindest."

Louis was sent for a blood test, then to a counter where he was issued with a set of overalls. He put them on and felt like an inmate. At least it was a short sentence. Eight days. Would Gillett believe the malaria story?

The supply sergeant who took his uniform noticed his sergeant's stripes.

"Don't s'pose you'll be needing these any more."

"What do you mean?" Louis asked.

"Ain't they gonna bust you?"

"Is that what your lot do?"

The supply sergeant shrugged. "Yep. That's what happens to our guys in here."

Demotion. He could be thrown out of Field Security, an infantry soldier, destined for Cassino. He turned to leave, his mind filled with more fears.

"By the way," the supply sergeant called out to him, "There's no rank in the pen. A guy can be a general and you wouldn't know it in these fatigues. Saves a whole lotta salutin'"

Outside the reception hut men shuffled around, smoking, talking, all in green. He was directed to a group of three long, low tents. Number three was for non US personnel, he was told. He entered through the flap and saw rows of canvas beds, men lying or sitting on them, playing cards, reading, smoking. Someone had set up an electric fan in a corner, but the place was still hot and there was a smell of men's sweat. He dumped his kit bag next to an empty bed, nodding to the men on either side.

"'ello mate," said one of them, a grizzled fellow. "First time here?"

Louis nodded.

"Oooh, you'll like it then. Nice hotel this. Hot and cold running water, American grub, the works. Pity about the sleeping arrangements though ain't it?"

The man on the other side laughed. He had his back to

them, but turned.

"Hello," he said, holding out his hand. "Welcome to our merry band. I'm Archie Farr and this one here is Lenny Fagin. He's a regular I'm afraid, but we don't think any less of him for that."

"Louis Nicholson!" It was an American sergeant, his head poking through the tent flap. "With me!"

Louis was led to another hut, marked 'LAB', where he experienced health education, American style. In a cubicle, an angry looking man with tiny round glasses and rubber gloves told him to take down his pants. The man scraped away with a toothpick at one of the sores on Louis' genitals. He jumped back at the sharp pain.

"Hold still won't you," the lab assistant said. "D'you think I'm enjoying myself here?"

The man ran a cotton swab over the weeping sore and wiped the fluid onto a microscope slide, telling Louis to button up his pants and wait. After a minute he took him to another cubicle to look down a microscope. He was told to fiddle with the focus knobs until he saw something. There were a series of red blobs.

"Your god damned polluted blood."

As Louis watched, a shiver went along his spine. A tadpole-like organism swam across his field of vision, pushing aside the blood cells with an alarming vigour.

"That's what's inside you," the lab man said, lighting up a cigarette. "Millions of 'em. Eatin' away at you. First they get yer balls, then -"

"Okay, I get the picture." Louis was irritated at the man's insistent, sing-song voice. This was clearly part of some scare tactic. The trouble was, it was working. He felt terrified.

The man ignored him as though reciting a text he'd memorised.

"Then they get into the rest of you and start spreading out. You'll get a rash all over, really gums up the works. Eventually you'll get it in your brain, drive you crazy. You married?"

Louis didn't answer, but the man asked again, so he said he wasn't. But the lab man wouldn't give up, continued on the basis that one day Louis would want to get married and he'd have to tell his girlfriend. She wouldn't want to do it with him, he'd be a real mess.

"How d'ya pick it up anyway?" Clearly this lecture worked best if the victim participated.

"None of your business," Louis said. "Are you done with me?"

The lab man exhaled and shrugged. "Just doin' my job. You'll need to come back here in three days, see what kinda progress you're making."

Louis walked out, banging the door shut.

As he was returning to the tent, he heard a bell go and men in the yard stopped what they were doing and started forming up in two lines, one shorter than the other. He asked around and discovered the longer one was for those with gonorrhoea. People in the clap line had it easy; they only needed four shots to his sixty.

He stood in line, thinking of the tadpoles inside him. Millions of them. Clearly something strong was needed to kill them all. He wanted to kill them all. Delete this pollution from his blood that threatened everything in his life, his position in the FSS, his relationship with Rob, his sanity, maybe his life itself.

When his turn came, he gave his name to a clerk who ticked it off on a list. A GI poked a needle into a small vial of amber fluid, sucked out the liquid and flicked the body of the syringe to release any air. His sleeve was rolled up. The GI quickly swabbed the area with antiseptic, thrust the needle in and squeezed. It was like a hornet sting, pain spreading into his whole shoulder.

"Is that really necessary?" he said after he'd recovered from the shock.

The heavy lidded GI who'd jabbed him was filling another syringe. He turned, looked him right in the eyes and shouted out "Next!"

Back in the tent he found Fagin and Archie Farr on their beds. Fagin was sleeping.

"If I were you," Farr said, "take it in turns, one arm, the other, then each buttock. The buttock ones hurt more but that way you spread them out."

"Thanks," Louis said, rubbing his arm. "How long have you got to go?"

"Hopefully I'll be out of here the day after tomorrow. My spirochete count is low already. I think most of them are dead - it's all I saw this morning, dead ones floating around, but they said you've got to take the full sixty before you get out. Better safe than sorry."

"Can I look at your arm?"

Farr obligingly rolled up his sleeve. The arm was a mass of swollen red blotches. The skin was breaking on one of them.

"I can't take much more there," he said. "I think the last few had better be in the bum. More surface area. "

"They're a bunch of sadists."

"True," Farr said. "But when you've got chaps like Lenny over there you can understand why they're like that. This is his third time. Keeps coming back. I'm not sure if it's because he can't keep his todger in his pants, or whether he's avoiding the front line. Either way, they feel they need to give us a hard time of it. Have you seen the chaplain yet?"

"I don't think I've been here long enough for that."

"Well, watch out. He'll give you a lecture. They try anything."

Farr winced and touched his shoulder, then added, "Thank god I'm not religious."

"Thanks for the warning," Louis said.

Then he saw the chaplain bearing down on him.

CHAPTER 21

He had rosy cheeks and shining eyes and his arms were loaded with pamphlets. Louis stood up to show his respect.

"Just arrived?" the chaplain said.

"Yes, sir, this morning."

"Thought I'd drop in on you. See if I can offer you a little succour."

"I'm afraid I'm not religious, sir."

"Ah yes, religion. But you have faith, don't you? You must have faith."

Louis considered this but couldn't respond.

"Do you believe in sin?"

"I suppose so. Perhaps."

"And goodness?"

"Certainly, sir. Yes, I do."

"Then you have faith."

The man was triumphant at this logical deduction. Louis wondered where this was going.

"And if you have faith…"

Louis saw that he was expected to agree.

"…you must believe."

It was another logical triumph. They were coming thick

and fast.

"The Italians. Too many opportunities for sin. You see that don't you?"

"I think I was just unlucky, actually."

The chaplain tried another tack. "Your mother. What would she say, do you suppose?"

"My mother's dead, sir."

"Ah yes. Well look, I'll leave you with one of these."

He handed Louis a pamphlet.

"I'll be here tomorrow," he said, his red face peering at Louis, "if you need to talk. God bless you, my son."

The time passed, punctuated by wake-up bells every three hours, blurring the line between night and day. The pain from the injections took a while to subside, only allowing brief periods of rest before the next bell. In between, Louis talked with Farr or Lenny Fagin, lay in bed, worried about the future and dreamed about the past. The bizarre environment, the absence of meaningful activity and the constant interruptions to his sleep encouraged his mind to wander. It was a kind of delirium.

As he lay staring into the night, the image of Susanna's baby was floating before his eyes; he remembered the feel of the child on his shoulder and his intense pleasure at that soft touch. Susanna was different in her own place, a mother, protecting and nurturing her child. The brash yet alluring sexuality she displayed in Capri and in his bed was another side to her. His diseased organ stirred, sending a sting of pain through his groin as he remembered her. Then his pain subsided as he thought again of her baby, sucking on her mother for the milk that gave her life.

Apart from a couple of brief, inconclusive encounters with Northern girls in Ellesmere Port, not going much further than kissing and groping around in underwear, Rob was the only other person he'd known sexually. Making love to Susanna was like being enveloped in a warm haven of perfumed flesh. With Rob it was totally different, and not just because he was a man; a passionate, muscular encounter, each of them eager and hungry for resolution.

Even in his diseased state he still had powerful stirrings at these memories. What kind of curse was this? He groaned and turned over in bed, trying to avoid pressing on his shoulder.

He imagined Susanna's baby growing up, finding her feet, running around. There were hordes of street children in Naples, barefoot, scrabbling for life. He remembered watching an American in the Galleria confiscate a tin of leather polish from a shoeshine boy. The boy was crying, his hand stretched out towards the tin, while the American lectured him on possessing stolen goods.

He hoped by the time Susanna's child was that age the war would be over and Naples recovered. Susanna would marry, live in a house, have a job, her daughter attend school in shoes and dresses. A husband perhaps. He must alert her to this disease she was carrying, get her into treatment. It wasn't her fault she'd...

He'd been asleep again. His mind wandered further as he listened to the breathing of rows of slumbering men around him. It was still an hour to the next bell.

When he was at school boys were beaten for masturbating. It would make them blind, give them epilepsy, weaken them, destroy their manhood. Several had been expelled for taking part in a group masturbation session. The headmaster must have decided this came too close to homosexuality.

Sexual contact between boys certainly occurred, but no-one was ever caught for it. He remembered, even as a pre-pubescent boy of ten or eleven, how boys would get into bed with each other, excited, and rub their bodies together. And one or two masters were suspect. Everyone sensed which ones they were. Some beatings had a definite sexual element, the master caressing the buttocks he was about to wound with a slipper or cane. Caning was the most brutal. Christopher told him one of his friends - was it Dashwood? - he couldn't remember - had actually shit himself during a caning.

His face flushed with the realisation that he'd been doing the chaplain's work for him. Sex and punishment, went together like a horse and carriage. Syphilis was a disease, an organism, a tiny wriggling organism trying for life, like the cats, the dogs, the feral children in the rubble of the ruined city, striving for existence in the only way they could. Religion had no place in explaining it.

He drifted back into sleep, then woke again with Peter Dashwood on his mind, the cigarette burns on his arm, not too dissimilar from the needle marks on Archie Farr, or indeed the punctures spreading over his own arm, his own stigmata. Something must have happened to Dashwood to cause such self-hatred. And the man's violence spilled over to harm others too.

A cool breeze came through the tent flap from the darkness outside. In the far corner, men sat around an upturned packing case, smoking and playing cards.

An image of Rob in hospital appeared in his mind, the time he'd overdosed on Benzedrine and alcohol. What if he'd fallen in love with a woman instead of Rob? They could have a baby together, perhaps a dark haired one, like Susanna's. He could see it in his arms, soft, warm, cherished.

Then he remembered Frank Lemaire, his sneering face during the scuffle in Vita's kitchen, and his heart began beating faster.

Why did he only want Rob? His obsession with him wasn't healthy. There were other fish in the sea. His relationship with Susanna proved that he could have a different life.

But then he took out a photograph of Rob kept in a secret place in his pocket book which he took out, staring at his face, feeling a powerful longing for his presence in his life, his voice in his ears, his touch.

Perhaps if he missed some injections they'd send him home? The six month treatment would then await him, whatever that was, but he'd be back in London, closer to him.

He dismissed the idea as soon as it entered his mind. He'd have to tell his father what had happened. He couldn't face that. And Rob would have nothing to do with him if he came home diseased. He'd have every right -

The bell rang and men stirred. He realised he'd have to go for the next jab, right buttock this time.

On Louis' second day Lenny Fagin departed. His place was taken by a lugubrious, silent French soldier who lay on his back, reading most of the time. Archie Farr was leaving tomorrow.

"What's next for you?" he asked Archie.

"Cassino," Farr replied. "Cassino, Cassino. And more Cassino. We've been going at it for months."

His face showed a mixture of sadness and resignation.

"Sometimes I'm ashamed of myself," Louis said. "Not having to fight."

"I wouldn't let it bother you."

Farr turned away and Louis fell back into thought. Farr had revealed he was a captain in the Guards. He didn't believe they'd demote him because of his disease. Too many of his rank had been killed at Cassino, so they'd need him up there for the final push. He'd been in love with the Italian girl who'd put him in the medical centre, had wanted to marry her, bring her back to England one day. But now, he wasn't so sure. Louis worried that Farr had a death wish. Men like that took unnecessary risks.

Louis feared combat. The prospect of demotion and ejection from FSS had forced him to consider it and he'd admitted that much to himself. When he thought of battle, he remembered his terror when the Germans had counter attacked near Paestum. And he imagined his brother's death under fire. Christopher still came to him in dreams, a presence he welcomed, but he didn't want to join Christopher in death. He wanted to live, to see home again. He wanted to preserve his skin.

He took the photograph of Rob from his wallet and looked at it.

"Who's the girl?"

It was Farr again. He hadn't seen the photo and Louis quickly put it back.

"Ruth. She's, she's my wife. We're married."

Farr grunted. "Long time no see, I suppose."

"Yes. It's been over a year now."

"And now you're here."

"I can't tell her. I just can't. She'd never -"

"Why make her unhappy," Farr said. "No point. People back home - they can't understand all this, this desolation."

Farr was clearly in a reflective mood, his arm sweeping to include not just the medical centre, but the whole of Naples, the war, all their lives together.

"It's the children that trouble me the most," Louis said. "In the streets. Just totally, completely, well…"

"Degraded?"

"Yes. That's it. Abandoned, most of them, running wild. By their parents, just lost. They die, you realise. I've seen them, seen their bodies. While the women throw themselves at us."

"Hm. I suppose you're right. Lot of little savages scuttling about the streets." Farr paused, then spoke again. "I was thinking about what you said about battle. I was afraid once, like you."

Louis began to object, but Farr silenced him.

"Perfectly normal reaction. Don't believe the man who says he has no fear. Well, not unless I say it." He laughed. "I've forgotten how to be afraid. You feel numb sometimes. Just want it to end, and you don't care how."

He lit a cigarette.

"You want to watch out for that," Louis said. "Could get you killed."

Farr drew smoke deep into his lungs and blew it out in a plume above Louis' head.

"You're giving me advice?" he said.

Louis smiled at this. "I suppose I am."

"Well, thanks for that. I'll try to remember not to get killed. And you, just you remember. Stay out of the fighting if you bloody well can. Get back to that girl of yours. Wife, I mean. You're not really married are you?"

"Yes, we are. Sort of."

"Sort of? What do you - oh I don't care. Wife, girlfriend. Get back to her in one piece. That's my advice to you, for what it's worth."

The six o'clock bell interrupted their talk, and they both tramped off to join the lines. After the usual stinging injection, Louis returned to his bunk and carefully lowered himself into place, avoiding pressure on his buttocks. An American sergeant poked his head through the tent flap and barked his name.

"Nicholson. Come with me."

He followed the man to the reception hut, a place normally forbidden to inmates. The sergeant told him to wait. They couldn't be planning to have him leave could they? He hadn't had enough injections.

A few moments later the door opened and Dashwood entered. This was a surprise. There was a strict rule; none of the inmates was allowed visitors. It was part of the punishment regime.

"How on earth did you get in?" he asked, getting to his feet.

"Look at you!" Dashwood said, laughing. "Turn around, let me see."

Louis displayed the letters on his back somewhat ruefully, while at the same time enjoying Dashwood's good humour.

"You must hang on to those Nicko. A souvenir from your time in Naples."

"I think you have to give them back when you leave."

"Fair enough. But seeing you there in those clothes...." Dashwood was grinning again.

"Yes, I'm sure it's very funny. How did you get in here? They told us no visitors."

Dashwood showed him a card. "This is a spot card. We've all been given them. Let's us go anywhere we want."

It was a folded booklet with a black spot on the front. Inside was a photograph of Dashwood and the following words:

> *The holder of this card is engaged in SECURITY duties, in the performance of which he is authorized to be in any place, at any time, and in any dress. All authorities subject to Military Law are enjoined to give him every assistance in their power, and others are requested to extend him all facilities for carrying out his duties.*

"That's handy," Louis said.

"They're new. You'll get one too, when you're back."

"But how can it work with the Americans? Surely it's just for the British."

"Nobody knows. I thought I'd try it out, and as you can see, it worked. They let me in. Mind you, I had to tell them it was part of an investigation, about which you had some crucial gen."

"Peter, that's ridiculous. You have got a nerve." Louis was laughing himself by now. "It's good to see you. It's no fun in here."

"No, I don't expect it is," Dashwood paused for a second. "Look old son, I owe you a favour. I've come to tell you, I've squared things with Gillett."

"How do you mean?"

"I've sorted out your problem. He still thinks you've got malaria. Very concerned about you as a matter of fact, even threatened to visit. I had to put him off. Said I'd see if you were ready for visitors, report back and everything. I'll tell him you can't handle it. Never knew the old bugger had such a caring streak."

"Bloody hell Peter. How did you do it?"

"Well, I know how the postal system works, don't I?"

"You don't mean…"

Dashwood tapped the side of his nose with his finger.

"Yes, I intercepted his post. The medical people were obviously going to write to him once they'd seen you. I knew that'd give the game away, so I got to the post room before him."

"You don't know how worried I've been Peter. I can't thank you -"

"No need to thank me old son. One good turn deserves another if you know what I mean."

Louis' mind was blank. What was Dashwood talking about?

"You remember, the report. In Momma's bar the other day. Got me off the hook. You signed it."

"Ah, I see." Louis had been worrying about that signature. This development tied the two of them together in mutual deceit, an uncomfortable feeling.

"I overdid it," Dashwood continued, "I know I did. But sometimes, when your blood's up…"

He was staring at the floor and seemed genuinely contrite.

"Very well," Louis said. "Look, thanks for this. I appreciate it, I really do. I'll be out on Friday, back on duty I hope."

Dashwood then helped him catch up on what had been happening in the unit during Louis' absence. It looked as if the battle of Monte Cassino was close to an end. A furious assault was beginning. If it fell, the road to Rome would open up, and they'd be moving on.

"About bloody time," Louis said, with considerable feeling.

Two weeks later he was packing his things to leave Naples. Army regulations restricted them to a small travelling chest and whatever he could carry in a kit bag. In Via Alabardieri he surveyed his room. It was surprising what he'd built up in - what was it, a year?

He'd leave the pile of newspapers. Gino could get rid of them. Give him something to do.

Spare uniform, brass polish, parade ground webbing. Still at the bottom of the chest where they'd been when he'd arrived. He resented the space they took up but he couldn't throw them out. Army property. He didn't know the punishment for losing them.

If you're sensible, you work through a list in your head. What do you need each day? Get up, clothes for the day, toothbrush, shaving set. Socks, underwear. Work: holster for the Webley, spot card. Should the gun go in the trunk? Would it still fire? He'd better wear it.

Leisure and pleasure: the gramophone records. He couldn't take many of them. The odds were they'd get smashed up, anyway. Paperbacks: quite a collection from the American PBS store. Any he hadn't read perhaps and the rest he'd give to Gino. He'd get a price for them. All the Italians were learning English now.

He sorted out the books and came across a German dictionary. He should pack it - he'd need it, eventually. Dashwood's German was better than his and he didn't want to depend on the man.

Susanna had left an empty bottle of perfume in his room. He picked it up and smelled it, drawing in her scent. Next to it, a tin of condoms, unused. He still had injection marks all over his shoulders and buttocks. They'd fade in time, the doctor had said. He opened the tin and looked at the folded rubber sacs, dusted with chalk. He should have bloody well used them. Snapping it shut he threw it into the trunk.

Gino was at the door.

"You leaving today, Signor Nicholson?"

"We're all leaving," Louis replied. "Those books are for you, if you want them."

He handed Gino a bottle of wine. What would happen when they all moved on? The soldiers had first destroyed the place, smashed up the buildings, bombed the harbour. Then they'd colonised it, filling its bars and shops with American money and the soldiers' raucous, desperate desires. Now the Italians would need to pick up the pieces, rebuild if they could.

"I'll be sorry to go," Louis said. He remembered the meals Gino had cooked for him and the others, miracles of culinary skill with rationed ingredients. "One day I'll come back."

Gino's eyes were watery. Books filled his arms, preventing him from putting them round Louis.

As Gino made his way down the stairs, Louis opened his wallet. A few extra dollars to compensate Gino wouldn't hurt. Rob's photograph was there. He looked at it for some time.

Another letter from Rob had arrived for him while he was in the medical centre. He went to the desk, picked it up, removed it from the envelope, read it once more, then folded it.

He walked to the bathroom along the corridor. Then he tore it up, throwing the tiny pieces into the toilet and flushing them far down, down through the building, into the Neapolitan sewers which discharged into the wide blue sea beyond the bay.

CHAPTER 22

"What did the letter say?" I asked.

Louis said nothing, but closed his eyes, his arms resting on the counterpane.

We stayed silent for a while. The sun shone through the window, warming the room. Cherry blossom filled the trees in the garden. Its annual display had just begun, the pink petals unfolding in profuse clusters. We used to go to Regents Park in the spring to see it. Louis would lift me to touch the flowers while Rob watched. I remember their coolness against the palm of my hand, their delicate colour against the blue sky.

Rob told me there was a pig farm in the park during the war. The police ran it as a club. Provided the coppers with bacon for breakfast; quite a treat during rationing.

"Do you want to see the blossom?" I asked. "Go into the garden?"

His eyes opened again. "I can see it from here."

I asked again: "Rob's letter? The one you tore apart."

He sighed. "He'd got another girl pregnant."

I felt a prickly sensation in my scalp, hearing again of a tiny presence inside this unknown woman, a scrap of her flesh and Rob's, what could have been.

"Actually, not another girl. It was the same one, Virginia, silly kid. Must have been obsessed with him to have another go. She couldn't hold onto the babies, though. She'd miss a couple of months and then have a miscarriage. It was her inescapable pattern."

"That's so sad."

"I suppose so. But I was furious, felt it was over between us. And he was going with Frank Lemaire again."

"How can you be sure of that?"

"He told me in the letter."

Louis' face screwed up tight as he relived the pain of his jealousy.

"Look Dad, you don't have to -"

He waved my words away.

"Frank Lemaire wasn't the only one, but he was the main one while I was away. He couldn't do without someone. Frank wasn't so special to him, but he was around." Louis paused, and then spoke with bitterness in his voice. "And I wasn't."

"What was he doing?"

"In the fire service. Things got complicated for Frank. They caught him looting."

"Looting?"

"Yes, pinching stuff. If there's a fire, the building's open to the elements. They'd hack their way in, he'd spy something, a ring, some money, and slip it into his pocket. Somebody must have seen him at it. They found jewellery under his bed."

"I thought he was a socialist."

"Ha! A self-centred bastard, that's what he was, and a thief. He got what he deserved. Six months in Wandsworth."

I got up. I didn't want Louis to get so upset.

"I'm getting something for myself," I said. "Do you want something? A sandwich? Tea?"

He turned his head towards the window.

"No, that's fine. You eat. Let me look at the blossom.

Happy memories, eh?"

I leaned over and kissed him on the forehead

In the kitchen downstairs I made myself cheese on toast and a cup of tea. Karen had been urging me on again and this time I thought she was right. It was time to ask Louis.

I climbed up the stairs with the food on a tray, apprehensive but determined. Silent next to Louis, I ate and drank, building up my resolve. After a last sip of tea I drew a letter out of my pocket and placed it near his hands.

"Who was Ellie?" I said.

Louis looked at the letter, then picked it up, opening the envelope to read what was inside, the paper trembling in his grip. Then he folded it with great care. His face showed nothing.

"When did you get this?" he asked.

"Last week. And now it's time for me to know about her."

"Eloise Bauer," Louis replied. "Ellie is a nick name."

"I gathered that."

Something in my tone of voice must have struck him, because he winced.

"I'm glad she's still alive," he said, closing his eyes.

Then I saw something shift in him and his eyes opened as he spoke again. "I wanted to tell you about Peter."

"No thanks. I'm interested in Ellie. You should realise that Dad. The letter…"

"What makes you think it's true?"

"Rob told me her name once. But I want you to tell me."

"But why do you want to know? What difference can it make to you? You've done your growing up now. Maybe when you were younger, but nothing can change now."

This felt like an admission, but I needed him to tell me outright.

"I've discussed this with Karen, Dad. I do want to know."

"Ah yes, Karen. You've been talking with her. Well in that case, yes, I'll tell you about Ellie. Just give me a moment."

Feelings of relief and anticipation flooded through me as Louis placed his fingertips together, bringing his hands up so that they touched his lips, then resting them on the blanket covering his lap. I couldn't quite believe I had reached this point with him, after all the years of silence.

"I met her in Vienna, in the street, 1945. I was with Martin Herz. Remember him?"

CHAPTER 23

When I was a child a man called Martin Herz used to visit us from time to time, with his wife Elisabeth. Louis had met him in Austria when Martin was a political officer attached to the American forces. When I knew him he was in the United States diplomatic service which involved occasional trips to London. He and his wife had no children. Elisabeth was an avid art collector and always gravitated to Rob's workshop where they spent hours discussing his work and the latest exhibitions. I think she even bought one of Rob's smaller pieces and Rob, hearing of this, insisted on giving her the maquette for his Helmet figure. It must be worth thousands now.

Rob liked making things for me too. Armies of little figurines in crazy poses made out of baked clay that I lined up on the floor of the living room. I used to fire nails at them from a toy cannon, break their arms off, send their heads rolling while Rob and Louis watched, laughing at my gleeful shrieks when I knocked another one over. I've still got a few in a glass cabinet at home. Karen jokes that they're museum pieces, calls them my 'Robert Gill collection.' I sure Elisabeth Herz would have liked some of them too.

The first meeting between Louis and Martin was in early June 1945 in Judenburg on the boundary of the Russian zone. To his surprise, Louis had been temporarily promoted to lieutenant after Gillett wounded his hand in an accident. Then he was attached to the official mission sent by the British, French and Americans to plan the zoning of Vienna. In Judenburg the Soviets put on a guard of honour for their visitors and there was a speech from General Rogov. The next day they'd be entering Vienna. Louis found himself next to Martin at the evening dinner and in between courses, toasts and speeches, they talked.

Martin spoke his American English with a hint of a German accent. "I was a kid here. My father's a Jew."

"Did they leave, you know, because…"

"Nope. Not that. It's a long story. How 'bout you. How d'you get those pips?"

"An accident."

Martin's eyebrows raised higher.

"It's a long story," Louis said and both men laughed. Then Louis swept his arm around to indicate the room. "What about this lot?"

The Russians had festooned the room with flags and were knocking back glasses of vodka in between speeches, with much merriment. Smoke filled the air and someone was plucking a tune on a stringed instrument while General Rogov beat out a rhythm on the table, his face flushed with good cheer. The visitors had given up trying to listen to the interpreters as the evening deteriorated. At one point Louis saw General Flory, Martin's boss and the leader of the mission, enfolded in Rogov's bear hug.

For a while the two men watched. Martin resisted the attempts of a cheerful Soviet officer to get him to swallow his vodka in one go. Louis succumbed and found the glass instantly refilled. And refilled again. And again. Soon he lost count of how many he'd had.

"Y'know," Martin said, "I do believe they get on better with our people." A group of British officers watched the proceedings from a distant corner of the room while the Americans talked, laughed and drank with the Russians. Then he added, "I spent time in Oxford. I know all about you British."

Louis' head span. "It was Cambridge," he said.

"No -" began the other man.

"I mean it was Cambridge that got me these." He pointed to the insignia of his rank. "Dashwood was too crazy and I was at Cambridge."

"You're not making much sense."

Herz pressed Louis' arm to the table and took the glass from his hand.

"You don't understand," Louis said. "I was Cambridge, you were Oxford."

"You need to go to bed."

"That's why they gave me the pips." Louis ignored the other man's pressure to stand. "Gillett was crocked. We were the only Cambridge men - Peter and me. The rest, all red brick. See?"

"I think I get it. Look, let's you and I skedaddle. The party's over."

Led by Martin, Louis stumbled out into the evening air where a wave of nausea overtook him. What had they been eating? A red soup concoction, pork, dumplings and pancakes, masses of wine, then the never-ending vodka. Where the hell did they get all that alcohol? His stomach couldn't cope.

The world circled faster around him and he bent down feeling nauseous until finally, irresistibly, most of his dinner came out of his mouth and cascaded onto the ground. Martin leaped back to avoid the splash. Louis coughed, spat, wiped his face.

"That's what happens when you drink with those guys." Martin was laughing again, slapping Louis on the back. "They're always gonna see you under the table."

Louis staggered, the other man's arm around his shoulders, across the square to the row of houses requisitioned for their use, up the stairs. The vomiting had stopped his head spinning. He thanked Martin, apologised.

"Hey, I've seen worse. Don't worry about it. See you in the morning."

Left to himself, Louis sat heavily down on the bed, tipped sideways and allowed sleep to take over.

Martin used to joke about that first meeting. If they broke out a bottle he'd always pretend to get Louis to drink more, using Russian words they'd learned, the two of them dissolving into laughter.

The next day in Judenburg, Louis awoke with a buzzing in his head and a dry mouth which he attempted to assuage with coffee. Once again, the quality of the Russians' supplies was excellent. Real coffee. It jolted into his system and by mid-morning he felt ready to face the day.

The convoy set off at noon. The French kept to themselves, straight-backed and serious in their vehicles, flying the tricoleur. But the Americans and British had no problem mixing and Louis found himself in a jeep with Martin.

"There should be more of us," Martin informed him. "They restricted our numbers."

"Why's that?"

"I don't know. The General thinks they don't want us snooping around too much."

The jeep drove over a large obstacle, throwing them up from their seats.

"Hey careful with this thing," Martin shouted to the driver.

They were on a ridge, the road winding down from Semmering where they'd passed a Russian checkpoint. Below them a wooded valley stretched out, with green fields in the distance.

Louis felt an urgency in his bladder. The coffee had been strong.

The convoy descended to the plain, snaking past farms and villages and coming to a turning where a sign pointed to Wiener Neustadt.

"They got it bad there," Herz said. "Aeroplane factories. I doubt if there's much left."

But whatever had happened there, they spent no time looking. The road widened, letting them pick up speed. Louis felt his hangover returning and his head hurt with the noise of the road.

"I need to piss," he said.

"Can't stop the whole show for that," Martin said. "Here, use this."

He handed Louis a battered water canteen.

"You sure?"

"Sure. When you gotta go…"

Louis unbuttoned and relieved himself. He was about to tip the liquid out when Martin reached over and took the canister from him, throwing it into bushes on the roadside.

"I've got another one," he said.

"Well that's a relief. In more ways than one."

Half an hour later, they entered the outskirts of Vienna.

Rows of high apartment blocks ran along either side of the road. One had crumbled, presumably bomb damage, but otherwise the buildings were sound. The people in the streets stopped what they were doing as the convoy approached. Men and women with grey faces and grey clothes, shopping bags, a few pushing hand carts, stood and stared. Louis watched a queue of women outside a shop alerted by the rumble of their vehicles, turning to see the sight, some waving at them. Martin looked straight ahead, absorbed in his own thoughts.

The convoy halted. There was a problem further up. The crowd got larger as people gathered, speaking to them, gesticulating, or sometimes just gazing. It was as if they were visitors from another world, objects of wonder to the grey ghosts surrounding their vehicles.

Louis saw a woman coming towards him, shouting something. She was dark, slim, wore a thin blue dress with a brown coat over it, a shopping bag on her shoulder. She'd pinned her hair back to reveal a beautiful face, features he was sure he knew.

He shuddered. He couldn't hear what she was saying. Her face floated in front of him, the vision around it blurred, his head swirling. He couldn't think, but only gazed at her. Every movement she made was the same.

The jeep lurched forward before she could reach him and the convoy picked up speed again and he lost sight of the woman in the crowds.

"What's the matter?" Martin said.

Rob had been there. His face, floating in front of Louis' eyes. It couldn't be him; Louis knew at some level that it was a woman he'd seen, but somehow it was him.

"Are you all right?" Martin asked again.

Louis recovered his wits. It was woman who reminded him of Rob, that was all. He hadn't seen Rob for two years. He must look at his photograph again and try to remember his features, fix him more firmly in his mind.

Martin was still looking at him with a worried expression. The American would think he was half mad if he told him. First pissing in his water bottle, vomiting on his shoes, and then...

"No, I'm fine. I just... just thought I saw someone I knew. I must still be drunk from last night."

He gave Martin a weak smile and the other man looked at him, puzzled.

"It's nothing," he continued, "Nothing at all. A coincidence."

The convoy halted in the city centre where Russians met them. Louis had to pull himself together and get to work.

They had six days to complete their survey of the city and then the Russians wanted them out of the place. While the generals sat in meetings to agree on zoning, timetables and headquarters buildings, Louis scouted out future accommodation for the occupying forces. It was a busy time. On the second evening he found Martin in an alcove in the bar and joined him when Martin beckoned to him. They drank a beer together and exchanged reports of their day. Then they fell silent.

"You got a picture of your girl?" Martin asked.

"I haven't got one," Louis replied, forgetting to say he was married, as he usually did.

"Thought you said you had one back home."

Louis couldn't remember what he'd said to Martin. He should stop this business of saying he was married to all and sundry. It led to unnecessary complications.

They fell silent again. Then Louis took a decision. "I'll show you a photograph then"

He took Rob's photograph from its secret compartment and handed it to Martin.

"That's her."

Martin looked at the picture and Louis took a large swig from his drink and stared, trying to gauge the small movements of the other man's expression. Martin seemed to choose his words with great care.

"Nice looking guy. You're very lucky."

And Martin smiled. It was a smile that sent waves of relief and gratitude through Louis and he realised tears were welling up in his eyes. What had made him trust this man? It was clearly an instinct that came from somewhere deep inside him, a recognition that here was a fellow human being to whom he could tell the deepest secret of his heart without fear. And his instinct had been right.

He tried to talk, but he couldn't get any words out. Martin handed him his handkerchief.

Then he told Martin, his voice quiet, about Rob, how he'd met him, about Vita, about Rob and Frank Lemaire, about Susanna. In fact, he spilled his heart out to the American, who was a wonderful listener, the best Louis had ever met. Martin, nodded, uttered words of sympathy and understanding, encouraging the torrent of words and memories.

It was so different from talking to Peter Dashwood, the only other man with whom he'd discussed his personal life. Not only was there the deception about Rob to maintain, but Dashwood was of a salacious turn of mind, still trying to get him to talk about his sexual experiences with Ruth Crossland whenever he scented the chance. At some level, too Dashwood pushed Louis away. Too often he'd signal his patience with Louis was over with that disgusting phrase, 'plenty more fish in the sea.'

"That's some tangle you've got yourself into there," Martin said, when Louis had finished.

"I haven't seen him for two years, but I think about him every day. I can't help it."

"Heartache. It's a tough one, and you've got the worst kind. You should try to see him."

"How can I do that?"

Martin pointed to the spot card. "That thing. Lets you go anywhere doesn't it? You could get a plane ride."

"I'll consider it," Louis said. "Look, thanks for listening. I don't usually -"

"That's all right. I know what it's like."

"Have you got anyone? Back home?"

"Back home? Where's home? I spent half my life here when I was a kid. Sure, there's someone, but I don't know where she is. Not any more."

"A girl?" Louis asked, smiling.

"Yup. A girl. A real girl for me."

They both laughed at this.

Martin was about to tell Louis more when a soldier - the man who'd driven their jeep from Judenburg - came into the bar and headed for Martin.

"Sir, I've got an urgent order for you to report to General Flory."

Martin knocked back his drink and got off the bar stool.

"Duty calls," he said, putting his hand on Louis' shoulder in a gesture of farewell. "I'll tell you some time."

He didn't get the chance to talk with Martin again before the Allied mission departed, the Americans and the French out to the west, the British to the south. On the road back to Klagenfurt Louis shut his eyes and remembered the conversation, feeling the relief that flooded through him still. There were good people in the world after all, people he could trust. Then he recalled the woman's face he'd seen in the crowd, the image mingling with his memories of Rob, so that the two seemed strangely indistinguishable.

CHAPTER 24

The next time he met Ellie Bauer she was in a Russian prison. He'd been on another visit to Vienna, helping smooth the way for the military administration, when they got reports of an English woman the Russians were holding. They'd discovered her living in Vienna. The Soviets disliked such anomalies. They ironed them out. The British could send someone to see her, but Louis must understand that her case was still being investigated.

The prison was a tall white building in a southern suburb of Vienna, barred windows at each level. A uniformed Russian woman ushered him through a double swing door into a room. It was being used for lectures, rows of chairs opposite a blackboard, desks lined up along one wall. He took a seat and waited. The room was quiet, insulated from the noise of the street by massive walls. There was a smell of disinfectant.

Steps sounded on the stone floor outside. They stopped and voices spoke in Russian. The door pushed open and a woman entered the room. Now he realised she was older than Rob, thinner, wearing a blue dress, her hair wild and a look of terror on her face. As the door closed behind her she half walked, half staggered towards him. Her eyes registered astonishment, and then relief as he got up and held out his hand to greet her.

"Hello, Mrs Bauer," he said. "You are her aren't you? You're British I think?"

At first she took his hand, but as he spoke her legs gave way. He put his arm around her, catching her, feeling her thin body against his, and lowered her with great gentleness into a seat.

It was the woman he'd seen earlier in the year, as his convoy drove past. Now he knew what she'd been saying. "Are you British?" she'd been shouting, "I am too."

He went to beg a glass of water from the woman at the entry desk, bringing it back for Ellie to sip as she recovered her composure. Her hand trembled as she brought it to her lips.

"I didn't know…" she whispered.

"Take it slowly. Drink."

"I didn't know what they'd do to me."

She was recovering from her fear.

"I thought…" But she couldn't finish.

Her body then stiffened and she sat up in the chair, firmer now. She downed the rest of the water.

"Lieutenant Nicholson," Louis said, shaking her hand which was still limp in his. "Look Mrs Bauer -"

She stood up as he spoke, turned away from him and walked over to a window that looked into an inner courtyard.

"Mrs Bauer, we don't have much time."

"Time for what?"

Louis realised he didn't know what he was going to do with her.

"Will you take me out of here?" She was returning to him, weaving between the chairs.

"I'm not sure. You've got to tell me about yourself. Fast. They'll be back for you soon I expect."

A shiver ran through her body making him feel

protective. She seemed cold in the thin dress. But he had nothing to offer her.

"What do you want to know?" she asked.

"Why you are here. Why they arrested you. What you are doing in this country."

She closed her eyes, drew her breath in and let out a long sigh.

"I am English. I come from Jersey in the Channel Islands. I met my husband there before the war and I came here with him. We divorced three years ago. I have been alone since then."

"In Vienna?"

"For the last year, yes."

"Why did they bring you here? What did they tell you?"

"I could ask you the same thing. Men came for me. They told me nothing. I thought, I thought... thought it was the end for me. You hear things. When they came for me again just now..."

His instinct told him she was an innocent bystander, a victim of Russian paranoia. He couldn't leave her here. Plenty of people disappeared, bundled into cars by the Russians, never to be seen again.

"We've got a chance Mrs Bauer. They let me come here. We must see what we can do."

A plan was forming in his mind. The only person outside was the Russian woman. Beyond her was the street. If he got this English woman past the desk, his jeep was just around the corner.

"Come with me."

She stood up. "What are you going to do?"

"I'll get you out of here if I can. Do exactly as I say."

She nodded.

"Put your wrist next to mine. We must make it look like we're handcuffed. We'll walk past them."

Louis took off his tie and knotted it around their wrists. It looked fake but he hoped to avoid close scrutiny.

Tied together, they left the room and into the reception

area where the Russian woman sat at her desk. She looked up as they approached, Louis holding up his spot card so that the woman's attention was directed at that rather than their wrists. It was all he could think of. He felt hot and his heart beat fast.

The woman inspected the card closely and nodded. She can't have understood the writing on it but it was obviously an official pass and the situation was clear: a routine transfer of a prisoner into British custody. Louis kept their wrists out of sight as she pushed a ledger towards him to sign. He made a show of fumbling for a pen with his free hand, at which the Russian let out a sigh, reached into a drawer and handed him one. He signed.

Then they were out of the building. It had worked.

"Quick. Get to the jeep. We need to get out of here."

"What did you do with her?" I asked.

"Got her out, of course. Out of Vienna. I got her back to the British zone and put her up at Sacher's for a couple of days. Then I stuck her in the boot of a car and drove her out, past the Russians at Semmering. No other way to do it."

It sounded like something out of a spy movie.

"It's hard to believe."

"It happened," Louis said. "It's how we had to do things sometimes. The woman at the desk didn't know what was happening, and on the car journey Ellie stayed very quiet and nobody thought to look."

"Didn't the Russians kick up a fuss when they realised?"

"Of course. But there was nothing they could do. She was one of ours. I got her accommodation in Klagenfurt where I was based. She got a job in the Labour section, translating documents and interpreting. She was good at it. I saw a lot of her and well, you know…"

"What?"

205

"The inevitable. We became close. I hadn't seen Rob for so long and I needed someone. She needed someone. That's how it happened."

Later that day, Louis and I decided to go for a walk on the Heath. I say 'walk' but in fact Louis was driving a mobility scooter. It was a brand new, bright red thing you had to plug into the wall to charge. It had a range of several miles, so we could go further afield than usual.

"I want to show you where Vita lived," he said.

I realised I'd never seen the home that Rob had known as a child. He hadn't taken me there and in my years of wandering Hampstead Heath I'd not set foot in the Vale of Health, even though it's only a half-hour walk from the house where we all lived.

The Vale feels private. It's a small village enclosed on all sides by Hampstead Heath, human settlement there dating from the eighteenth century, taken over by writers, artists, political radicals and poets in the nineteenth century. Now, in the midst of the city, it provides the pleasures of English village life to its wealthy residents. There are no shops and the road leading there is a dead end. You wouldn't visit the place unless you had business with someone.

We climbed up the side of the Heath on a tarmac path which turned to rougher stones and then earth and gravel. The wheels of the scooter were small and the surface bumped Louis around a lot so stopped for a while and looked over to the boating pond. You can't see the women's pond from there because it's surrounded by a screen of forest.

"We go left here," Louis said, guiding his scooter along an avenue of trees and then up across a grassy area, children playing on swings nearby. We stopped at a small lake lying below the Vale. Houses lined its banks, grass lawns flowing down to the water's edge.

"That's where they lived," Louis was pointing straight ahead.

I looked to see which house he meant. A modern block with white balconies, about six storeys high, dominating the terraced cottages next to it.

"The flats," he added, pointing again.

"But that's modern. Where do you mean?"

"They built the flats later. A fire destroyed the house."

"I'd no idea."

I felt disappointed. I'd built up a picture in my mind - the conservatory, the studio, the garden.

"Was it a rocket, a doodlebug I mean, those things at the end of the war?"

"No, it was later. They think it might have been a gas leak, maybe a pipe that got dislodged or cracked by the bomb that fell in 1941, but no-one really knows."

"What set it off?"

Louis shrugged. "I wouldn't know. Perhaps Vita lit a cigarette. It destroyed the whole house as well as the one next door."

The implication slowly dawned on me. Vita was in the house, the house that was completely destroyed.

"You mean -"

"Yes, she was there. It happened in the night. Rob was staying at Frank Lemaire's place. The neighbours said Vita got out but went back to save the cat. Smoke inhalation. They had to dig her body out of the ruins."

Until then I'd never known how my grandmother had died. I imagined a tall woman in her nightgown, hair flying loose, standing in the street at night. She desperately watched her beloved house going up in flames, neighbours around her, breaking away from them to run inside, searching through the flames and smoke. She fought against the heat of the fire, gasping for breath and finally collapsed. The images gripped me.

"Come on, let's go," Louis said. "This thing's battery won't last forever."

As we retraced our steps across the Heath, Louis told me that Rob had salvaged a few of his bronze pieces from the rubble. The fire ruined his maquettes, drawings, tools, everything else in his studio.

"He was devastated," Louis said. "He and Vita were very close. But it was also difficult for me."

"Difficult?"

"Things had just started with Ellie. I'd put Rob out of my mind at last. This was something that drew me back to my old life at just the wrong moment. I should have taken leave, gone home to see him. But I didn't."

He'd stopped the scooter to talk so we were under trees.

"It didn't help that Frank was involved. Otherwise I might have made the effort."

"What did Rob do?"

"I found out, much later. The first few days were terrible. You can imagine. He blamed himself, said if he'd been there it might not have happened. Perhaps Vita left the gas on by mistake. Or he might have stopped his mother going back into the house. And Rob had nowhere to live. Staying with Frank wasn't an option, although he bedded down there for a few days. It was a dreadful time for him."

Back at the house Louis parked the scooter at the basement entrance. I had to carry him up the stairs to the kitchen. He said he felt very weak. I put the kettle on while he went to the toilet. Soon he'd need help with that.

"Go upstairs will you?" Louis asked, "I want you to get something."

He told me to find a yellow plastic folder from the trunk in his room. I brought it to him and he rifled through it, taking out a letter.

"Read this," he said. "One of the few I ever received from him. Your grandfather. I kept it as a souvenir."

I took it from him. It was short.

Dear Louis,

I hope you are well. I have a little stiffness in my back but am otherwise fine.

I write to inform you that your friend Robert Gill is now lodging with me at our home. Since the unfortunate incident with his mother he was unable to find alternative accommodation.

He is much relieved to be here and has taken your room. He will pursue his artistic activities in the basement, where there is space for fabrication. I trust this arrangement will meet your approval.

We attended Mrs Gill's funeral yesterday. As you may imagine, it was a solemn occasion.

I must thank you for your recent missive. The Carinthian countryside does indeed sound most pleasant. The weather here is fine for the time of year.

We look forward to your eventual homecoming.

Your affectionate father, etc

James Nicholson.

"He wasn't much of a letter writer," I remarked.

"No, he wasn't," Louis said. "That's a pretty representative example. Did you see the postscript?"

I looked again. There was a handwritten note below the signature:

PS: Robert reminds you of the need to locate Kurt. I can only report this request. He says you will understand its meaning.

"Kurt Reich? His Austrian brother?"

"The same. The one who stayed behind when the aunt's family left for America in 1939. No-one had any idea what had happened to him."

"How could you find him in that chaos? Even if he

survived."

A look of professional pride came across Louis' face.

"I was good at finding people. I thought I could locate Kurt Reich. If, as you say, he survived."

"It's nice that your father looked after Rob," I said.

"Yes, I suppose he had a heart of sorts."

"Well, it was very decent of him."

"I think he was lonely. He lived on his own after Mother died, with me being away. He liked having Rob there. It suited them both. Rob set up a studio in the basement. And slept in my bedroom, of all places!"

"So there we were," he said later, in the kitchen, sipping tea and eating a biscuit. "A bomb went off in Rob's life and he ended up here with Father, living in my room. And a bomb went off in my life too: I met Ellie, your mother."

CHAPTER 25

The affair with Ellie started because of a lost boy. Norman Gray brought him into the office. He was about ten or twelve years old, dark-skinned, dressed in filthy clothes, a grey jumper tied around his waist. He was excited, gabbling away in a language Louis couldn't place.

"I think he's a gypsy," Norman said.

"Why'd they let him in?"

"I don't know. But look at him will you? He's trying to tell us something."

The boy opened his rucksack and rummaged inside. Alarmed, Louis got up, took it from him and searched it for himself. There was clothing inside, scraps of food. Something sticky at the bottom gave off a rotten smell. Louis withdrew his fingers from it sharply as the child came forward, pointing at a pocket on the side. It contained a photograph booklet with just one picture: the boy with his family. His parents were posing stiff and straight in a photographer's studio, the boy between them two or three years old, his hair brushed smooth.

He was still talking, pointing to the picture, trying to explain something. As Louis listened he realised it was a

French dialect, though not one he'd heard before. He and Gray tried for a while, but got nowhere. Odd words, too few to make sense. The boy stopped, realising he wasn't getting through. He picked up his rucksack and turned to leave, at which point Gray grabbed him.

"Not so fast young man," he said. Then to Louis: "We should find someone who can speak his lingo."

The boy tried to tug himself away but was held firm. Eventually he stopped struggling, sat on the floor of the office and cried.

"I can't deal with this Norman," Louis said. "Let's take him to Hut C. Someone'll look after him there."

Hut C housed the Labour section where Ellie worked. They marched the boy downstairs and out of the building. Ellie worked in a corner of the hut, five other women behind typewriters in the centre of the room. Louis could have let Gray take the boy away, but he was curious about his story. And he wanted to see Ellie.

She looked up when they entered and a broad smile crossed her face. Louis liked this about her. She welcomed people, drawing them to her warmth. The boy sensed it too and headed for her, telling his tale again in the incomprehensible language. The women stopped work and the men stood and watched.

Ellie's head was bent to listen to what the boy was saying. To Louis' surprise she said something and the boy appeared to understand, responding with a flood of information. As he sensed that she understood him, the boy became less agitated and the torrent of words eventually dried up. Ellie smiled again at him. Then he dropped his rucksack onto the floor and stepped towards her, at which point she enfolded him in her arms and he held on to her, tight, as if she were his mother.

"He's from Algeria," she said.

"How did you understand him?" Louis asked.

"He speaks French. Well, a type of French. I could hardly follow it though."

It was a French patois common in the Channel Islands, but delivered with the boy's strong accent.

"What's his story then?" Gray asked.

The boy was not a gypsy. He was an Algerian Arab whose parents had been working in Guernsey when the Germans invaded and sent the family to camps in France. At some point his parents had been separated from him and when American troops liberated his camp he'd gone in search of them. He'd heard they had gone to Austria.

Louis spoke. "How old is he?"

Ellie asked the boy who'd now recovered and was sitting next to her on a chair eating a biscuit.

"Ten," she said. "He's big for his age."

"I wonder where his parents are."

The adults fell silent for a moment, pondering that issue.

"He'll need looking after," Louis said. "Norman, can you find the lists and see if there's anyone in our DP camps? Get the boy's name, his surname. Arab names can't be so common."

"And if they're not listed?" Ellie asked. "What will happen to him then?"

"We'll put him in the Child Welfare place at Hietzing. They'll make inquiries, liaise with the French. There must be someone in his home country."

It was the usual bureaucratic solution. Systems would process the boy, look after him, meet his basic needs and get him off their plate. The boy now stood in front of them, staring at the two men, understanding nothing of their plans.

"He can come to my place," Ellie said.

"You can't look after him."

"I know how to look after children. That Welfare place…"

Louis knew what she meant. It was a barn, filled with lost, damaged children. Some would never find their families. Others didn't want to, if they had any sense. The children there fended for themselves, the adults overwhelmed by the numbers.

"Well, if you're sure. We must get him registered though. As living with you, that is. Norman, could you see to it?"

Louis left them to sort out the arrangements. That morning he thought of Ellie cradling the boy's head, comforting him. He wondered at the tenderness she showed, about where it came from, and who she really was. And he remembered the feel of her body falling into his arms when they first met.

"What happened to the boy?" I asked.

"He stayed with her for about a week. Then we found his parents."

"That's fantastic!"

"Told you I could find people, didn't I? Yes, he was a lucky little blighter. Enterprising too. He'd walked all the way from France to get to them. They were in a DP camp in Villach a few miles away. They must have been pleased."

Louis had been in bed since our walk on the Heath two days before, too weak to leave the house. The palliative care people had been to visit, asking questions, promising support. It was the beginning of the end.

"She really impressed me at that point," he said. "Ellie could switch on the charm. It was infectious, and it got to me. I fell for her because of that."

"The way she was with the boy?"

"That was the start of it. But it went beyond that. She was just good with people. She had a child of her own you know, a daughter, living with the husband's family."

He thought more about Ellie in the following week. When they found the parents, he decided to go to her personally with the news, using the opportunity to ask her out for a drink. She declined, saying she couldn't leave the boy alone, but after they'd reunited the child with his parents Ellie was free. He took her to a restaurant overlooking the Wörthersee where they sat on the balcony drinking wine.

"That boy, what was his name?" Louis asked.

"Samir. But I called him Sam. He didn't mind."

"I've been thinking about how he walked across Europe to find his parents. I wouldn't have done that."

When he was the boy's age, Louis had been at boarding school, sometimes fantasising about getting away from the place, making his way home under his own steam. But his parents would only have sent him back.

"Didn't you love them enough, your mother and father?" Ellie asked.

He felt confused. "Love? Oh no, different situation. Don't know why I'm comparing myself…"

She smiled and they both took a drink from their glasses, looking out across the lake. Coloured lights flickered on the opposite side, their reflections moving on the water and they heard music and voices.

"What's your daughter's name?"

"Anna. She's nine. It was her birthday last month."

"When did you last see her?"

"Three years ago. I miss her terribly."

"How did it happen, separating from your husband?"

Ellie didn't reply, turning her head away to stare at the water.

"You don't have to tell me."

"No, it's all right."

She turned back and placed her elbows on the table between them.

"I met Michael in Jersey. He came there to find work. You know how things were then."

"I'm not sure I do" Louis said.

"There was nothing for him in Austria. He was in the hotel trade and they were closing everywhere. The

Germans - they'd stopped coming for skiing holidays."

She took another sip of wine.

"But his parents wrote after we had Anna. Things were picking up in Zell-am-See. The tourists were coming back."

"When was this?"

"1938. After the changes."

"Weren't you worried?"

"What about?"

"The political situation."

"I don't think about those things."

Louis found it hard to understand how she could have started a new life in Austria after Hitler had taken over. Didn't she realise?

"We lived with his parents at first. He had a job in the mountains - the dam at Kaprun - organising food for the workers. But it wasn't right. It was a tiny house and, well, there was his mother. We didn't get on."

"What was the problem?"

Ellie hesitated, fingering her glass.

"Michael had an affair."

At this point the wine glass fell over. Her fingers had lost their hold on its stem. Wine spilled onto the table cloth. Louis reached over and set it straight.

"His mother hated me for being foreign." Ellie pursed her lips. "And she's a Nazi, a bloody Nazi through and through."

She was in the grip of her feelings now and the rest of the story came out fast: her husband, encouraged by his mother, had taken up again with a childhood sweetheart and then Ellie discovered they were having a full blown affair. It was an intolerable situation, so she left him.

"Where did you go? What about your daughter?"

"They kept her. That family of his, they knew everyone in the town. I was the outcast, the foreigner. There was nothing I could do."

Her shoulders slumped. "She's probably forgotten me

by now."

Louis reached over and took her hands in his.

"I went to Vienna. Then the Russians came. You know what happened then."

He felt a surge of compassion. He was sure he could help reunite her with her daughter, just as he'd helped the boy find his parents. Above all, he understood that he wanted her.

The affair began a week later after a garden party at the officer's club. He walked her back to her flat and she invited him in. They both knew what would happen. But her lips were unyielding when they kissed and her body felt hard against his, ungiving. When he entered her she gave a gasp which he thought might be pain and he withdrew. He was disappointed.

He asked her how she was feeling. Hadn't she liked it? What was the matter?

She said things had happened to her in Vienna that she couldn't talk about. It wasn't his fault.

But it played on his mind.

CHAPTER 26

In the early spring of 1946 Louis was in his office at the Klagenfurt headquarters of the Section he now headed. A middle-aged couple were ushered in. It was Herr Fischer and his wife who owned the Gasthaus on the Wörthersee where the rest of the Section were billeted. Fischer was a rotund fellow who ran an efficient establishment, his wife managing the kitchen. They looked worried as they lowered themselves onto the plain wooden chairs opposite Louis' desk.

"Good morning Herr Fischer, Frau Fischer. What can I do for you?"

The woman started. "It's our daughter…"

This was a fifteen-year-old called Maria who served the tables at the Gasthaus.

"What's the matter with her? Not ill I hope?" Louis smiled encouragement at the couple who were tongue tied, the wife looking at her lap, her fingers fidgeting with a handkerchief.

The husband burst out. "They touch her, your men, touching my little girl. You must stop this!"

The Fischers were reasonable people, placid, solid, not given to hysterics, but the man's face shook with feeling as he spoke. His wife pressed her hands harder into her lap.

"If the men are -"

"We wish you to talk to them Herr Nicholson, tell them." It was Frau Fischer who was on the verge of tears. "They cannot do this. She's a child."

Louis saw their point. He'd have to warn the men off the girl. He didn't want trouble. It wasn't Naples where parents sold their daughters to the highest bidder. The Klagenfurt locals were cut from a different cloth. Or they weren't as hungry, he reflected, looking again at Herr Fischer's wide girth.

"I'll do it this evening," he promised. "As soon as I can get away."

The couple shook his hand, thanked him, clearly embarrassed, and shuffled out.

Paperwork, whose volume had increased since peace had broken out, occupied Louis for the rest of the day. Denazification was in full swing, so the unit were spending much of their time working their way through arrest lists, knocking on doors, questioning suspects. Photography studios were a good place to start. The Nazi hierarchy had liked to have their pictures taken, and the photographers kept the negatives, filed by name, in case of repeat orders.

Louis had to examine the reports written by members of his unit, recording interrogations and vettings. Many civilians wanted jobs with the military administration, so Field Security had to screen them for any political involvement under the old regime. And there were displaced persons to process, people applying to travel into the frontier zone with Yugoslavia where partisans and criminal gangs still operated, feeding off the chaos.

It generated mountains of paperwork, much of which came across Louis' desk, so he was often there late into the evening, grateful his own quarters were only around the corner.

Louis picked up another file and opened it. A questionnaire, filled in with tiny black handwriting. A series of idiotic questions about someone's political involvement, the answers all lies. He couldn't bear it and shut the file.

This was all just putting off his confrontation with the men. He remembered joining the unit in Oran years before, the awe he had felt towards the men he now commanded. This evening he needed to assert authority over them, get them to do his bidding. The prospect was daunting.

It was a warm night. He drove over to the Gasthaus where he found most of the men outside, sitting around tables. A couple of them played cards. Norman Gray sat separately, reading. He saw Peter Dashwood, drinking beer from a tankard. In a corner, Lofty Elliott was strumming something on a guitar. Louis missed this relaxed camaraderie. They were here, sharing rooms in the Gasthaus, while he lived in an officer's apartment in town, luxurious but alone.

"Hello chaps," he said as he walked into the courtyard. "I need a word with you."

He was about to start when young Maria Fischer herself came out of a doorway, blonde, large breasted, a tray in her hand, and bounded towards him.

"Lieutenant Nicholson!" she said with a warm smile. She wore a dirndl, traditional Austrian dress, and she exuded a healthy, youthful ardour with her every movement. Louis saw the men eying her. Norman Gray, inscrutable as always, looked up from his book, raised an eyebrow, and turned back to his reading.

He declined her offer of a beer. He'd not be staying. She smiled and pouted disappointment simultaneously, as if he'd wounded her without in any way affecting her fondness for him, and went back indoors. This was, indeed, a young woman sending out powerful messages, perhaps unaware of the effect she was having, or maybe just enjoying the power it gave her over the men, whose lecherous responses she'd not yet learned to treat with sufficient caution.

"As I say," Louis repeated, "I need to have a word with you. Gather round."

The men moved towards him.

"It's about Maria Fischer," he began, his voice lowered so the family indoors wouldn't hear his lecture. "Her parents saw me."

There were a couple of sniggers, suppressed when Louis stared at the culprits.

"Do you know her age?" he asked.

No-one answered.

"Do you know the age of consent?"

The silence continued.

"She's fifteen. That's what she is. Fifteen. Get that into your thick heads. If any one of you violates that girl, the sky will fall in on that man. Your habitation will become a dungheap and you will be better not to have been born. Is that understood?"

He looked around the assembled company with what he hoped was a commanding gaze. The men adopted thoughtful expressions, nodded, murmured assent, and returned to their tables. It had worked and Louis was relieved it was done. Then he heard a voice of dissent.

"Y'know you can't put toothpaste back in the tube."

A ripple of laughter went around the courtyard. It was Dashwood, who swayed as he stood, holding his beer.

"What's that supposed to mean?"

"If the horse is bolted," Dashwood said. "Stable door. You know what I mean."

"Come outside with me Peter. It's time we had a chat. Put that drink away won't you?"

Louis' promotion meant that Dashwood had been passed over even though he had far more experience overseas than Louis. He'd said nothing, but Louis knew he resented it.

In the street outside they faced each other.

"Are you drunk?" Louis asked.

"No more than usual."

"Well Peter, you need to explain your last remark. What have you been doing with that girl?"

"Didn't say it was me."

"So are you planning to rat on someone then?"

"Of course not. It was a joke. Bit of fun. Don't take it so seriously old man."

Louis felt angry. He didn't like being obliged to chastise the men. But they were a hard-working, competent and, above all, disciplined team and he meant to keep them that way.

"It's not funny. Not in the tiniest bit. Especially not in front of the others. Its... its insubordination."

Dashwood found this hilarious.

"Insubordination? Me? Faithful old Peter? You're having me on."

"I mean it Peter. And I'll have you on a charge if I find out you've touched -"

At that point something snapped in Dashwood. A murderous look crossed his face.

"A fucking charge? You're joking. You little prig..."

He lunged at Louis, his beery breath following him so that Louis almost retched. The punch didn't connect as Louis stepped aside and pulled the other man over. Dashwood fell onto the road, arms splayed to break his fall, then groaned and turned to sit with his legs out, his head in his hands.

This shocked Louis. A brawl of this sort was a serious matter if he acted on it. Attempting an assault on a superior officer. But Dashwood was once his friend, so he bent down to him, thoughts of rank out of his mind.

"Are you all right?"

Dashwood didn't reply and Louis realised, much to his surprise, that the other man was sobbing. He remembered the time at school when Dashwood had cried after Louis had climbed onto his back in a play fight. Everyone knew Peter Dashwood didn't cry, yet here it was again.

"Come on Peter," he said, gently helping the man onto his feet. "Let's take a look at the lake."

They walked to the shore and watched the moonlight shining on the water.

"I haven't touched her, you know."

"That's a relief."

"She sits on everyone's laps. She's a little flirt. A tart. I wouldn't be surprised if -"

"Forget it Peter, I don't want to know."

"Look, I'm sorry…"

"Forget it. We've all been working too hard."

It had been tough time for them. Sending the Chetniks over the mountains had been the worst. One of them had made it back and told them Tito's people had stopped the train over the border, ordered the men out and opened up on them with machine guns. The FSS men who'd rounded them up, Louis and Peter Dashwood included, were disgusted, with their orders, with the war, with everything about what they were doing. Then, after a few days, people had recovered, got on with it. That's what you did in the army.

"I didn't want this command," Louis said. "If you'd got it -"

"I can't see why they passed me over," Dashwood said, his resentment surging. "I was in North Africa for months while you were standing around in Liverpool or wherever it was, doing nothing."

"It wasn't quite -"

"And dash it all, I'm older!"

Louis had to suppress a sudden urge to laugh. It was as if they were still schoolboys, discussing who ought to become a prefect.

Louis had guessed the real reason for Dashwood's being passed over. He drank too much, so hangovers sometimes interfered with his work and his punctuality. And people sensed the simmering violence in him. The leader of a Field Security Section needed a cool head and a steady temperament. And Louis wanted the men to like as well as respect him.

"There's nothing we can do about it Peter. I didn't ask for it, but I'm doing it to the best of my ability. I won't pursue anything with you but just don't play silly buggers with me again, especially in front of the others. Are we agreed?"

Dashwood looked at him, subdued, then without warning flung his arms around Louis, burying his head in his shoulder.

"Yes, yes," he said, his words muffled by Louis' clothing, "I agree."

Then, abruptly, Dashwood broke away and marched back to the Gasthaus.

Louis stayed behind, stunned by the outburst. Dashwood could be strange, unpredictable. He shrugged his shoulders and walked to his jeep.

The following day Dashwood knocked on the door of his office.

"I want a transfer," he announced.

His old friend was still very worked up. But Louis wasn't inclined to make any concessions.

"I mean it," Dashwood said.

"I'm sure you do Peter. Take a seat."

Dashwood sat down hard, folding his arms across his chest.

"Is this about last night?"

"I knew you'd think that."

"What am I supposed to think?"

Then Dashwood relaxed, unfolded his arms, leaned forward so that his elbows rested on Louis desk.

"I'm sorry about what I said, okay? Too much to drink, and…"

Louis waved his hand to acknowledge the apology.

"It would be better if I get out of your hair,"

Dashwood continued, "There are opportunities in Vienna."

Louis had heard. Vienna was fast becoming the hub for the British military intelligence effort as the Soviet threat became more evident. They were recruiting the brightest and the best from FSS units in the south of the country. Louis wasn't sure Dashwood was in that category, but he could see that life could be simpler if he transferred.

"It'll be a step up for me too," Dashwood pointed out. "Make up for…"

"Yes. I understand your disappointment. Well I won't apologise for that again. I didn't ask for this command, they – "

"Damn it, just do this thing for me, will you? I need a recommendation from my, my commanding officer. We'll both do all right if it falls the right way."

"I'll see what I can do. Fill in the forms will you? Then I'll put it through."

Satisfied, Dashwood stood up and shook Louis' hand.

After he'd left, Louis sat back and reflected on his old friend's request. Dashwood had spied an opportunity to get a leg up in the military hierarchy, denied to him when Louis was promoted above his head. This was important to Peter, whose father was no doubt disappointed he'd only made it to sergeant. He'd be at the heart of things in Vienna. Though he had no similar ambitions, Louis felt a twinge of jealousy. Why should the man's bad behaviour be rewarded? He'd have to think more about this request.

And he had other things on his mind. There was Rob's reminder to find out about Kurt Reich, his half-brother who'd stayed behind when his family left the country before the war. He might put out a few feelers, see what he could do.

CHAPTER 27

Kurt Reich was a mischling, the son of a Jewish parent. If he had survived, then the obvious place to start was on the displaced persons lists. There were several DP camps in the British zone housing a shifting population. The lists weren't perfect, but they were a start.

The camp for Jews was troublesome from a security point of view and Louis had been there several times. The local people resented the better provisions the Jews received. There'd been a riot when fresh milk supplies had dried up, but deliveries continued for the camp. And it was a Zionist hotbed, the people keen to get to Palestine, something the British authorities opposed.

Louis approached Norman Gray for help, but he was sceptical when Louis talked him through the problem. He pointed out there was no reason Kurt should be in a DP camp. Plenty of mischlinge had survived the war. He could still be in Vienna, and even if he was in a DP camp, he'd be more likely to be in the American sector where they had ten times as many Jews.

So Louis called Martin Herz. The American was helpful as ever, promised he'd put someone onto it and call him back if they found Kurt on their lists although he observed that Kurt Reich could be a common name.

Herz was right about the name. Gray found two Kurt Reichs on the British lists. One was over fifty, but no age was given for the second name, so Louis decided he'd better investigate.

He drove through a series of well-kept villages towards the mountains, rising high, eventually reaching a grassy plain with rows of wooden huts. Once, barbed wire and guard towers had surrounded the camp, but these were had been dismantled and a low perimeter fence put in their place. Louis stopped his car outside a reception building and the British commandant came out to meet him. He explained his business while a crowd of curious young men gathered around his jeep. These men were short, unshaven, thin but filled with an intense energy. They were survivors.

The commandant addressed them.

"Where is Jossel?"

An older man with a grizzled beard and dark eyebrows pushed forward through the crowd. Louis knew him from earlier visits: Avram Jossel, the group's elected leader. A powerful looking fellow, he'd been through Theresienstadt, Mauthausen and its labour camps where he'd worked on the defensive wall the Germans had thrown up in the East to halt the Russian advance.

Louis explained why he'd come. Kurt Reich wasn't in trouble but he needed to find him.

Jossel sighed. "We have two by that name."

"Describe them, would you?"

"Why should I help you?"

"Can we go somewhere?" Louis indicated the crowd of men around them and Jossel eventually nodded, saying Louis should follow him.

He led him to a hut, at the end of which was a room set aside for Jossel's use. There was a stained table in the corner, strewn with canned foods, paper bags, half-opened food packets. An enormous slab of butter lay wrapped in the centre of this debris, presumably destined for the black market.

"Kurt Reich is a relative of my wife," Louis said. "Her brother. She'd like me to find him."

Jossel's eyes widened at this news.

"A personal inquiry? Well then, I can help. But mind you -"

Louis held up his hand. "The Kurt Reich I'm looking for would be about twenty-five by now."

"That one? He's no longer here. He left a month ago."

"Where did he go?"

"To the American zone. He'll not be coming back."

DPs weren't allowed to travel between zones without a permit, but Louis knew they did anyway.

"What can you tell me about him?"

Jossel shrugged. "He has a beard. Spectacles."

"I mean who he is, what he believes in."

"He's a patriot," Jossel said. "He has ideals. He will go to Palestine, like the rest of us."

Jossel wouldn't expand. Louis tried to get him talking about the young man's history, but the camp leader denied knowledge of this. A thousand people were there and he couldn't keep up with all of them. It was no good seeking out Reich's friends. They wouldn't talk to Louis. Jossel was only talking because he was a helpful sort. Louis should ask the Americans.

Louis tried anyway, going to Reich's hut where he met a wall of silence. Yes, they knew him but no, they could not say why he left or where he'd gone.

The best option would be to go back to Klagenfurt and wait for Martin Herz's report. Reich might be on the American lists.

But when Martin's report came through, it offered no leads. Louis felt at least he'd tried. He'd report that to Rob, and he could hope for news through some other channel.

The following week Louis received orders to assemble a group of three men under his command, to leave within the hour, equipped for several days with clothing and personal weapons. They were to proceed to Mallnitz, eighty miles north west of Klagenfurt, where they'd be joining a larger force being assembled by a Major Smith-Allison whose purpose was to investigate the sabotage of a military train.

He selected Norman Gray and Lofty Elliott and then, after some hesitation, Peter Dashwood. He felt mildly guilty that Dashwood's application for a transfer was still on his desk. Anyway, Dashwood had the best command of German.

They were housed in the buildings of a military ski school. Mallnitz was in a cul-de-sac at the end of a long valley, on the British side of the border with the American zone, to which it was linked by a railway tunnel. The train had been derailed on the British side.

The village was sealed off and the field security men spent three days scouring the place for information, interrogating residents, searching local farms, questioning people from the surrounding area to discover if they'd seen strangers. It was frustrating, weary work, the local people less than forthcoming, reluctant to help the former enemies of their country.

Then Gray had some luck. A Gasthaus owner reported that two men carrying large rucksacks had visited his establishment the night before the explosion. Smith-Allison had brought a forensics expert with him who prepared identikit pictures from the description of the men. One of the pictures showed a man with beard and spectacles.

After that breakthrough, they received information that the Austrian police on the American side had caught a man coming down from the mountains. He was armed with an automatic pistol and the Americans were holding him for illegal possession of a weapon. Louis selected Dashwood to come with him through the tunnel to Bad Gastein for an interview with the prisoner and, if possible, his extradition to the British zone.

Before they left, Smith-Allison gave them a stern warning. The suspect was a Jew and American policy on Palestine opposed the British view, being in favour establishing a Jewish state, so the matter was sensitive. He told them they'd need to remove their badges of uniform and replace these with 'Press correspondent' bands on their shoulder straps.

They passed the site of the derailment and saw that the damaged train had been righted and towed away, leaving uprooted bushes scattered on the ground. The saboteurs were either amateurs or hadn't intended to cause much damage as they'd put their charges on the outside edge of the track, only causing the engine to tip over and lean against the hill. Had they placed their explosives on the other side, it would have tumbled down the mountain.

In Bad Gastein, American military police met them and took them to a young man in a cell. He sat on a wooden chair, staring through a barred window. His appearance was consistent with both identikit pictures, but that was hardly proof of anything as the pictures were crude. He had no beard, but wore glasses. He gave his name as Isaac Goldstein and he denied involvement in derailing the train. He was exploring the mountains, for the pleasure of it. He'd needed the firearm as there were dangerous people everywhere.

Dashwood was conducting the interview. The man's voice was rough and throaty, speaking in an accent Louis found hard to follow.

"He's from Vienna," Dashwood said. "Leopoldstadt."

"What happened to him?"

"He says he was released from a labour camp in Gusen. Now he's in an American camp in Bad Gastein. Out for a walk in the mountains." Dashwood snorted in disbelief.

"Some story!"

Louis agreed it wasn't very likely. "We can check his story about coming from the Bad Gastein camp."

"I need water," said the man, speaking in English. "Water and food. I've had nothing for six hours."

"You understand English." Louis said. "Why didn't you tell us?"

"You might have asked," Goldstein replied.

"I'll get you something," Louis said. "Sergeant, you carry on."

He went to find food and drink. The US Intelligence Corps building in Bad Gastein was extensive, but eventually he found a canteen where he picked up a sandwich and a bottle. When he got back, Dashwood was standing over the suspect who was now kneeling on the floor, his hand holding his face, blood dripping through his fingers.

"You bloody idiot Peter. What have you done?"

Louis moved over to Goldstein and lifted his head. He had a cut beneath his left eye where he'd been hit and a venomous look on his face.

"Is this how you British treat Jews?"

There'd be an almighty row if Goldstein reported this.

Dashwood protested. "He needed some encouragement. The man's lying through his teeth."

"Don't you realise Peter?" Louis snarled, "He's in American custody and we're here on sufferance. They'll go mad."

Goldstein spoke in English again. "Clean me up and I will make no complaint."

Both men looked at him, surprised.

"If you leave me alone," Goldstein added.

He continued, speaking slowly, as if explaining to two children.

"You can inform the Americans that you have interrogated me, and you have no further questions. I will make it easy for you."

Louis thought for a moment. There was nothing they could do. The man had them in a corner.

But Dashwood was furious. "Give me a minute with this blighter and I'll soon -"

"Shut up Peter. You've done enough damage." He turned to Goldstein. "We're finished here."

Goldstein nodded, satisfied.

"A handkerchief please."

He held his hand out, beckoning to Louis, who produced one from his pocket. As they left, he was dabbing his face.

In the train back through the tunnel there was silence between them. Then Louis spoke. "That's the last time I take you on a security operation."

There was no reply and Louis was too angry to say more.

On the British side they reported to Smith-Allison that there was nothing doing with the suspect. Since the investigation had made no further progress they were to go back to Klagenfurt.

Entering his rooms that evening, Louis felt exhausted and demoralised. Things couldn't carry on like this. He'd have to have a proper talk with Dashwood, but it would have to be later in the week because for now he was tired, needed a wash and a sleep, wanted to see Ellie.

His absence had led to a pile-up in the paperwork and it was all he could do to process the urgent matters, so it was ten days before he had time to consider Dashwood again. He stiffened his resolve for the confrontation and went in search of him.

It was a Sunday, a day off, but Louis didn't think it could wait any longer. First, he looked in the Fischer's Gasthaus, but Dashwood wasn't there. He was up in the mountains, Lofty Elliott told him, at a hunting lodge where he often went at weekends.

Louis got the directions from Elliott. The lodge was in the hills near Wolfsberg and after passing through the town he stopped to gather his thoughts. He could have given Dashwood a bad report, so bad he might have been kicked out of the Section. Dashwood would never forgive him, but Louis wasn't sure he cared any more. This talk was going to be his last chance to reform himself.

A drink would help stiffen his resolve. He'd passed a hostelry on the way out of town and he retraced his steps to it. The building had the long sloping roof typical of the area, ready for the winter snows, window boxes decked with flowers in early bloom at every window sill. On entering, he heard men singing a marching song. He stood in the doorway and watched a group of five or six men banging their fists on a table in time to the song, making the beer tankards jump.

One of them noticed him and fell silent, prompting others to turn and look at Louis, who was in uniform.

In the ensuing hush one of men picked up his beer and raised it in a greeting, saying "Grüss Gott," a gesture of peace.

Louis smiled back. "Sorry to bother you gentlemen," he said in English and prepared to leave.

But another man then turned and rose unsteadily to his feet. It was Peter Dashwood who, like the rest of them, had dressed himself in a brown jacket and plus fours.

"Louis! What are you doing here? Come and join us."

Louis felt he must accept a drink. It wasn't the right atmosphere for the confrontation he had planned. Singing had stopped and the men were friendly, relaxing again as they saw the new arrival was no threat to them. But as he sipped his beer, Louis knew he'd have to do something about Dashwood one of these days.

Dashwood offered him a second drink. They'd be leaving for the lodge soon. Louis could come with them if he liked. He declined, saying he had to get back to Klagenfurt.

"What are you doing up here old man?" Dashwood asked again. "By God it's good to see you having fun for once. Work far too bloody hard if you ask me."

"What were you singing when I came in?"

"Oh, one of their songs you know. They've got plenty of them."

Then he started again, his beery breath blowing over Louis, his fist banging the table. "Die Fahne hoch! Die Reihen fest…"

It was the SS marching song.

The other men looked alarmed. One laughed nervously, touched Dashwood's arm and wagged his finger at him to get him to stop, which he did.

"Just a song, Louis. Get's your spirits up. We should have more songs you know. These chaps know how to enjoy themselves, eh?"

"Peter, let's go outside. I need to have a word."

Dashwood scowled. "Oh not again. Not bloody again. I'm just about - "

"Come on Peter. It won't take long."

Louis led him out to the street, sat him on a stone bench and stood over him with his legs apart.

"It's about what happened in Mallnitz."

"Oh that. I thought we'd had that out."

"No we didn't. And it's not just about Mallnitz. It's -"

At this point a furious look appeared on Dashwood's face. He shouted, stabbing a finger at Louis.

"You little shit!" he yelled. "You piece of shit. You come up here and disturb me with my friends on my day off. Can't you fucking leave me alone? For one day?"

Louis went cold and spoke through clenched teeth.

"You need to listen Peter. If you won't listen -"

"Well then I won't fucking listen, will I?"

Dashwood stood, waving his arms about. Louis stepped back but Dashwood continued to yell at him.

"I'm sick of listening to you. You're a little upstart, always were. At school too, a pathetic whinger, sidling up to me and your precious brother. You can fucking well listen to me for a change."

"What could you possibly have to say?"

"Wouldn't you like to know?"

"Spit it out then."

"That girlfriend of yours."

"What about her?"

"She's a whore, that's what, a tart, a prossy, an out and out....and I can prove it."

Louis hit Dashwood in the face. It wasn't a hard blow, but it was enough to make the man slump back onto the bench, holding his cheek. People emerged from the restaurant, to stare at them.

"You fucking hit me."

"You deserved it." Louis breathed heavily, his face red with anger.

"She's a tart, all right. And believe me, I can prove it."

"I don't want to know."

"I'm sure you don't, but the Vienna office -"

"Have you been going behind my back?"

"You should be more careful who you get involved with. Vienna told me all about her."

"I said I don't want to hear this Peter. We're here to discuss your behaviour."

"That's not what I'm up here for. I'm on my ruddy day off and you come up here…"

Now all the hunters were in the street, the Gasthaus owner too. Louis realised they were making a nasty scene. It wouldn't do.

"This isn't the time or the place," he said. "We'll discuss this when you get back. Tomorrow. When you've sobered up."

Dashwood was spluttering a reply to this but Louis shouted him down.

"No more! That's it! You can go with your Nazi friends."

Louis couldn't resist this last jibe. He knew the hunters

were not likely to be active Nazis. They might have been once, but now... They were just local country people, bending with the prevailing wind.

In Klagenfurt the following day, Louis waited for Dashwood to show up, but to no avail. He could have sent someone to fetch him, but decided it wasn't worth the bother. He didn't want to hear him talking about Ellie again. And he knew, now, what he'd do about Dashwood's request for a transfer.

CHAPTER 28

"**S**o what did you do about it?" I asked.

Louis had just had a bath. One of the MacMillan nurses was helping, although she shouldn't have done. Someone lower down the mysterious pecking order of the caring professions was supposed to do it, but she was fond of him. She was called Brenda and she said he kept her amused. Louis could be very charming with women, even at his age.

"I didn't recommend him, if that's what you mean."

"So you decided to put up with him?"

"No, not that."

I waited for him to explain.

"I wrote a disciplinary report on him and sent it further up the food chain. He was scuppered after that. I told them everything I knew about him. In the end it got him kicked out of FSS."

"That's pretty vicious."

"Yes, I suppose it was. But it was the right thing to do. His behaviour was compromising our operations."

I've come across difficult, aggressive people at work, but never been in a position to do much about them. You just have to avoid them, humour them, rub along with them somehow. It's different in the military, I suppose, where they can be slapped down by discipline from on high. For me, Peter Dashwood's episodes of uncontrolled fury spoke of an immense inner pain which he exported onto the victims of his violence. In spite of myself, a small part of me felt sorry for him.

"Was that the end of his army career?" I asked.

"I don't know. He was transferred back to England. Probably got demobbed. We lost touch. Problem solved."

Louis must have seen the look on my face.

"He was a liability, damn it. I had to do it. It was just a shame it had got so personal. If I'd recommended him for Vienna he would have made a mess of things again, and that would have reflected on me. I couldn't do it. And I couldn't keep him in the unit. So I stopped protecting him. I told the truth."

Brenda came to say goodbye. She's a lovely woman and, like Louis, I'm very fond of her. She kissed him on the head and I saw her to the door, thanking her for the care she showed to my father. When I got back he'd closed his eyes but when he heard me settling down nearby, they opened.

"I had a wonderful time with Ellie that summer," Louis said.

The sun coming through the window of his bedroom must have reminded him of his time in Carinthia, fifty years before.

"I liked her company. She was such a lively person, always interested in what was going on, always involved. Fantastic warmth with people, so she made a lot of friends. We used to swim in the lake at the weekend, all very joyful and free after the troubles I had to deal with all the time at work. She taught me so much about music too."

"Music? I thought that was Rob."

"Oh no, Ellie came first as far as that was concerned. She'd been crazy for music in Vienna. Went to everything she could. We had a gramophone and she found records from somewhere. We spent evenings listening and she explained it all: who was playing, the composers, conductors, everything she knew. Once Die Fledermaus played in Klagenfurt - a touring company from Graz. It was one of the best nights of my life."

Louis and Rob had always had the radio on, the third programme if it was music. They went to concerts, got opera tickets, attended the Proms every summer. I didn't like thinking about Louis sharing this pleasure with someone else.

"And we just drove around. It's a beautiful place, Carinthia. The name, you know? Carinthia - like a female version of Corinth, mythical somehow, a dream. You should go there one day."

"I will."

Louis went on with his reminiscences. One day they travelled to Udine across the border, accompanied by Norman Gray who'd been there several times before. Norman had a knack of knowing his way around wherever he was. He led them to the fruit market where they found piles of fresh produce selling for next to nothing, stalls with gaudy knitted jackets, ribbons, straw hats, scarves, all of which delighted Ellie. It was a garrison town for the Eighth Army and the restaurants and shops were buzzing.

"Men used to look at her in the street…"

But then Louis stopped.

"You're not so keen on this," he said.

"It's not that. It's just -"

"I know. I can see how you feel. Me going on like that about her. I was just trying to convey to you, well, that my feelings for her were more than simply affectionate, at that time at least."

The child in me surfaced then, the child who had loved my other father. "But what about Rob?"

"Rob," said Louis, taking in my distress. "Rob was in my thoughts. Of course he was. Always. But I still wanted a way out. You can't imagine what things were like in those days, the filth in the newspapers about men like us, the anxiety, worrying my parents would find out."

"No, no," I objected. "I'm -"

"Susanna helped put me on a different path. And then Ellie. She was a remarkable woman and I really thought it might work. It was only later that I realised there was a bit more to her than met the eye."

"How do you mean?"

"I mean there was a sense in which Peter Dashwood was right. I don't think she was a prostitute, but she was playing a game with me. What she said about sex, for example, how true was that? She said things had happened in Vienna - well you know what happened there, don't you?"

"The Russians?"

"Yes. She was dropping hints about being violated by them. Obviously it made me feel sorry for her, but that was the point, wasn't it? That's what she wanted me to feel. When I asked her to say more, she suddenly didn't want to talk about it. To this day I don't know the truth. She'd been through a heck of a lot, on her own in that country. She couldn't have survived without working out how to influence things in her favour, by fair means or foul."

"Did you learn that from her too?" I asked, laughing now, relieved that his memories of Ellie were not all idyllic. "How to manipulate people?"

Louis smiled. "No, not entirely. But you could say she got me started. She helped me lose my blasted innocence. I have to thank her for that."

CHAPTER 29

One day in October Louis received a telephone call from Martin Herz. It concerned Isaac Goldstein, the suspected rail saboteur. The Americans hadn't been able to pin anything on him so they let him go. He was a DP in Bad Gastein and Isaac Goldstein wasn't his real name. He was called Kurt Reich. Perhaps Louis would like to see him?

Louis was planning to stay at Ellie's place that night. He'd been away in Vienna for several days and he'd missed her. She lived in the top floor of a house in Jergitchstrasse.

A delicious smell filled her apartment. She'd cooked rabbit stew for him and he showed her a bottle of wine he'd got from the NAAFI stores. The electricity was down that evening so they ate by candlelight.

"Where'd you get the meat?" He indicated the stew.

"The garden. Do you like it?"

"Oh, yes. It's fine. Very nice…"

Louis was taken aback. The hutches in the garden were kept by the Austrian owner of the house who still had permission to visit the place to feed and look after the rabbits there, which he bred for the pot. Louis had seen Ellie stroking them, holding them in her arms, smiling, as

241

if she were holding a small child. And now they were eating one.

"Herr Steiner said it would be fine to have one."

"That's very good of him considering we kicked him out."

"Oh, we get on well," Ellie said. "He's found somewhere. These people, they all have relatives in the country."

Louis picked a small fragment of bone from his teeth and took a sip of wine.

"Afraid I've got to go away again for a few days."

"So soon? You've just got back."

"There's nothing I can do about it."

"Where this time?"

"Bad Gastein. The American sector."

Ellie stiffened at this news. She had been badgering him to take her into the American zone. She wanted to contact her daughter, Anna. She couldn't get a permit to go there alone.

"You can come with me if you like," he said.

"Oh Louis, you're a darling. You've no idea how much I've missed her. It's been so long. They don't let her answer my letters. Just to see her would be so wonderful."

"We'll find her," Louis said, his heart warming to the idea. "Bad Gastein first, then we'll go to Zell-am-See. You can be my interpreter."

They made love that night in the narrow bed. Afterwards she fell asleep but Louis lay next to her, disappointed and guilty that, once again, he seemed unable to give her pleasure. She made him feel she was only doing it for his sake.

The next day he told Norman Gray where he was going and drove off to pick up Ellie. The road to Bad Gastein took them away from the Wörthersee, past Villach and along a valley that became increasingly narrow, the mountains rising high around them. Ellie was in a good mood, the breeze blowing through her hair, singing English music hall songs. The road climbed up the side of the valley, taking them towards snow covered peaks.

At a high point they stopped to look at the view.

"So are you going to tell me about this man we're seeing?" Ellie asked.

"He's called Kurt Reich," Louis said. "It's a personal thing, actually. I know his mother."

"His mother? I thought this was about your work."

"I suppose I was embarrassed."

The story was working. All his stories skirting around his relationship with Rob seemed to work these days. He was getting used to it. Vita was a family friend, he said, who had asked him to find her son who had a Jewish father.

"The father went to America. His sister looked after the boy in Vienna. I don't know if he ever met Vita."

"They said I was one," Ellie said.

"What?"

"A mischling. A half Jew. But I put them right."

She said there'd been some kind of investigation of her ancestry after things broke down between her and her husband. His family were trying to pin something on her, drum her out of town, but they'd got nowhere. She'd left Zell-am-See on her own accord. She seemed proud of that.

He looked at her. Her hair was nearly black, her skin browner than most Austrians. Once again, he was struck by how familiar her appearance was, but this time he remembered Vita, not Rob.

"Mediterranean," she said, noticing his gaze. "My family's from France. My mother was dark."

So what was Ellie? French, English, Austrian? Whenever she revealed something about herself he felt he had more questions for her.

They drove on and soon approached Bad Gastein. The place had been a ski resort before the war and had a lot of spare accommodation. The DPs were housed in a collection of requisitioned hotels and other buildings dotted around the town. They went to the address Martin Herz had provided and the concierge directed them to a hospital on the outskirts. She said Reich would be there.

"Is he ill?" Louis asked.

He worked there, the woman said. He was a medical orderly.

They found him on a ward, sweeping the floor. He'd broadened out, Louis thought, lost some of his hungry appearance. And he had grown a beard.

As they approached a look of recognition came across the young man's face.

"You!" he said.

"Yes, it's me," Louis said, smiling and reaching out to shake his hand. Kurt Reich hung on to his broom.

"Don't worry. We're not here to arrest you. No trouble. Just to talk."

"Who's this?" Kurt was indicating Ellie.

"This is Mrs Bauer, my interpreter. We're here on other business. Thought we'd drop in on you. I've some news that will interest you."

"What news? Why do you come here?"

"Is there somewhere we can talk? Here it's…" Louis gestured at the patients all around them.

"I must ask my supervisor. Wait here."

While he was out, Louis looked around the ward. It was a light room with newly whitewashed walls and ten beds, each with chairs next to them, only half the beds occupied. The hospital had the air of a well-run place.

Kurt came back and said he could give them a few minutes. They went outside, into a garden and sat on a bench.

"So, what is this about?"

Louis was struck, once again, by the man's perfectly correct English. There was clearly no need for an interpreter, but Kurt didn't seem to mind Ellie's presence.

Louis studied his appearance. He didn't look like much Rob, being short and stocky, muscular. His dark hair curled and he had the beginnings of a beard. Louis realised he took after his father, Willi Reich. Like him, Kurt's cheeks were rosy and he even had the same thick hair on the back of his hands.

"This is a fine hospital," Louis said.

"It is very nice. And my work here is most useful of course. But can we proceed please? I am busy."

"It concerns your mother," Louis said.

"My mother? What do you know about her?"

"Vita. Vita Gill. She's your mother, isn't she?"

Kurt's face was impassive. He sat back on his bench in an exaggerated pose of relaxation before he replied.

"How do you know this? Who are you?"

Louis explained, for the second time that day: Vita was a family friend. She'd asked him to find Kurt. He was pleased they'd finally met. As he spoke, Louis sensed Ellie next to him, her eyes darting between him and the other man, listening intently.

"Well then," Kurt said. "You have found me. What now?"

Louis had not been looking forward to this moment.

"I'm sorry Kurt. I, I may call you that, may I?"

Kurt nodded.

"The request, I mean, Vita's request. Well, it was -"

Louis couldn't think how to start.

At this point Ellie intervened, leaning over to put her hand on Kurt's arm. "What Louis is trying to tell you is that your mother has died, Kurt."

"Dead?"

"Yes," Louis said, "I'm so sorry. To have such bad news. She died earlier in the year."

Kurt stood and walked away from the benches. He went over to a stone balcony and remained there for some time looking out into the distance, while Ellie and Louis waited.

When he came back, he was calm.

"How did she die?"

Louis told him about the fire. Then he added, "But there is also good news. Robert was not in the house. He's fine."

"Robert? Who is Robert?"

"Your brother."

"Ah, yes… Robert."

Louis saw that Kurt was troubled although he was holding his feelings back. He went on to say that Rob shared his mother's concern for Kurt's welfare. Rob would want to know how he was, what his plans were. And, Louis thought, he too would like to know the man's story.

He looked across at Ellie, then spoke.

"Look, we're staying here tonight, moving on tomorrow. I can see this is a lot to take in. And you have your -

"My work, yes, I must do my work."

The man was in a daze, confused by the unexpected resurgence of his past, as much as the news of Vita's death. He needed time.

"Can we meet this evening?" Louis asked. "When do you get off?"

Kurt agreed to meet them after work. He'd come to their hotel.

That evening, in the hotel, Kurt had put on a clean shirt and jacket. He was good-looking, Louis realised, like his parents. Like Rob.

As they sat around a restaurant table, Kurt told them about himself.

In 1938 he'd not wanted to go to America with his aunt, Esther, who'd brought him up in her family. He'd never felt he really belonged with her. Her own children had a greater share of their mother's attention than he could ever command. His father, Willi, had hardly visited him as a child and he had no contact with Vita. He didn't know his parents' story, but he heard of Willi and his escapades, as Esther used to speak about them, despairing at her brother's endless confrontations with other psychoanalysts, horrified at his sexual adventures. He thought of his father as a wild man, a crazy animal, a bully, and was glad he saw little of him.

He was aware of the political currents sweeping through Germany and Austria during that time. Most of his friends at school were other boys of mixed parentage, or they were non-Jews, Aryans. He didn't like mixing with Jews as they reminded him of his father.

Esther had asked him to come with her to New York, but he'd refused, opposing all her arguments. He'd persuaded himself he had a different destiny. As a mischling he would be safe from persecution. And anyway, once Esther had left who would know what he was? How could anyone even be sure Reich was his father?

"What do you mean?" Louis asked. "There must have been papers, certificates. The records will have shown -"

Ellie intervened again. "No, Kurt is right. These things could be hidden."

Kurt gave Ellie a curious look, then said, "Mrs Bauer is correct. It could be hidden."

He paused.

"And anyway, my mother was loose, what do you say in English, a loose woman?"

As he said this, his face flushed red. Yet he gripped his fists tight and said, slowly, "Many men could have been my father."

Louis looked again at Kurt, reflecting again on his physical similarity to Wilhelm Reich, but he said nothing.

After Esther had left, Kurt applied to join the Wehrmacht. Many of his friends were doing the same, even the mischlinge. Especially them, in fact. They had a variety of motives. People said Jews were cowards, so some intended to prove this wrong by becoming heroes.

Others believed they could hide in the army, perhaps help their Jewish relatives in civilian life.

But Kurt was different. He filled himself with Nazi ideals, persuading himself he would help make Germany strong again, restore his homeland to its rightful place. When Hitler had marched into Austria his heart had surged with delight at the prospect of re-unification. He decided he despised his Jewish family, his aunt Esther, running around like a frightened rabbit, making arrangements to leave, like a rat leaving a sinking ship. He'd be on the winning side for once.

When he signed up, he had to fill in a form recording his racial heritage. He proudly wrote 'Aryan.' In the medical inspection, he said his circumcision was due to a growth that needed excising. A doctor came along, inspected him, pronounced that the operation was consistent with the story. He thought he was safe.

He took part in the invasion of Poland. Later, he was sent to France. One victory after another. The army was his new family.

Then the decree came to kick mischlinge out of the army. Again, he thought he was safe but then one of his school mates ratted on him. The Gestapo looked into it and found the case against him to be proven. His new family expelled him, just as he'd been expelled by Vita, Willi and Esther, and he was alone again.

Louis noticed that Ellie was paying Kurt rapt attention. Her eyes were wide and glistening with tears.

"What did you do? Where did you go?" she said.

Kurt had served a three-month term in a military prison for falsifying his record and then, set loose, had gone from town to town seeking work. The story reminded Louis of Ellie, wandering around the country after her divorce, another outcast.

Kurt ended up in a hospital for injured airmen, sweeping floors. Then, in 1943, they'd drafted him into Organisation Todt and sent him to work in the stone quarries near Gusen. There, he'd got into a fight with a supervisor and was punished severely for it: he was sent to Theresienstadt, again working in the hospital there, such that it was. People went there to die, not to get well.

And during that time he'd thought hard about where he belonged. The hospital work made him realise that he was a man, not a confused boy, and that he had something to offer to the world. Looking after the patients in Theresienstadt, he learned how to give some of them hope, some of them comfort, some of them only companionship as they neared their ends. He stopped thinking of all the things he was angry about and started thinking of other people. He decided that one day he'd become a doctor. And he wanted to go to Palestine with the people he'd met in the DP camps. They were his family now. He was proud to call himself a Zionist. As he reached this point in his story, he fixed Louis with his gaze.

"I had nothing to do with your train. And that man of yours, the one who hit me. Is that how you British behave? You're meant to be better than the Nazis, are you not?"

"That man will be disciplined," Louis said.

Kurt snorted scornfully.

"I'm sure Louis believes you about the train," Ellie said. "Don't you, Louis?"

Louis nodded. There was no point pursuing Kurt about the train incident. No-one had been hurt.

It was getting late. Kurt thanked them for their concern and for pursuing Vita's dying wish. One day he'd travel to England to meet Rob. For now, they should assure him he was fine. He now had a purpose in life. He was happy.

Before he left, Louis wanted to wish him well. He found a memory of something he had once read. He thought it was a Jewish saying, or an Arab one, he didn't know which, but he said it anyway, hoping that a jocular tone would help it come across well.

"I wish you a long life, then, and many children."

Kurt had risen from his seat at this point, but now stiffened and spoke these bitter words: "I have made an oath, a most solemn one, that however long I may live I will never, ever produce a child. The world has enough children."

And with that, he turned and left.

CHAPTER 30

Louis had a visit from a researcher today. She said she was a Senior Research Officer with the Tavistock Institute, evaluating the palliative care programme he was receiving. Could Louis answer some questions? His replies would be anonymised and the results would help other people. He could opt out at any point.

I got him up and sat him in the living room for her visit. The researcher was very young for one so senior, her hair in braids tied in a bunch with coloured beads, balancing nervously on the edge of the sofa. She asked him to rate his pain on a scale of one to ten, the quality of the care he received, his quality of life.

I think it was the last one that did it. He looked puzzled, then amused.

"The quality of my life? Ah, now that is a big question. I'd need to think about that."

"Take your time," the researcher said.

Then a harder look came across his face and he said he wasn't sure, after all, that he could do this. He suggested she leave and he'd consider pursuing this another day, when he was stronger.

She looked disappointed, but managed to say that she

quite understood, gathered herself together, and left.

After she'd gone I commented, "That was rather harsh on her, Dad."

"Yes, I know. But I'm afraid I haven't got time for that sort of nonsense. I'd prefer to talk to you if I have to go through this dying business."

I protested, but he held up his hand to stop me.

"We might as well face facts."

I went to make him a drink. The revelations about Ellie had been intriguing, but I knew there must be more. I wasn't born until 1950, but the events he was describing must have been in 1946, the year after the war ended. So their affair must have lasted a long time. Did they return to England together? I wondered what Rob might have thought of that.

When I came back, bearing mugs of tea, he continued.

After their meeting with Kurt, he and Ellie drove to Zell-am-See to search for her daughter. It was a picturesque little town on a lake, all whitewashed walls and sharply sloping roofs. Once again they registered at one of the many hotels. The place was very luxurious, brocade curtains everywhere, hunting trophies on the walls, leather armchairs dotted about in the lounge. They were the only guests.

The first afternoon they went to Kaprun, a nearby village, to talk to an old friend of Ellie's who greeted her warmly. But she had news that shocked Ellie. Michael Bauer had married again. They were living in new housing on the outskirts of the town. He and his wife had produced another child. Ellie trembled when she heard this, sat on the step outside her friend's home, her head in her hands. Louis helped her into his car and they drove back to the hotel where Ellie instantly complained of having a splitting headache. She went upstairs to lie down.

When they went out the next morning to look for the

family they encountered a conspiracy of silence. No-one was at the address they'd been given and the neighbours claimed to know nothing of the family's whereabouts. After lunch at the hotel they walked to the Rathaus to make further inquiries and drew a blank. Ellie knew where her ex-husband's girlfriend had once lived, but there was nobody in. Again, the neighbours said they knew nothing. By this time it was late afternoon but bright sunshine still struck the houses around them, the light reflecting from the white walls and dazzling their eyes.

"I've come across this before," Louis said, squinting, as they stood in the road outside the house. "Nobody knows where anyone is as soon as a policeman asks questions. I should have changed out of uniform."

"I think it's me," Ellie said. "They know me in this town. They're all on her side."

"Her?"

"His mother. Everyone knows her. They all know what happened between me and Michael. She's been telling lies about me. The man in the hotel - he knew me as soon as we came in. He's spread the word. No-one'll help us."

"We'd better visit the dragon in her castle then," Louis said.

"I can't go there. I can't face her." Ellie looked terrified. Michael Bauer's mother was clearly a force to be reckoned with.

"We have to if we're to find your daughter," Louis said, trying to sound gentle, encouraging. He put his arm round her as they walked back towards the hotel.

"Not today though," Ellie said, stopping to face him. "Could it be tomorrow? Please, tomorrow? I can't do any more today. I'm exhausted. My head hurts."

"Why don't you lie down at the hotel," Louis said. "I can go for a stroll."

But Ellie hadn't finished. There was a pained expression on her face.

"Look, I'm not sure this was such a good idea," she

said. "Anna is nine years old now. She's probably forgotten me."

"No, no, of course she hasn't."

Ellie shook her head, her fists clenching and unclenching as she stood before him. "I can't help thinking she might be better off where she is, with her new family. Seeing me will only disturb her."

Louis objected to this, held her to him, stroked her hair, tried to soothe her. A woman with a shopping bag glanced over at them and tutted, so that Louis released Ellie. It had been a long day, he said, she was overwrought, would see things differently in the morning. Anna needed her, he was sure.

She pulled away from him, saying once again that she was exhausted and wanted an early night.

That evening Louis sat in the hotel lounge thinking about what Ellie had said. The man at the reception desk, who Ellie thought had spread the word about them around the town, busied himself with paper work. He was short, bald, obsequious. Louis wondered if she was right about him.

After a while he walked to the nearby lakeside, went along a path at the edge of the water and looked across at the lights of houses on the opposite shore.

Her attitude puzzled him. She'd been so concerned to reconnect with her daughter, but when it came to it she was morose about the prospect, even reluctant. This fear of confronting the husband's parents - what could it signify? Ellie was no shrinking violet. He'd once seen her slap a man's cheek when he got too close for comfort. And if her story was true, a weakling wouldn't have survived what she'd been through.

He stopped where the path ran out and lit a cigarette. It was now getting dark, but he could still see the white of the mountain peaks in the distance.

He thought about Ellie's daughter. What could she have made of her parents' divorce, losing her mother, the new family she was now in? His thoughts turned to all of the lost children he'd encountered, the street urchins in Naples, the German lad in Benevento who he'd saved from the firing squad. Then the Algerian boy they'd reunited with his parents. And Kurt Reich who was still, surely, some kind of abandoned child, searching for a family to whom he could belong. Not for the first time he wondered why people had children if they couldn't, or wouldn't, look after them.

As he looked over the lake he remembered again the feel of Susanna's little girl on his shoulder that time he visited her in the Piazza Olivella. He was surprised at the surge of feeling it produced in him.

And then he thought of Christopher, his brother, a child who would never be coming home to his parents. He still carried the stone in his pocket.

He threw his cigarette into the water and started back. It wouldn't do to dwell on these thoughts.

"I can tell you the exact day I lost my innocence," Louis said. "It was when we went to the Bauer's house the next morning."

He'd finished his tea and I took the cup from his hands.

"We found the grandmother there," he continued, a far-away look on his face as, once again, he cast his mind back over the years. "her name was Ilse Bauer, a hard-faced character. I don't blame Ellie for not wanting to see her. The hatred oozed out of the woman's eyes as soon as she saw Ellie on her doorstep."

"Why did she hate her so much?" I asked.

"I've no idea. I can't distinguish any more between what Ellie told me and the impressions I formed for myself."

"What did Ellie say?"

"That the woman was a Nazi. That she hated her for

being foreign. That she was jealous of her for taking up with her son. That, at least, might have been true. "

"Did you find Anna?"

"No, we didn't. We never found her, at least not on that trip. Ellie did get in touch eventually, but only much later, after our lives had changed."

"And your innocence?" I asked. "How did you lose that?"

Louis laughed at this. "Oh yes, my innocence."

On her doorstep, on which she stood glaring at them like a guard dog, bristling with suspicion and hostility, Ilse Bauer had claimed her son and his new family had gone away, she couldn't say where. Louis shoved past her into the house to check on her story. There was nobody else there.

Ellie entered in his wake and Ilse remained nearby, fuming, making sarcastic remarks. At one point, Ilse said they could take Anna's doll, which was on a shelf. Anna had no use for it now.

This really affected Ellie. She begged her to say where her daughter was. But Ilse looked as if she enjoyed seeing Ellie on her knees. Louis felt like hitting the woman.

Then the older woman went to get some papers, which she gave to Ellie, saying they belonged to her. Ellie looked at them, gave out a little cry and sank to the floor, the papers falling from her hand. Louis thought she had fainted, rushed over to pick her up and half carried her out of the place while Ilse Bauer stood watching the scene, a satisfied smile on her face. As they went down the path the woman came after them, the documents in her hand.

"Here, you forgot these," she said, thrusting them at Louis.

Back at the hotel, Ellie lying on a sofa in the lobby area, Louis read the papers. They were official documents, issued by the Nazi authorities in 1942. They recorded Ellie's agreement that she'd have no further contact with her two daughters, Anna and Maria, after her divorce, and that the father, Michael Bauer, would now look after them. She'd signed it.

So there was another child. Louis had no idea at first why Ellie had never mentioned her, but over the course of that morning, and in the car on the way back to Klagenfurt, he gradually got the story out of her. And what he learned changed his feelings towards her. Ellie never thought about Maria. She had expunged the child from her mind.

"She was a very difficult baby," she said, slamming the car door shut after throwing her bag on the back seat. "I couldn't look after her."

"Difficult? How difficult can it be to look after a child?" Louis had seen too many abandoned children and he couldn't get them out of his mind. He felt angry with the parents of these children and he was angry with Ellie now.

"She was looked after well," Ellie said. "A farmer's family. Michael pays them."

"And how old is she now, Maria?"

"She must be six years old."

"Must be? You mean you don't know? The age of your own child?"

At this, Ellie too lost her temper. "What gives you the right? The right to judge me? What do you know about me? What I went through? Leave me alone about my children. How can a man like you, any man, understand?"

Louis fell silent and started the car, driving through the town and onto the open road. He couldn't respond to what Ellie had said without saying that he wasn't like other men. Who knew what further revelations a statement like that would lead to? It was best to keep quiet. Hers was a murky story and his silence meant that more came out as they drove on. She'd been unhappy after the birth. She couldn't feed the baby. All of Michael's sisters had been treated the same way when they were babies, looked after by peasants in the country. It was what the townspeople did with their children. Maria would be living with Michael and his new wife now.

"And the document? It says you agree that you are not fit to be a mother to them. That you renounce your rights over them as a parent, that…"

"I was made to sign that." Ellie was shouting at him now, crying, so that he was worried about the car going off the road and slowed down. "They forced me. You've no idea what it was like. You, the conqueror, that's what you think you are, coming here and lording it over us."

Louis didn't reply, but drove on, clutching the steering wheel with tight hands. A conqueror? Him? Had she forgotten how he had rescued her from the Russians? He'd been her saviour. And then she'd become his lover, a beautiful woman he was proud to have on his arm, one who he had saved.

But now he saw her in another guise, as a mother, and he judged her and found her sorely wanting. She had unfairly preferred one child above another, giving Anna all her love so that none was left for Maria, whom she had abandoned to the uncertain care of others. At the back of his mind he knew his feelings were driven by something he didn't fully understand. He knew only that he felt enraged about discarded, unwanted children, and that he was angry with Ellie.

At any rate, he couldn't trust her any more. How could he when she'd hidden this from him all this time? Caught up in the feelings of the moment, he doubted her story about how she'd come to be separated from Michael Bauer. He began to wonder whether Peter Dashwood had been right about her. Perhaps she really had been a whore in Vienna.

It never crossed his mind that he had kept his own secret from her.

When they got back to Klagenfurt he dropped her off at her place. Louis was miserable and he could see Ellie felt the same. They both knew it was the end of their affair.

CHAPTER 31

When he went to work the next day, Louis found Ken Gillett in his office, sitting in his chair, examining a file.

"Morning, Nicholson," he said as Louis entered.

"Good morning, sir," he said, trying to recover from the surprise. He hadn't seen the man since Italy.

"I'm back," Gillett announced, his hand giving a theatrical flourish to indicate a chair in which Louis should sit.

"Yes, sir. Welcome back."

"How have things been?"

Louis gave a brief report.

"And how are things with you?"

"Very good, sir."

"I've been talking to Colonel Fortnum. You've done a good job while I've been away. Congratulations."

"Thank you, sir."

"I'll be taking over now."

Louis knew not to show any disappointment.

"I expect you'll be disappointed," Fortnum said.

"Oh no, not at all, sir. The Section has missed you," Louis replied. "How's your hand?"

Gillett leaned back in his chair, his right hand held up. He flexed his fingers.

"Much better, thank God. Mind you, the docs nearly chopped it off."

When Gillett had left, his hand, injured by the accidental firing of a gun, had been extraordinarily swollen. An infection had raged through it and he had a fever.

"Penicillin," Gillett said.

This gave Louis jolt.

"Ever heard of it? It's the new thing. Works like magic."

"Yes, I believe I have heard of it."

"Works a treat. Mind you, it involves a lot of jabs." Gillett guffawed at this. "Hell of a lot. Had a bloody sore arm."

Louis remembered.

"How long did it take?" he asked. "In the hospital, I mean."

"A couple of weeks and I was right as rain."

Louis wondered what Gillett had been doing all these months if his hand had recovered so quickly, but didn't ask.

"I think that's enough about me," Gillett said. "I've some news for you."

"News, sir?"

"Yes. Good news. You're to be promoted. Congratulations once again, Captain Nicholson."

Gillett held out his hand to shake. There was more.

"But we can't have two of us running the show, can we? So you'll need to move on."

After the first rush of pleasure at his promotion, this hit Louis hard. He'd got used to the Section. His style differed greatly from Gillett's. The men liked this. Louis liked it. They all worked better that way. Once again, it was best not to reveal his feelings to Gillett.

"May I know where I'm going?" he asked.

"The colonel will brief you. He's expecting you. Pop

round there would you?"

Louis got up to go.

"Oh, and I'll need this office now. If there's anything you want…"

"I'll come back this afternoon," Louis said. "Clear the place of my personal - "

"Jolly good. You can brief me on outstanding matters. Let me know what Fortnum has to say. I am interested in, you know, your welfare and all that." He gave a brief smile.

Expelled from the office that had become his home over the past few months, Louis went out into the corridor. He felt lost. The army was unsentimental about attachment. You did what you were told and hoped for the best. Gillett was a career soldier, not a conscript like Louis, so must be ambitious. But whatever he'd been up to since he left the Section in Italy, it hadn't brought him any advancement. This must have disappointed him; perhaps he was also envious of Louis going up in the world.

Colonel Fortnum was with another man in civilian clothes. He was introduced as Major Bellingham and informed Louis he'd flown out from London the previous day. They both congratulated him on his promotion.

"I've been studying your file," Fortnum said. "I see you're married."

Louis nodded.

"You haven't taken much leave, have you?"

Louis agreed he hadn't. He could have flown home on a couple of occasions, but had either not taken the leave or driven into Italy with Ellie for a few days.

"Your wife not want to join you out here?"

There were married quarters available for officers with wives.

"No sir, I don't believe she does."

"Why not?" Bellingham asked, leaning forwards.

"Well sir, she has her work…"

Fortnum started to speak, but Bellingham wasn't finished.

"And your brother?"

"My brother? How do you -"

"Died in Spain I understand."

Louis nodded.

"A member of the Communist Party, wasn't he?"

Louis hesitated at this, but then answered, "Yes, he was."

"And you?" the Major continued, "You were never -"

"No sir. I was not."

"Why do you think he joined, went to Spain?" Bellingham asked.

"Well, sir, I've asked myself that many times. I think it was some kind of rebellion. That was part of it. And he liked an adventure."

As he spoke, Louis was thinking that Christopher had another, more personal motive: his desire to be admired.

"What was he rebelling against, would you say?" Bellingham asked.

"I hope it won't sound trite, sir, but I believe he was rebelling against our parents."

"Hmm. I imagine they weren't too thrilled about that," the major said.

"No sir, they were not." Then he commented: "You know a lot about me."

Bellingham smiled. "We do our best. Look, I might as well put our cards on the table. I understand you've done a good job with 93 FSS."

"Thank you, sir."

"A bloody good job actually, clearing up over here. But things are moving on now. The Russians…"

"Ah yes, the Russians," Louis said. He sensed where this was leading.

Bellingham explained to Louis that the world was changing. The British government needed men like him in a new role, something very hush-hush but important. It would involve a return to England. He'd be learning Russian, undergoing special training. Would this be of interest to him? He couldn't tell him much more at this stage, but the work was stimulating and he'd be well suited to it.

"I'll need time to think about it, sir," Louis replied.

Bellingham nodded, said he understood. He could have a couple of days, but he'd be going back at the end of the week. If Louis agreed, they could return on the same flight, so he'd learn more then.

It didn't take Louis long to decide. The alternative was hanging around in Klagenfurt without a role, with three months to go until he was demobbed. Then it was back to England anyway, to an uncertain future. He'd no idea what he'd do with himself in civilian life. The offer sounded intriguing. He'd travel back with Bellingham, take it as far as it went. Back to England. Back to Rob.

CHAPTER 32

Inevitably, there was a distance between them. He had been away for so long - almost three years - and there was still the spectre of Frank Lemaire. And, for Louis, there were the memories of Susanna and Ellie. He needed to do something about Ellie, draw a line under things. It would hurt her, but there was no other way. A month after he got back he wrote, telling her he had a wife in London, saying he was sorry he'd not told her before, and that they were reconciled now. He said he'd do what he could to help her and he hoped she might understand. There was no reply.

And Rob and he were not reconciled. He continued to live in the house as a lodger but he and Louis had very different lives. His father clearly thought that nothing was amiss, happily accepting the presence of both men. The old man pottered about the house in slippers. He'd given up his medical practice now, spent half his time in an armchair in the living room, smoking a pipe, dozing next to the radio. Maybe he expected all male friendships to be pretty uncommunicative.

Rob had taken over the basement for his work. Louis didn't go there, using the front door to avoid entering the house through the workshop. He didn't ask Rob what he did there, but he heard the noises he made, the knocking of a hammer on a chisel, the rasping sound of a file being run across wood or stone.

They sent him to SOAS again, where people came over from the Slavonic studies unit in Senate House to teach Russian. He took to it better than German, enjoyed the shapes the language required of his tongue, teeth and lips, its musical cadences. His instructors complimented him on his accent. He'd do well.

And he started work in a building near St James's Park, beginning the career that was to absorb his energies for the rest of his life. They told him he'd need a cover story, so he had business cards printed. The world knew that he was a stockbroker.

Things at home were awkward. His father continued to believe he and Rob were good pals and gave every sign that he welcomed their presence. But conversation was strained when they were all together. The atmosphere around the dinner table was especially difficult.

He noticed that Rob had become much more serious. He now wore a jacket when he wasn't in his workshop, replacing the coloured jumpers and cravats he'd used to display his younger self, and he'd cut his hair short, giving him a more masculine appearance. But his face still showed the same lovely softness that Louis had always found attractive and which, even now, produced pangs of longing in Louis, which he immediately tried to suppress. When they talked about Vita's death Louis offered sympathy, which was accepted in a restrained, quiet way. He knew there were further depths to Rob's feelings, but he kept them locked up. They never mentioned Frank Lemaire.

The result was that he found reasons to stay working late, eating out or sometimes going for long walks through the city before returning home. But he couldn't do that every night. When he was home for an evening meal, it was often a relief to finish and retire to his room.

Late one evening, three months after his return, he lay on his bed reading. He heard a knock on his door. It was Rob.

"Can I come in?" he asked.

Louis sat up. Rob shut the door quietly behind him and sat opposite him. He must have been in his workshop all day. Stone dust made his hair look grey and he noticed Rob's hands were rough, the nails chipped and broken.

"I think we need to have a talk," Rob said.

Louis nodded and waited for him to say more.

"I don't think I can stand this much longer." Rob pressed his hands together.

"I've been thinking of taking a flat," Louis said.

A pained look crossed the other man's face, but then he gathered herself together and spoke in a soft voice.

"Yes, that might solve things."

"But it wouldn't, would it? My father. He'd wonder why. He'd be…he'd be disappointed."

"We'll just have to face that."

Rob sounded certain, but looked miserable.

Rob's response surprised Louis who then regretted having spoken about the idea of his leaving the house. After all, it was his home and his father's, not Rob's. Why should he leave and Rob stay? Surely Rob had some money from Vita? Rob was the one who ought to leave, set up shop somewhere else.

He almost started saying it, but then stopped himself. Rob was good for the old man. His father liked having him in the house during the day, chipping away at his stones, coming up the stairs to sit with him over cups of tea when he needed a break, making his lunch. They'd become fond of each other. If he left, Louis would be out at work all day, sometimes away for long periods. His father would sink back into lonely, introverted depression.

They'd been silent for a minute or two. Then Louis looked up and asked, "What are you actually doing down there in the basement?"

"You've never been there, have you?"

Louis shrugged in apology.

"Come now," Rob said. "Come on."

It reminded him of how Rob used to be, how he would pull him away to see the things which excited him, the spark of his happiness and enthusiasm lighting up Louis' own feelings. But this time, following Rob down the stairs, he felt apprehensive.

"We're going to take a look," he said to his father as they passed the living room where the old man sat reading a paper and smoking his pipe.

Rob opened the door to the basement and they descended the stone steps. Bare electric lights lit the room, which was large, taking up the whole of the ground floor. Objects of all sorts filled the place, stone blocks, half-finished sculptures, tools, shelves crowded with bottles along one wall, a huge mirror. Louis picked up a rolling pin.

"What's this doing here?"

Rob laughed. "You wrap emery paper round it. It smooths off the surfaces."

A figure emerging from a stone block reminded him of sculptures he'd seen in Florence during the war, Michelangelo's figures of slaves whose twisted bodies seemed to be wrenching themselves free of the constraining grip of the marble from which they were carved.

"Nothing's finished?" he asked.

"That's because they've been taken away. I've got an exhibition. My first."

Rob smiled with pride. Louis realised he'd not shown enough interest in Rob's work to ask how things were going.

"You can come to the opening. It's next week. Henry will be there and you can meet him. They'll all be there."

Moore had turned to drawing during the war. Louis

had seen an advertisement for an exhibition of his work at the Tate. The poster showed rows of huddled people sheltering from the Blitz in tube stations. He'd meant to go there when he got the time.

Rob was still talking, telling him about the other artists he'd been meeting. Hampstead was filled with them: Gabo, Hepworth, Nash. He knew them all.

As Rob talked, Louis moved to a table and leafed through a sketch pad. The charcoal drawings were plans for the shapes Rob planned to create in stone. They differed from those Louis remembered seeing at Vita's house. There, the bronze statues had been angular, sharp-edged. Now, smoother lines flowed across the pages. He stopped at an image showing a broad-bodied creature sitting on the ground, its head bending to examine its lap, in which lay an oval stone, a deep indentation in its centre, like an eye. The face of the creature was a blank and there was movement in its body, drawing his gaze around its shape.

Rob stood close, reaching over and brushing Louis' arm to point at the drawing. "That one's in the exhibition."

Louis moved his hand away from Rob's touch.

"I'd like to see it. No more bronze?"

"One day. It's still hard to get the materials."

As they leafed through the book Rob continued to stand next to him, talking about drawing being the basis of his art, praising his teacher at Hornsey, Anthony Coxon, who had instilled discipline into his sketching. He kept turning pages to show him new drawings and Louis began to find Rob's warm presence next to him disturbing. He moved away, trying to find something else to look at and admire.

Sensing this, Rob drew aside a curtain and lifted an object from the shelf behind, placing it on a surface near Louis. It was the beaked figure from Vita's studio, with the head like a gun.

"I saved this from the ruins," Rob said. "You can have

it if you like."

Louis paused, running his fingers over the jagged ridges of the sculpture. "What happened that night, Rob?"

Rob put the bronze figure back on the shelf and drew the curtain.

"I'll tell you," he said. "Have you seen enough? Let's go upstairs."

Louis' father had gone to bed, and they sat in the living room as Rob told him about the events leading up to the fire.

He'd spent the evening with Vita. Frank Lemaire was there too. They'd all been drinking. At about nine, he had offered to make them all something to eat and had gone off to cook some eggs in the kitchen.

"What was Frank doing there?" Louis said, unable to suppress his irritation.

"He'd been released from Wandsworth. I was seeing him again."

Rob spoke flatly, not meeting his eyes.

"He said he needed to get back to his place in Willesden. He asked me to go with him."

At this point Rob started crying, his hands over his eyes. Louis felt the urge to go over to him, but didn't move.

"If only," Rob sobbed, "If only I hadn't gone."

"But you did, didn't you?"

Rob took his hands from his face and looked at him, wounded, tears smearing the white stone dust on his cheeks. Louis felt a pang of regret that he had been so harsh.

"What happened exactly?" Louis asked. "How did the fire start?"

"Don't you see?" Rob said, his voice now desperate. "Can't you see?"

"No, I can't. See what?"

"It was the gas. When I went to cook the eggs. I must have left the gas on."

At this, he sobbed again, his body curling up so he lay on the sofa, his legs bent and his shoulders shaking. Louis sat for a while, watching him, trying to piece things together. Then he knelt on the floor next to Rob and, cautiously, placed a hand on his back. His other hand rested on Rob's hair, feeling the stone dust between the strands.

He stroked Rob's head. He told him he couldn't know for sure. The gas leak might have come from anywhere. And anyway, how could they be sure it was gas? He found himself saying many other comforting things until the sobbing stopped.

Eventually, when he was still, Rob turned around to look at him. Louis felt something warm and familiar unfurling inside him Then it was too much for him, so he drew his hands away, got up and returned to his chair.

"And Lemaire?" he said.

"Frankie?"

"I don't like that name for him," Louis snapped.

Rob sighed. "I think it's time I told you about him."

Louis rolled his eyes up at this, but he listened nevertheless.

"I met Frank on my first day at Monkton Hill. He was older, from another school where he hadn't got on."

Louis snorted.

"He had so many friends, other boys. Girls admired him too. I was really impressed. He seemed daring, always up for -"

"How old were you?" Louis asked.

"Thirteen. He was sixteen. It was exciting, knowing him. He paid me a lot of attention. It was nice."

Louis wasn't sure he could listen to any more.

"No, stay. I must tell you. Please. He, he invited me one day. Invited me to go for a walk. It made me happy. I suppose I was flattered. An older boy."

Rob looked down at his hands, his pitted fingernails.

"He got me away from the school buildings and kissed

me. I liked it at first. But then he forced himself on me."

"What do you mean?"

There was a long silence as Rob continued to look at his hands. He picked at a fingernail, then looked up at Louis with sadness in his eyes.

"I didn't want him to do it. I told him I didn't, but he did it anyway. He took it much further than I wanted. It hurt. It hurt a hell of a lot."

Rob began to cry again.

"The bastard," Louis said quietly, the rage rising in him. "The bloody bastard."

Louis remembered Frank's grinning face, the time they'd fought in Vita's kitchen. He wanted him there, now. He'd smash his face in.

"Did you tell anyone?"

Rob screwed up his eyes and rubbed them with his fists in an angry movement. "There was no point telling the teachers. No point at all. Some of them got up to things themselves, with us, with the children I mean."

"I see," Louis said. The memory of children in Naples flashed across his mind, girls and boys who offered themselves to the soldiers, had sometimes offered themselves to him.

"I told some of it to Vita in the holidays," Rob said.

"What did she do?"

"Nothing. She did nothing."

At this, Rob's face dissolved again and he couldn't speak. Louis took a handkerchief out of his pocket and gave it to him. Rob blew his nose, his eyes red from crying.

"Vita said, she said…"

But he couldn't go on and Louis sat next to him to put his arm around Rob's shoulders as he sobbed. After a while he again tried to speak.

"Vita said it was, it was…"

"What did she say?"

"That it was time I got started, that Frank had done me a favour."

Rob spoke these words in a tiny voice, as if forcing himself to remember. Again the story was too much and his head lowered as he shook with tears.

"She told me… She said it was bound to hurt if we did it like that. Advised me to go for something a bit less, well…"

Another image, a memory of Vita flashed across Louis' mind, her flowing clothes, rich brown hair, her stature. He imagined her next to Rob, telling her child these things. It disgusted and horrified him.

"I didn't know what to think. I hadn't enjoyed doing it with Frank. It was horrible. But Vita was my mother, she made me wonder…"

"What?"

"If I'd been wrong to feel that way. You see that, don't you? She'd always had this view that sex was a healthy thing and that it was good for me."

"Surely you didn't believe her?"

"I didn't know what to believe Louis. I couldn't, I just couldn't…"

Rob was crying again. Louis gave him time, and he told him more.

After speaking with Vita, his feelings about what Frank had done to him began to change. His sense of being violated diminished. When he returned to school, Frank wanted more, but this time Rob had the confidence to tell him not to go so far. Nevertheless, Frank was very rough with him.

The relationship became known about in their small circle and it gave him a way into a group of older boys, though if one tried to touch him, Frank bullied them away. This gave Rob the feeling that he had powers over these boys, although he knew it was only because he was Frank's property.

"He dominated me," Rob said. "I was so young. I understood so little, and Vita…"

"She should have protected you."

Rob didn't reply.

"And you see that's why I behaved that way when I was with you," he said. "Can't you see?"

Louis didn't know what he was talking about.

"I've thought it through since Vita died. I've done so much thinking."

"I'm glad to hear it."

"Highbury, all those people. The men. I -"

"I don't want to hear much more of this," Louis said. He couldn't bear it, wanted to block up his ears. The pain he'd been through, all these years, because of this man and his dreadful mother. And the pain Rob had been through, now that it was coming out. It was too much for him and he couldn't, he wouldn't make sense of it.

But in spite of this barrier made by Louis after their first talk, their reconciliation had begun. Over the next few days Rob said more about what had happened and Louis discovered that he was able to listen to the stories that were coming out, enough to know that his love for Rob was returning, and to realise that it was even stronger and deeper than before.

Frank Lemaire had continued to make demands on Rob, ones he'd found impossible to resist. He'd hated himself for it. But then he would remember what Vita had said. Something must be wrong with him if he didn't like it. So he persuaded himself that it was all right, that this was how things were when you had to grow up. He stopped being able to distinguish between what he wanted and what others wanted him to do.

Louis tried to tell Rob that Vita had been a terrible influence on him, but Rob defended his mother. He pointed out that Louis' own parents would have thrown a fit if he'd told them a similar story about a relationship with another boy. Vita's attitudes were progressive, whatever harm they'd done.

Louis didn't buy that. Right now, he could only think of it as abuse, with Vita as a willing accomplice.

Rob told Louis he was a far better man than Frank or any of the other men he had known in his days as an art student. He'd always known Louis loved him and that he ought to love him back. In fact he had loved him, always, but couldn't admit it while this addiction raged inside him. It was an uncontrollable thing. It was only after Vita died that Rob found the strength to finally break off all contact with Frank. He had no idea where Frank was. He never wanted to see him again.

During this time, which Louis thought of as their second great encounter before the start of their lifelong devotion to one another, Louis went to the opening of Rob's exhibition at the Warren Gallery. He introduced Louis to Henry Moore. Anthony Coxon, Rob's old drawing teacher, greeted Louis warmly. People milled about, issuing admiring comments. Rob was the centre of attention.

Excluding himself from the gaggle that surrounded Rob, Louis looked around, impressed to see how the sketches in the workshop had been translated into stone and wood. They were semi-abstract pieces, their curving, flowing shapes suggesting organic origins, mysterious depths.

Louis then came to a sculpture in the centre of a room. It was a huge piece in white marble, easily the height of a man. He wondered how it had been transported from the studio, it was so large. It was the realisation of the sketch he'd paused over for so long when he first visited the basement, the creature seated on the ground, looming over the indented oval stone in its lap, like a predatory bird. The smooth marble shimmered in the artificial light of the gallery.

He looked back at the crowd around Rob and managed to glimpse his face, animated as he responded to the circle around him, flushed with excitement, his eyes glistening. And at this moment Louis finally accepted that he would love this wonderful man for the rest of his life.

CHAPTER 33

This morning I had a call from Brenda, the MacMillan nurse. She was in tears.

"Louis is dead," she said.

My father is dead. I repeated the phrase to myself, my lips moving, but with no sound.

Then I realised Brenda was still on the phone, saying things I couldn't hear.

"I'll be over straight away."

She said she'd wait, so I put the phone down.

Then the shock hit me. Without a word Karen came and put her arms around me. After a while she said we could go to Louis' house together. She would drive.

Brenda opened the door. She'd been watching for our arrival. Her eyes were still red.

"I found him this morning, in his bed. He must have died during the night."

We went upstairs and I entered the room while the others hung behind. Brenda had arranged the covers so that only his head was visible, resting on the pillow, his face peaceful, eyes closed. I bent down, kissed his forehead, and finally felt something break in me. I began to cry.

How could he go like this? There'd been no chance to say goodbye, to tell him... but what did I want to tell him? I realised I didn't know.

Karen came into the room and over to my side. Together, we smoothed his hair and straightened the already-straight counterpane. I said I'd like to be alone with him for a while, if that was okay.

I sat with him all of that morning. His stillness changed gradually, so by the time I was ready to leave he was no longer my father but was, instead, my father's body. The small, cold body he'd left behind. I covered his face and went down the stairs.

Brenda knew what to do. Phone calls were made and the doctor came to certify the death. He said he'd seen Louis the week before, that it was probably his heart. Apparently chemotherapy can weaken the heart.

Brenda wanted to console me, telling me he hadn't got so long to live anyway. I said I'd have liked more of him and she said she could understand that. I think she'd have liked more of him too.

Then it was about arranging the funeral, a cremation at the place in Golders Green. Everything was very efficient and unreal. People had to be invited, a reception arranged, endless small decisions made. It was eerily similar to organising a celebration, a birthday party or a wedding. In fact, the man who took the service insisted on calling it a 'celebration of Louis Nicholson's life'. I found it hard to see it that way. Right now, I could only feel a deadening sense of loss. There was nothing to celebrate.

He could have been buried in Highgate Cemetery. He used to joke about it when we went there, as people do, to see the graves of the famous. "Not too close to him," he'd say, as we stood opposite Karl Marx, or "I wouldn't mind being near her," as we looked at the grave of George Eliot. But we opted for Golders Green where he'd put Rob, next to Vita. Recently I discovered Freud's ashes are there too. You can have a plaque in the memorial garden there, but we decided on a bench in Kenwood. They have them all over the Heath, inscriptions to the deceased 'who loved this spot.' It would have Louis and Rob's name on it, together.

The funeral was nothing like Rob's. On that occasion, the great and the good of the art world had flocked to the event. There were even press there, waiting outside to photograph the guests and at the reception in Burgh House people had to stand in the street, too many of them to fit indoors.

After Louis' funeral there was a reception in a place we hired, just off Platt's Lane. Brenda was there, Karen of course, some distant cousins from Scotland who I'd never met. They said they were from his mothers' side of the family. I've no idea how they heard of his death.

As I made my rounds, accepting condolences, I saw an antique gentleman in a wheelchair. He was almost prehistorically old, a tiny homunculus wrapped in layers of tartan blankets, wheeled in by a cheerful young man who announced he was his carer.

I stopped to say hello and the old man slowly withdrew an arm from under a blanket and reached out to shake my hand. Once we touched, I felt his other hand enclose mine, which he held all the time he spoke to me, as if I might try to get away.

"Anthony Coxon," he stammered.

"Mr Coxon insisted on coming," said the carer, a happy smile on his face. Then, awestruck, "He's a hundred and one."

It was Rob's drawing teacher. I was about to congratulate him on his great age, but he shook his head and pulled me closer, so he was speaking directly into my ear.

"He was a brilliant student," he said in a whisper. "The best I ever had. I was proud, proud to…"

He trailed off, apparently exhausted by the effort and I smiled warmly at him, thanking him for coming, thanking him, in a way, for his great gift to our family.

The carer took this as a signal and indicated it was time to get Mr Coxon back to his nursing home. It wouldn't do for him to be out too long.

I wandered over to a table where we'd put the flowers and cards. There was one from Rob's brother, Kurt Reich, sent from Israel. He'd gone there after the war and become a doctor, working in a hospital in Tel-Aviv. He and Rob had seen each other occasionally, and I'd met him once when he came to our house.

Another was from Martin Herz who apologised for being unable to travel. 'To my old comrade in arms,' he'd scrawled on his card, 'my best wishes for your continuing journey.'

The next encounter was with a more sprightly looking fellow. He looked to be about the same age as Louis had been, before the cancer had started taking its toll. His hair was still dark though that could have been the effect of cosmetics. He had a classic Roman nose, giving him a rather superior look.

"Tony Bellingham," he said at my shoulder as I examined the cards, and I found myself shaking another hand.

"I'm very sorry for your loss," he added. And then, by way of explanation, "I worked with your father. Sad to see him go, but extremely pleased to be here."

It was the man who had recruited Louis in 1946. I wondered if he might talk about their secret lives.

"Louis told me about you," I said.

"Good things I hope?"

"Well, I don't know. Not a lot. But he described your first meeting - Klagenfurt?"

Bellingham's eyebrow moved upwards. "He told you that?"

"I'd appreciate the chance of a proper talk," I said,

"one of these days. I know he wasn't -"

"Wasn't supposed to, no. Quite right."

"Could we meet?" I asked.

"I'm not so sure," Bellingham said. "Sorry."

This was particularly childish of him. Both of them had retired from the service years ago. Books had been written about what they were up to during the Cold War. What harm could be done by a little personal reminiscence?

Bellingham must have sensed how I felt.

"He was bloody good, you know, did important work."

"That's nice to hear."

"Ellesmere Port," Bellingham said.

"What about it?"

One of his eyebrows raised in surprise. "Ah, so he really didn't tell you so much, did he?"

I waited, hoping for more. I sensed that he was dying to let it all out.

"Your father. Very good at creating legends."

"Legends?"

"Very useful. If someone needed one, supplied it just like that, fully formed, utterly convincing. Saved people's bacon a few times. Damn good at it. Should have been a writer."

He gave a little laugh, then added: "We weren't all rabid right wingers you know. Not like they make out in the books. A good range of political views in the service. Broadminded."

I remembered. Louis and Rob were internationalists, liberals, supported closer links with Europe. Rob even went on Ban the Bomb marches.

"What did you know about Rob?" I asked.

Bellingham shrugged. "Everything."

I must have shown my surprise.

"We knew everything. Not a problem."

"What about those other Cambridge men, the spies - you know."

"Oh, Burgess, Blunt, all those people. The ones in the books. A different story. Your father: not the same thing at all. We did a calculation, decided he was safe. By that time he was pretty useful to us, so we did a deal."

"A deal?"

"Well, you know what things were like in those days with men of that sort. We made sure they were protected, the pair of them, him and Gill. Protected you too, when you came along. Couldn't have one of our best men getting upset by the authorities."

"Me? What do you mean, protected me?"

Bellingham gave me another long look and his hand went to his moustache, his fingers twiddling its tip.

"Perhaps we do need to have a chat," he said.

Bellingham stayed until everyone left. I told Karen I'd walk home. We found a seat in the garden while the caterers cleared up inside. It was like a John Le Carré novel, the spymaster meeting his source for a secret exchange. Except the source was now Bellingham, the spymaster.

In the 1950s there was a police crackdown on gay men. Every now and again I'd sensed fear in the house. Rob would take me aside and have a talk. I told my school friends what he told me: my mother had left Louis; a housekeeper looked after me when he was out; Rob was my uncle who lodged with us. It was drummed into me. And we did have a housekeeper for a while, a woman no doubt chosen for her discretion, although I wasn't fond of her.

Indoors, someone dropped a plate and cursed. A woman saw us in the garden and shut the glass door into the house. Bellingham was talking again.

"The child welfare people," he said. "Took you away."

I gasped. The half remembered visit to the hospital with Rob, the smiling faces of Mr and Mrs Baker. The hot chocolate. My longing to go home.

"Rings a bell, does it?"

Bellingham was peering at me.

"The Bakers," I said in a small voice.

"You really do remember. Remarkable."

"Who were they?"

"You were four years old. They looked after you. Nice couple."

"Looked after me?" I could feel something horrible rising inside my stomach, a thing that had been there for too long, lurking.

"Calm down, old boy." Bellingham stood up and stepped away from the bench, then turned around and spoke.

It was 1954. Louis had come into the office in a terrible state and went straight up to Bellingham's floor, saying I'd been taken away from them. Something had to be done about it. Rob was going crazy with anxiety and grief. He was going mad too, couldn't think about anything else, didn't give a bugger about work anymore. It could go to hell unless they could do something. Bellingham said he'd never seen Louis in such a state. Told him to slow down, start from the beginning.

I'd had a fever. Rob was in charge while Louis was away somewhere. Everyone worried about children with fevers in those days: it could be meningitis, even polio. He took me to the doctor, and I ended up in the hospital for a night. I was crying a lot and Rob said he'd stay. Louis came back, so the two of them were with me then, next to the bed, each of them holding one of my hands and trying to cheer me up.

This sparked off a lot of sniggering amongst the nurses, who weren't used to a pair of men behaving like this. An almoner came by, nosing around with that fake sympathy social workers exude, asking where my mother was. She must have sensed something. They had their guard down, you see. I was pretty ill, and they were worried. I don't know what sparked it all off. Perhaps they let their hands touch, or gave each other a hug. Perhaps it was just a look, or the way they seemed together. Whatever it was, it aroused the almoner's suspicions and the whole thing went on from there. A doctor said I should stay another night.

Then the alarm about my illness was over and I was ready to go home. Rob went to pick me up. The next thing Louis knew, this almoner woman and a policeman were at the door. Rob was with them, in tears, saying they'd taken me away. I was being looked after by some good people, the woman said. Louis thought the policeman looked awkward about it, to do him credit, but the almoner: she was a piece of work. A Catholic. On the doorstep bristling and superior, condemning them.

It went on for weeks while Louis tried to keep his cool and carry on with work. He was eventually allowed access, but not Rob. Louis had to see me under supervision, in case he did something with me. Aylesbury was where the Bakers lived and one of them always had to be present. Apparently I cried desperately when I had to say goodbye, begging to come home. They had to peel me off him. It must have reminded him of those times he was sent away to school, beseeching his mother to let him stay at home with Christopher.

After one of those visits he decided he couldn't take any more. His career, everything, what did it matter? He'd fight this, take me away from the Bakers by force if need be and damn the consequences. Go abroad with me and Rob. Find somewhere.

It was Rob, poor old Rob, usually the wild one who followed his feelings, who pulled him back from this. He had the idea: speak to your employers. They'll pull strings for you.

"So is that what you did? Pull strings?"

Bellingham was fingering his moustache again. The

caterers had finished their clear-up in the house and stood around inside, waiting for us to go.

"It was awkward," Bellingham said. "The Home Secretary. Couldn't let it reach him. Clashed with his moral crusade against…"

"Against men of that sort," I said, irritated.

"Yes, quite. But we needed Louis. Bloody awkward."

"And you did it. You got me home."

Bellingham nodded, then beckoned me across the lawn and through the house. It was time to leave.

In the street outside, before we parted, he said more.

"We put a stop to it. Sent a woman. A cover story."

I remembered her. She stayed with us for a couple of years, playing jazz records in the attic and smoking a lot. Rob and Louis said she was a housekeeper, but I don't remember her doing anything around the house. It sounds silly, I know, but sometimes I wondered if she was my mother, paying us a secret visit. Then, they didn't need her anymore, and she went. Now I don't even remember her name.

Bellingham was speaking again. "One day someone'll write a book about homosexuals in the service, but it won't be me."

"I've always wondered how much Louis hid from me," I said, hoping for more. People in the service kept secrets even from their nearest and dearest. Told them tales, invented legends.

"Well, he was bloody good at making up stories. Men like that often were. Sign of the times I suppose. Why we liked to use them. Pity things have changed from that point of view. No need to lie anymore."

Bellingham gave a little laugh at his own joke. I reflected that the deal, as Bellingham called it, cut both ways: the service could remove their protection, throw Louis to the wolves if he ever threatened to step out of line. They were using him.

"But the main thing: he was a linguist and a patriot."

Bellingham was speaking again. "All we needed. If you knew what he did for us, you'd be proud of him."

He clearly wasn't going to tell me more. Important parts of my father's life would always be hidden from me and I couldn't help resenting that. I looked into Bellingham's face. His moustache was flecked with spit. It was a military moustache, cleanly clipped. He'd probably had it when he first met Louis, and had it ever since, part of his implausibly youthful appearance. But the spit was the give-away. Time and age were taking over.

"I'm already proud of him." I smiled and moved away.

A few days later I was walking across the Heath to Kenwood House. I needed to talk to the park administration about the memorial bench. I chose the route I always do, past Rob's monumental sculpture.

It sits on a plinth in a wooded area, a replacement for one of Moore's that was stolen in the 1980s. The thieves must have driven onto the Heath with a lorry in the night. It was never recovered and is thought to have been melted down for scrap. Moore said he was too old to make another one; it was time someone else had a go.

I must hope no-one melts down Rob's sculpture. It's formed from two huge bronze pieces, shaped like figures, their upper halves leaning into each other, touching at various points. The delicacy of their touch contrasts with their vastness. It's called The Three of Them, which is a little mysterious until you get close. When I pass by, I always reach my hand through the railings and stroke the small oval shape lying between the figures. It has a deep indentation in its centre, like an eye looking out at me. Sometimes I wink back at it.

The people in Kenwood were helpful about the bench and I felt cheerful for the first time in days. The sun was mostly out and there was a warm breeze, so I went downhill along the eastern edge of the Heath, past the fountain at the bottom, past the women's bathing pond. I chuckled as I looked at the notice: "Women only. Men not allowed beyond this point."

Further down, the boating pond is fenced off and there are huge earthworks on the hill behind, to do with building a new flood defence system. Corrugated metal barriers have been sunk deep into the pond floor, so the lower half can be drained. As the water level has sunk, various objects have emerged, old bicycles, a child's scooter, that sort of thing. But the real trophy has been a complete, though rusty, Ford Cortina, dating from the 1970s. Local papers have carried photos of the strange sight. No-one can explain it.

A man was taking a picture of it through the fence, his wife next to him, a large woman on a mobility scooter, just like the one Louis had. They noticed my curiosity, and the woman told me how it had got there.

"It was this bloke," she said. "He was cheating on his girlfriend. Had this car, loved it, spent every bleeding weekend polishing and kissing it, never thought a moment about her."

"Because of the car, you mean? How he felt?"

Her husband interrupted. "No, Lisa's not explaining it very well, she means -"

"Oy, shut up you. It's my story."

She hit him playfully on the hand.

"What I mean is," she continued, "he loved his bloody car and he loved another bloody woman too, that's what I mean."

"Clear," I said. "How'd it end up here then?"

"Well, she found out didn't she? He used to say he was out at night fishing, you know, you must have seen 'em."

I had, men in green tents, camped next to the ponds, staring grimly into the watery distance, waiting for a bite. I didn't realise it went on all night.

"Bloody morons if you ask me, but anyway, that's what they do. So he said to her 'I'm going fishing' but she thought why's he dressed up like that then? He's got his best shirt on."

"'E went fishing in his best shirt," the man said, laughing. "'E did. Bloody idiot."

"So anyway, she found out he was meeting her up here, taking the floozy to that women's pond over there for a bit of quiet you know what, so she got all her girlfriends together and they took his precious bloody car and drove it up here, pushed it into the ruddy pond didn't they."

"That's how it got here," the man said. "Pushed it in they did, pushed it right in. And now we've come up to see if it's still there, and there it is in broad daylight."

"Years later. Got her revenge, didn't she?" the woman said, crossing her arms, her bottom lip quivering.

"You don't want to upset yourself," her companion said, his hand moving to her shoulder. She put her hand up to his, patted it.

"Thanks for telling me," I said. "It's a funny, no, it's a sad story. Well, funny and sad. How do you know all this?"

The man laughed. "She can tell you."

But she was blushing.

I thought I could tell them a story about the ponds too, but I said goodbye and walked on, along the pathway between the trees, thinking of my young fathers, hand in hand, stealing through the undergrowth.

When I got home there was a message on the answer machine. Ellie had returned my call. She wanted me to come and see her.

CHAPTER 34

The house in Salisbury was large, white and Georgian, built at the corner of two roads. Like ours, there was a lion's head doorknocker, but I pressed the bell.

She took a long time to answer. When the door opened an elderly woman stood before me. She had thin hair tied back tight, her eyebrows just pencil lines. She'd smeared bright red lipstick onto her lips so that her mouth looked like a wound.

The mouth smiled, and the face transformed into a person.

"Hello, Christopher. Thank you so much for coming," Ellie said, looking me up and down. "So nice to see how you've turned out. Come inside."

She took me to the back of the house. French windows led to a garden where there was a large mulberry tree, planted on a man-made hummock, its branches spreading wide over a lawn scattered with red, squashed berries. She saw me looking at it.

"I used to collect the fruit, but now it's too much trouble."

She indicated an armchair and asked me if I wanted

coffee but I declined, so she sat opposite me, near a large fireplace, smoking a cigarette. On the mantelpiece there was an antique clock, richly decorated in red and gold, whose pendulum swung slowly behind a glass front.

"I couldn't come, you know," she said.

She was talking about the funeral. I'd invited her, but she hadn't replied.

"That's all right. It was -"

"I couldn't," she said again.

She turned her head sideways, passing a hand across her forehead as if to sweep away her feelings.

"I was in Vienna with Maria."

"Your daughter?"

"Yes, for a month. Maria's son was getting married."

"That must have been nice for you."

"I won't be going over there again," she said, her face hardening. "They'll have to come to me."

Framed photographs on the surfaces in the living room showed there were more children. She told me about them. There were four of them from her marriage to Richard. One of the boys had died. Another was a librarian somewhere north of London. The third, a girl, worked in a university. She didn't know what the fourth was doing now. Somewhere south of London, she thought. They'd fallen out.

"Do you see much of them?"

She made no response except to wave a hand, as if it didn't matter.

"What did he say about me?" she asked.

It was a direct assault. My first instinct was to tell her something bland, non-committal, but then I decided I'd not come all this way to skirt around the truth, so I told her: "That you were lovers."

Ellie grunted, shrugging her shoulders. "Lovers? He used that word? What else did he say?"

"That you broke up."

"What did he tell you about that?"

Here my courage failed me and I tried to change the subject.

"Do you have much contact with your daughters then, in Austria?"

"I've already told you. I returned last week after staying with Maria in Vienna. Anna too. They come here, I go there. We are very close."

"So you got back in touch?"

She evaded this. "What did he tell you about why we separated? I want to know."

I took the plunge. "He told me it was the second one, the younger one -"

"Maria."

"Yes, Maria. He told me, said it was something to do with her. What he found out."

A pained look crossed Ellie's face and in a quieter voice she asked, "What did he think he found out?"

"Well, just that she existed. That you hadn't told him about her."

"And?"

"That you hadn't looked after her enough."

Ellie winced. "And I suppose he told you I was a terrible mother? That's it, isn't it?"

"I'm not sure I'd put it like that... But he was very fond of children."

"Typical Louis. I can't believe he still thought that, after all these years, after I explained, and after what I did for him."

"He said they'd been taken away from you. There was a document."

"Oh, that bloody piece of paper. It was the Nazis: they forced me to sign it. Let me tell you, Christopher, let me tell you. Oh, God, he condemned me, but he had no idea, no idea what things were like for me. He had no right."

Now she trembled with rage.

"I'm sure he didn't mean -"

"Of course he meant it. Your father was a bloody

finger wagging, small minded moralist, a hypocrite too, with no experience of life. A man! An absolute classic man. Didn't take the trouble, didn't listen. Yet he judged me and found me wanting."

I tried to object, but she hadn't finished.

"How can he still think that? And say it to you?"

Our meeting had taken a disastrous turn. I hated what she was saying about my father. He couldn't defend himself. I wanted to get up and leave her to her ranting, her recriminations, walk out of the door and never come back.

"He doesn't think it anymore," I said, feeling hot, tears forming in my eyes. "He was a good father, and I miss him very much."

Ellie looked hard at me.

"I was forgetting. I'm so sorry. Christopher, my dear, I have so much to tell you, about him, about Robert and, oh dear, I suppose you need to know about me too. You mustn't leave here with, you know, the wrong ideas."

I nodded my agreement. She had a low voice, but it was strong and she looked past me as she spoke, out to the garden, out to the mulberry tree.

After Louis left, Ellie had realised she was on her own once again. She decided she wasn't going to moulder away in Klagenfurt. It was time she got her life back together. She applied to get her British passport back.

It wasn't straightforward, though. The application sparked off alarm bells in the Home Office and enquiries were set in train. They wanted to know what she'd been doing in a Nazi country all that time, what her political sympathies were. She had to undergo several interviews and was told the police in Vienna would be looking into her background.

Peter Dashwood had interrogated her, and had been very hostile. Louis was wrong about him being sent back to England. At first, he was transferred to Graz, to get him out of Louis' hair while the high-ups were thinking what to do with him. But they must have been short staffed, or perhaps he had people arguing his case for him. When Louis returned to London, Dashwood, as the only other Cambridge man, had inherited his position as head of the FSS unit in Klagenfurt. It must have been very gratifying for him.

Ellie's application took months to process and, in the end, was turned down. They gave her no reason. It was another blow, but as usual she picked herself up again, discovering she could apply for a visa to come to England as a foreign tourist. And this solved her problem. She came to London and, as it happened, the authorities never pursued her when the visa ran out. She was under the radar once again, just as she was in Vienna under the Nazis.

And when in London she sought out Louis.

At this point the anger on Ellie's face was replaced by a smile.

"He was a kind man, your father, whatever his other faults. He said he'd help me. He had already written me a letter of recommendation to the Home Office when I applied for naturalisation. It wasn't his fault it didn't work. He helped me find a place to live too, in Bayswater."

It was my turn for an assault. "Did you have an affair with him in London? That's what I always thought. That Louis had an affair with someone."

She started back in her chair.

"What makes you think that? No, as a matter of fact I did not."

With Louis I had waited too long, let him get away with too much. I took the letter she had written to me, the one I had shown to Louis as he lay in bed looking out at the cherry blossom, and gave it to her.

"This is what you sent me."

She took the letter and studied it, as if she did not know what it contained, frowning as she held it, her hand shaking a little, before putting it on the coffee table between us.

"Is it true?" I asked.

Now Ellie's eyes were filling up. A tear formed and trickled down her cheek. She wiped it away.

"Why do you think I invited you here?" she asked. "I wanted to see you. I wanted to tell you."

"What exactly were you going to tell me?"

I could see her choosing her words very carefully at this point.

"That I gave you to them. That I made you. That you are mine as much as theirs"

My face flushed.

"Is that how you see it? You gave me to them?"

I got up and went over to the French windows. Outside, it was raining. The red mulberry stain on the grass would spread, leaching into the soil.

It was true then: this woman was my mother. I had known it to be true for a long time, ever since Louis had reacted to the letter, but I needed her to say it.

I returned to Ellie. "Why didn't they tell me anything about you?"

"I don't know. It was important to them. I can't say why."

I'd asked them of course, who my mother was, but they'd always skirted around the subject. I'd never even found out her name. I remembered Louis handling the letter, his reluctance to open it, then finally reading it. There'd always been some reason why he couldn't speak about it: he was too tired, he'd get to it eventually. I saw now that he'd been putting me off, and for the first time I felt angry.

"It was Louis," I said. "He's the one who didn't want me to know who you were."

"You may be right. Or perhaps it was a promise he made to Rob, a way of having you all to themselves. They never discussed it with me."

"It was Louis. I'm sure of it. His side of the family: they all managed difficult subjects by clamming up. He probably swore Rob to secrecy."

Ellie shrugged and I could see she really didn't know. I'd just have to get used to the idea that my two fathers had this conspiracy between them, one that excluded me.

For a moment I wasn't sure I wanted to discover any more about these people, my parents' generation years ago, their lives, loves and rivalries. I remembered what Louis had said to me when I showed him the letter. What difference could it make to me now? I'd done my growing up. Nothing could change.

But I still felt angry. They'd kept the truth about Ellie from me all these years, thinking that the passage of time would remove the purpose of knowing about her. All they had to do was wait. Yet it did still matter to me, and always would. No-one stops wanting to know.

"All right," I said. "Explain away."

"Do you want that coffee now?" she asked.

I wasn't sure, but she went into the kitchen to make one anyway, leaving me alone. As I sat waiting for her I looked around the room again. There were some framed drawings on the wall that seemed strangely familiar, images of the sea, of wheat fields, one with a great stone monument in its centre, like one of the statues on Easter Island.

I closed my eyes and waited.

CHAPTER 35

When Ellie came to London in December 1947 Louis had been back for eighteen months. She'd been in touch with him by letter and he'd arranged a room in Bayswater for her. But when she got there, she didn't pursue him. She wanted a new life, free of old entanglements.

At first, she found work painting flowers onto perfume bottles. She made a friend, Clare, in her lodging house and they explored London together. Clare had come to the city from the North of England; Ellie had never lived there, so it was new to them both. Even in the winter fog and postwar austerity, with bomb sites still marking every street, there was a great deal to enjoy. They weren't far from the pubs and bars of Soho. The theatres were open. Music was in the air. When spring came, Clare suggested riding lessons in Hyde Park and they found themselves alongside soldiers from the Horse Guards, young men far from home. Things were looking up for her.

But money was a problem. The perfume factory didn't pay well, and she struggled to keep up with the rent. Clare advised her to contact Louis to see if he could help.

One Saturday afternoon she took the tube to Belsize

Park and walked up Haverstock Hill to the address he'd given. It was two years since she'd seen him. The day was warm and the trees in the street still had the yellow-green leaves of spring, light shining through them so they looked almost transparent. The houses in Hampstead Hill Gardens were surprisingly large. She hadn't realised he was so well-heeled.

She knocked and waited, worrying, wondering about the changes she might see in him.

But it was another man who appeared, smiling, white dust in his hair.

Then Louis was in the hallway, his face fuller than she remembered, but otherwise the same. He looked shocked, but then put out his hand to shake hers, a formal gesture that jarred with her. "It's good to see you Ellie," he managed to say. "This is Rob."

"So you knew Rob too."

"Of course. We became great friends. He helped me find a job."

Ellie got up to open a drawer below a bookcase, bringing out a large colour photograph which she handed to me.

"We had it enlarged."

My father stood between them, grinning, his arms around the two of them: Rob and Ellie, also in high spirits, Rob's hair blowing across his eyes. The picture had been taken on the south bank of the Thames with the Houses of Parliament behind them. Rob and Ellie were very alike, Rob a little taller, but both with the same dark hair. Rob's eyes were bright and his face happy, an energetic, confident man. It was wonderful to see him looking so young and handsome.

"We met a photographer who took pictures of tourists. Louis paid him for a colour print, but it was worth it."

"You should put it on the mantelpiece," I said. "How

was it, being with them?"

"They were unassailable as a couple. I sensed that straight away. My presence wasn't going to separate them if that's what you think."

"No, I didn't mean that. Just, well, it must have been awkward."

"It could have been, but Rob made sure it wasn't. He was so friendly, and he knew all about me and Louis, but it didn't trouble him in the slightest. He had a contact, someone who imported artist's materials, took me to his office in St Martin's Lane, and the man gave me a job. Rob and I went for a drink afterwards to celebrate. I used to go to his studio to watch him work on my days off."

I wondered if the friendship with Rob had been so uncomplicated. "Was he really so -"

"You don't believe me?"

She turned and pointed to the drawings on the wall behind her.

"He gave me those."

I got up and looked again at the pictures. Close up, I could see they were his. The line, the sweeping strokes. He'd even signed one.

Ellie watched me.

"I ended up being more a friend to Rob than to Louis. Louis took a while to relax when I came round, until he realised things were safe. I suppose, well, I suppose I lost interest in him. Rob was a lot more fun if the truth be told."

She had a point. Rob's smiles were frequent and always full of feeling; Louis too often had to force his smiles into life.

"What else did Louis tell you?" she asked.

I sensed a great deal lay behind her question. I told her he'd said nothing about her being in London, but I knew how things were in Klagenfurt.

She stiffened. "What did he say about Klagenfurt? About us?"

"Well, he was -"

"I adored him, you know."

Surprise must have shown on my face, but she continued.

"In Austria I thought he was the love of my life. I'm not sure I ever loved anyone else as much again."

She paused as we absorbed the confession. I considered Richard, her husband. He was dead now, but she'd been with him a long time, had children by him.

She read my thoughts.

"Richard? You're worrying about him? He was a meal ticket. And he knew it too, took me on all the same. Pathetic."

She had a contemptuous look on her face and her teeth were bared. They were yellow, one of them twisted in the gum. I looked away.

"And Peter Dashwood. Did Louis ever get to the bottom of that one? I bet he didn't." Her voice dripped with contempt. "Did your father speak about him? That so-called friend of his."

"He told me a fair amount," I said. "Sounded like a nasty piece of work."

"He poisoned Louis' mind against me. And he did his best to stop me coming back to England."

"How did he do that?"

"Peter Dashwood wrote a report saying I'd led - what was the phrase again?" She screwed up her face to remember, "An 'immoral life'. That's it. Said I'd entertained soldiers in my flat in Vienna, cosied up to the Germans, then the Russians, and then the British. He made it sound as if I was soldier mad. A common prostitute."

I thought of what she'd told me about her and Clare, pursuing soldiers in Hyde Park, but put it out of my mind straight away. She was getting worked up again.

"He recommended they turn down my application, and that's what they did."

"How can you be sure it was him?"

"He told me! The pig told me. He took great pleasure in doing that."

I knew Dashwood felt jealous of Louis' advancement through the ranks, but was he also jealous of him about Ellie? Did he want Ellie for himself?

I shared these thoughts with her. She listened patiently, waiting for me to finish before she spoke.

"No, it wasn't that."

"How can you be sure?"

"I just know."

I looked at her but she didn't explain herself.

Then she said: "I saw him in London."

"Who?"

"Peter Dashwood. He'd left the army."

She gathered herself before continuing, her bright red mouth twisted into something approaching a smile.

"It was in Soho, passed through on my way to work every day. An interesting place. Do you ever go there?"

"Yes, Chinese -"

"Oh, It's changed I suppose. In those days, well, I expect you know."

I did. We went there as schoolboys to look at the sex shops.

"There was a bookshop near Royalty Chambers - extraordinary things they sold. I remember some of the titles. The Sex Life of Ancient Rome, Pleasures of the Torture Chamber. And there were queers everywhere. They used to promenade up and down the street. People visited Soho just to stare at them."

She must have seen the look on my face

"You don't like the word. Well, it was a queer place, in more senses than one. Fun, actually. I enjoyed it."

"What was Dashwood doing there?"

"He hadn't come to gawp at the passers-by, had he? I was at the book stall one evening and I glanced up - recognised him straight away. I think he knew who I was too, but he pretended I was a stranger."

"So you didn't say hello."

"You don't understand, Christopher. He was with another man. They were coming out of one of those clubs. He was just taking his arm away from the man's waist as they stepped out into the street. You couldn't mistake it. Peter Dashwood was a fairy, just like Louis."

"Don't call him that," I said.

Ellie shrugged. "All that time, it wasn't me that Peter Dashwood wanted. It was Louis, who couldn't see it. But it was obvious, even in Klagenfurt. It was the way he looked at him. Norman Gray realised it too. I discussed it with him, actually."

I remembered the older man Louis had described quietly reading books in the corner while the others drank and played cards.

"Did you see his arms - Dashwood's?"

"You mean the burn marks. Louis told you about them, did he? He told me too but no, it all happened very fast."

She paused while I absorbed this news.

"As a matter of fact, I think Peter Dashwood had been interested in Louis for years, well before I arrived on the scene. They went to school together, didn't they? But he shouldn't have punished me for falling in love with your father. He told Louis I was a ruddy prostitute, and then he informed the world at large. Louis believed him, too. That's why it ended between us."

This wasn't the only reason Louis had changed his opinion about Ellie, but I kept quiet.

"I'd have been a hopeless prostitute," Ellie now said, giving a little laugh. "I never liked sex all that much."

She looked at me, challenging me to be shocked.

"If you know all this, you must have seen Dashwood again," I said.

"Yes, we bumped into each other occasionally after that. Once his secret was out the tension between us seemed to go. Even had a few drinks together. I almost forgave him for what he did to me once I understood what was behind it. Felt sorry for him I suppose. He was a disappointed man, drank too much."

"Disappointed?"

"He didn't last long in Klagenfurt. Louis' report eventually caught up with him and there was some kind of inquiry. It was a blot on his record, so he realised he'd be going nowhere in the army. He got out, went back to civilian life."

"What did he do?"

"A debt collector, pursuing people for unpaid rent. Lived somewhere in south London. Spent his weekends in Soho, drinking and chasing after boys, ruminating over what might have been, blaming Louis for his troubles. Miserable old sod."

We talked on for a while. I asked more questions about her children and got the impression she saw very little of them. She spoke with more warmth of her daughters in Austria, but she repeated what she'd said at the start of my visit: it was the last time she'd be going over there. She was too old to travel.

Then, in mid-sentence, Ellie fell asleep. I'd noticed she had a mug of something going which she sipped as she talked, though she'd only brought coffee for me. The smell of alcohol came off it and, now that I looked more carefully, I saw a box of pills on the table.

Frustrated, I got up, opened the French windows and went into the garden to look at the mulberry tree. It must have been very old, metal bolts going through its trunk to hold it together, the shaft covered with a rough growth of bark. The remains of a tree house clung to a branch, bits of wood nailed to it, a piece of rope rotting away. I imagined children there, playing around the tree, climbing it, and wondered what Richard, her husband, had been like, the family that must once have filled the house with life.

I decided I didn't like Ellie. I felt glad Louis and Rob had taken me from her.

As soon as this feeling surfaced it felt like a betrayal. Ellie wasn't that awful. I could only imagine the times she'd lived through, the things she'd had to do to survive. And she was my mother.

I heard a noise and went inside. The mug had fallen onto the floor and Ellie was stirring, her eyes opening as she heard me near her.

"Must have dropped off," she said. "It's these things."

She indicated the pills.

"My escape route. One day I'll take too many. Everyone should have one."

"Have what?"

"An escape route."

Then she smiled sweetly as if we'd been discussing the weather. "Will you have some lunch?"

We ate in the kitchen, a large room with an Aga stove keeping it warm, too warm in fact. There was a spacious table, covered with books, papers, magazines, in which a small space had been cleared for one person. She shoved them aside to make room for me, gave me sandwiches from the supermarket and offered me a glass of wine which I declined. She took a drink for herself, and then another one.

"We all used to sit around this table," Ellie said with surprising gentleness, "when the kids were young. Now it's just me."

Once she began the job in St Martin's Lane, Ellie spent more time in Louis' house at Hampstead Hill Gardens. She liked to watch Rob at work and to meet his artist friends. She even took lessons in drawing at the Slade, which ran evening classes.

Rob sympathised when she heard of her separation from her Austrian daughters. Together with Ellie's boss, the man who owned the artist's materials business and was a little in love with Ellie, they cooked up a plan: her boss would travel to Austria and seek them out. It wasn't a very satisfactory encounter, the family he met was defensive, worried he'd take the children away, but it was a first contact and that had made Ellie very happy.

As they spent more time together, Rob began to confide in her. He told Ellie about Vita, his own history with men, his masochistic relationship with Frank Lemaire. Ellie in turn described her own childhood and her experiences in Austria. The friendship between them deepened.

Then Rob began to tell her about the longing Louis had for a child, the sadness they both felt that they would never have one of their own. They couldn't make one between them and they'd never be allowed to adopt one. Shortly after that conversation, one evening, Louis visited Ellie in her room in Bayswater.

"He had a proposition for me," Ellie said, smiling at the memory. "And I agreed."

CHAPTER 36

They decided to do it by artificial insemination. They first consulted Norman Haire in Harley Street, but he was getting on in age by then, cutting back on his practice. He told them William Bolitho, a gynaecologist, was the right person for the job. Bolitho was completely open-minded, an active member of the World League for Sexual Reform, with experience of the latest techniques.

It was embarrassing for all three of them, sitting in the consulting room with Bolitho, planning to make a baby. But the doctor seemed at ease with the situation, unusual though it must have been even for him. His outline of the practicalities was so matter of fact, making it sound as if they were going to boil an egg, or change the wheel on a car, that they relaxed. He said it was best done away from the clinic, at their home. They'd feel more settled there and that would increase the chances of conception.

When the time came, Louis and Ellie went upstairs with Bolitho. Rob said it was better he wasn't around, so went out: he had important business to conduct, a new exhibition.

Bolitho directed Ellie to lie on a bed in the spare room

while he waited in the corridor with a syringe. Louis should go to his bedroom. Bizarrely, Louis was supplied with a jar and postcards of naked women that Bolitho assured him often helped the man produce what was needed. Louis must call him when all was ready.

But Louis couldn't do it. The postcards were hopeless. Absurd poses of women in diaphanous Edwardian robes, faces painted white, their large bottoms or breasts thrust towards the camera lens. And the thought of the doctor outside in the corridor, syringe at the ready, was simply too comical. Try as he might, nothing would happen. He was very embarrassed about it.

"What did you do?" I asked. I was wide eyed, listening to this bizarre story of how I was conceived.

"That, I am afraid, would be telling," Ellie said, as if she hadn't told me enough.

I was born at the Royal Free in Islington. Louis was present at the birth and after a few days they returned to Rob and the house in Hampstead.

"So now you know," Ellie said. "That's how it happened."

"Didn't you," I started, "Did you, I mean, did you find it hard?"

Ellie closed her eyes.

"Yes, it was hard. Very very hard. Hard to make love to him again and oh, so hard to give you up. But I still loved Louis at that stage and I was very fond of Rob, you see. I wanted to make them happy. I haven't made many people happy in my life. Perhaps I've not been such a wonderful mother. But I do know how to produce babies!"

She gave a little giggle at this, so I smiled too as I considered what she'd said. She'd described Louis as the love of her life. If that was true it must have been heartrending for her, to have Louis again and yet not to have him, and then to have his baby.

"So it really is the best of both worlds for you, my dear.

You're born, which is to be welcomed, and you get looked after by very nice parents. It was all very sensible."

She'd adopted a breezy tone.

"How long were you with me?" I asked.

Ellie's face fell at this and she didn't answer while she lit another cigarette, her hands trembling slightly.

"How long?" I repeated more gently.

She looked up. "Three months. You had to be weaned. I had to show them how to do things."

She inhaled deeply and blew the smoke out sideways.

"Then he made me leave."

"What do you mean?"

"He made me. Louis did. I think he realised I wanted to stay with you. With them."

"How did he do that?"

"Persuasion. Then threats when that didn't work. Threats. Said he could get me deported back to Austria - I was here illegally. I told him I wasn't, but I knew he could get me sent back all the same."

I was appalled.

"In the end I had to agree. He gave me money. Rob was crying. I had to leave you with them. That's how I ended up here."

I found myself standing up. I walked over to her chair and put my arms around her. We held on for a long time.

Secrets are peculiar things. The more secret they are the more you burn up with the desire to know them, but when they're revealed they lose their magic. I looked at Ellie, sitting back in her chair, gazing out of the window into her garden. Her husband was dead, her children far away, and I felt her loneliness.

She asked me to make another cup of coffee for us. She felt too shaky. I brought the cups to the table.

"You know, what I've told you is just one version of events," she said.

"How do you mean?"

"I could have told you a different story."

I said I was hoping she'd been telling me the truth.

"What if I said I came to England to take Louis back, tear him away from Rob? What if I said he loved me more than he loved Rob, that we had a real affair? That he stayed with Rob out of guilt. That I fell pregnant, and he took the baby, paid me off. Would you believe that?"

I thought about it.

"No," I said. "No, I wouldn't believe that."

"That's the trouble, isn't it?"

"Trouble?"

"Working out what to believe. Where the truth lies."

She was rambling now, her coffee spilling onto the table. I got up to get a cloth and wiped up the spill. Perhaps she was teasing me. If so, it was cruel of her.

Ellie told me another thing before I left. Louis had cleared out his mother's room when he returned from Klagenfurt and found a canvas bag there, containing things Louis' brother had with him when he died: a ring, a notebook, an identity card, photographs. It must have been sent back to England after he was killed.

There was one more item in the bag, and Louis had given it to Ellie when she handed over her baby. She'd like to return it now.

We were outside in the garden by then, admiring the mulberry tree. She went back into the house to fetch the object.

"He said this was precious to him. I'd given him something precious, and he wanted to give me something back that was more than just some money. Not as good as my gift, mind you, but I should keep it for ever as a reminder. But I think it's now time to return it. You, Christopher, are most certainly now its rightful owner."

She handed me the object. It was, in fact, two objects, two halves of an egg-shaped stone. One half had travelled to Spain with my uncle Christopher, the other half with Louis to Italy and beyond. The two halves still fitted together perfectly.

ABOUT THE AUTHOR

Julian Gray is the author of Interrogating Ellie, a novel based on the true story of his mother who lived in Nazi Austria during the second world war. She appears again in this novel. He has written numerous non fiction books under another name.

Visit:
www.interrogating-ellie.com
to learn more

PLEASE REVIEW THIS BOOK

Hi there...
I have a quick favour to ask you...
Amazon uses reviews to rank books AND many readers evaluate the quality of a title based solely on this feedback from others.
To put it simply: Reviews are very important to an author like me!
So, if you've enjoyed The Sins of my Fathers, or even if you're still working through it, could you take a minute or two to leave a review on Amazon? Even a sentence or two about what you like really helps!
I really appreciate you taking the time to read the book and I look forward to seeing any feedback you may have in the review section.

PRAISE FOR JULIAN GRAY'S
INTERROGATING ELLIE

"This is one of the best-written books I have reviewed...
Everything about Ellie works and we root for her against
the odds." Historical Novel Society

"'Interrogating Ellie,' is a thoroughly human story, told by
an author who draws us on to a moving and masterly
conclusion. One of the best books I've read this year."
(Ann Victoria Roberts – Amazon reviewer)

"Tremendous story about a young woman who confronts
and survives enormous and often terrifying adversity - at
many points, I felt that I would just have given up - its
quality is enhanced by it being, if not biographical, at least
based on a real person and a true story. It is very well
plotted and written and a real page turner." ('Al' – Amazon
reviewer)

"I finished reading the book last night and wanted to
congratulate you on a most gripping read. I was totally
involved/immersed in the story and characters and found
it very difficult to put it down every night. The fact that it
is based on your mother's life makes it very moving and
meaningful. It is a fitting tribute to her great spirit and will
to survive those awful times. (S.A. – Amazon reviewer)"

"A must read which compels you to want to research and dig deeper." (Gillian Ashton – Goodreads reviewer)

"Gray's book on World War II isn't cloak and dagger resistance movements and it isn't focused on the concentration camps. It's more like reality, reality that probably was for a lot of women in that time and in that place. That is what makes it beautiful." (Nicole Overmeyer – Goodreads and Netgalley reviewer)

"An amazing story !" (Ilse Landemann – Goodreads reviewer)

Visit Amazon to purchase / borrow *Interrogating Ellie*

USA
https://www.amazon.com/Interrogating-Ellie-Julian-Gray-ebook/dp/B00SIA1UBM

UK
https://www.amazon.co.uk/Interrogating-Ellie-Julian-Gray-ebook/dp/B00SIA1UBM

Visit:
www.interrogating-ellie.com
to learn more